A K

He pulled himself [illegible] at on the side of the be[illegible]

"John," she protes[illegible] herself up on her elbows, staring at his shadow in the darkness, unable to believe he would leave her. Not now.

"I came to say goodbye," he said hoarsely. "I didn't intend for any of this to happen. I only wanted to say goodbye. To kiss you one last time."

"I was sure you had come to tell me that you loved me and wanted to stay."

"I can't stay," he said. He raked his hands through his hair and walked away from her. "You know that."

"And you don't love me."

"I can't love any woman," he said rigidly. "Not now. Not when what I'm doing is so dangerous and uncertain.

"I'm doing you a favor, Lida," he whispered. "You might not think so now, but believe me, blue eyes." He walked quickly across the room and took her shoulders, pulling her close for one last kiss. Her mouth clung to his, sweetly, desperately.

"Forget you ever met me," he murmured as he turned to walk out the door . . .

Raves for best-selling author Clara Wimberly:

"Marvelous . . . A powerful testament to the triumph of the human spirit."

—*Romantic Times* on *Tomorrow's Promise*

"An uplifting, moving treasure that will be reread through the years. Unforgettable."

—*Affaire de Coeur* on *Kentucky Thunder*

CLARA WIMBERLY

ZEBRA BOOKS
KENSINGTON PUBLISHING CORP.

ZEBRA BOOKS are published by

Kensington Publishing Corp.
850 Third Avenue
New York, NY 10022

First Printing: June, 1996
10 9 8 7 6 5 4 3 2 1

Printed in the United States of America

To strong women everywhere who have faced the prospect of leaving home because of a man's love.

Acknowledgments

A special thanks to Patsy Mullet and Matt Nojonen of the Holmes County Public Library for their generous help and patience. Also thanks to Alma Kaufman of Millersburg, Ohio, for sharing her experience and knowledge.

One

Spring 1862
Walnut Creek, Ohio

Lida Rinehart couldn't sleep. She blamed it on an approaching storm that lit the skies outside her family's big farmhouse, and the distant thunder that rumbled and rattled over the Ohio countryside.

She slipped out of her bed, going to the window for what seemed like the hundredth time. She was worried about her brother.

"Where are you, Ephraim? Where are you?"

Quietly she opened her window, letting in the warm breeze that carried the fresh scent of rain into her room. The wind was growing stronger as the storm approached. Lida had hoped her brother would be home before it hit, but now she doubted it. It must be past midnight, and she was concerned about how much longer Ephraim could continue these secretive all-night outings before their father found him out.

Or before something happened and one morning Ephraim didn't make it home before time for chores.

By now Lida was almost frantic with worry. Ephraim was her younger brother, her only brother, and she supposed her concern had something to do with having to care for him as a child. She didn't know what she would do if anything happened to him. She was even afraid that he might be thinking of going against their Amish beliefs and joining in the Civil War that had torn the country apart for the past year.

Just this morning, she had asked him outright about his secretive night activities.

"Ephraim, please . . . won't you tell me? What is it you do? You are not thinking of going English are you? You know mama and papa would die if you did." Lida had taken hold of Ephraim's shirtsleeve, tugging at the material and forcing him to look at her.

She thought even now of how handsome he was, with his dark hair and beard and pale blue eyes. No wonder all the young girls of Walnut Creek giggled when he drove past in his buggy, or stood staring at him on Sunday morning during church services.

"Me?" he said. "Go English? *Nein,*" he'd said, laughing. "And you are a great one to talk. You are the only one in this family who has ever been called to public confession."

"I was only a girl then," she said, resisting a smile at his teasing.

"Sixteen," he reminded. "Not so long ago."

"Four years is a long time. Now that I'm a fussy old maid of twenty, no one can accuse me of being too strong-willed to please the church deacons. I have behaved very well recently." Lida's blue eyes sparkled with mischief as she joined in her brother's bantering.

"Oh, but you are still strong-willed and independent in your thinking," he whispered, leaning close and tugging a strand of long blond hair from beneath her crisp white prayer cap. "I can see it in your eyes. You still hate being told what to do, Lida. You always did. Papa says it's the worst fault of all the worldly ones. God expects us to be nonconforming to the English life, but he does not expect his people to be independent within the church."

"Especially women," she said with a stubborn lift of her chin. "I have always believed that if *you* had been the one accused of independent thinking, nothing would ever have come of it."

"Ah," he said, grinning. "You see, it still bothers you, even now. Papa says you shall never find a good Amish boy to marry you if you continue being so stubborn and independent."

"And who says I want to marry . . . a good Amish boy or anyone else?" she countered. "Besides, you are changing the subject—purposely I suspect. I want to know where it is you go at night and what you are doing. You know how worried I am about you."

Ephraim's face changed then—the fun suddenly gone, replaced with a solemn look she'd rarely seen before. His stubborn look shut her out, and that was something Lida wasn't used to.

"Ephraim—I'm afraid for you."

"Don't be, *Liebling,*" he said, putting his arm

around her shoulders. "I can take care of myself. And if it will make you feel any better, I will tell you this, what I'm doing is for a good cause."

"Good cause!" she scoffed. "If it is so good, then why can't you tell papa what you're doing . . . or me?"

"Because I'm sworn to secrecy," he said. "It is very important that no one know about the—there . . . I've almost said too much because of you, my prying sister. I don't want you to know anything more. What you don't know, you can't repeat, and I would never ask you to lie for me."

Lida's heart fell as she heard his words and saw the solemn expression on his handsome young face. What did he mean? And why would anyone ever question her about her brother's activities?

Lida's daydreams about the morning vanished as lightning lit her room. Thunder followed, rattling the windows and causing her to jump. The wind blew the curtains away from the open window and she could feel the spray of rain coming in as well.

Quickly she ran to the window, pushing down on the sash and closing it. It was then she saw a movement past the house out toward the barn. She frowned and stared harder through the panes that were being splattered by rain.

Someone was going into their barn. She could see the faint glimmer of a lantern and the outline of someone leading a horse through the doorway.

It was Ephraim, it had to be. But she was sure that someone else was with him. And Lida intended to find out who it was and what they were doing at the barn in the middle of the night.

She pulled a cape around her shoulders, not bothering to bind her hair or put on a cap. She had to get to the barn before Ephraim came inside and whoever was with him had a chance to leave.

Quietly she slipped out into the hallway, her footsteps muffled by the sound of the storm that raged around the farmhouse. Once she was past her parents' room, she began to hurry, going down the enclosed stairway and through the house toward the back.

The wind howled so loudly in the trees that surrounded the house that she could hardly hear the sound of her own footsteps. It blew her raincoat away from her body, whipping about her gown and allowing the rain free access. Her hair fell about her face as she stumbled and tried to pull the hood down far enough to shield the rain from her eyes.

Lightning flashed dangerously near, followed by a loud clap of thunder that Lida felt reverberate through her entire body. She thought she would never reach the safety of the barn, even though it was no more than a hundred yards away.

Once she was safely inside, she hesitated, pushing her wet hair back and drying her face as best she could with the edge of her cape.

The barn felt wonderfully dry and welcoming. Even the warm mingled scent of the farm animals and hay was reassuring somehow. She stood for a moment, allowing her eyes to adjust to the gloom and staring toward the back of the barn where a faint glimmer of light appeared. She was certain she heard voices coming from that direction.

She moved toward the light, being careful not to make any noise or to disturb the animals in the stalls. It was a complete shock when she suddenly found herself captured by strong, hard arms, and felt a man's hand clamp over her mouth, pulling her head back against his chest.

"Who are you?" a deep voice growled. "What are you doing here?"

"Wait . . . wait. Let her go. It's only my sister." A light flared as Ephraim lit a kerosene lantern and hung it on a nearby post.

As the man's hands released her, Lida whirled around, staring with furious, blazing eyes at Ephraim and the stranger who had grabbed her. There was a sheepish apologetic look in her brother's eyes, but she was too angry to care. What did he mean, sneaking into the barn this way, bringing a stranger who treated her in such a manner? And from the looks of him, an English stranger at that!

She turned to the tall man who'd held her, staring into eyes that smoldered a misty gray color in the dim light—eyes that were the color of stone, and every bit as cold and hard. Black hair and dark skin seemed to indicate a heritage of some ancient tribe. Yet the serious gray eyes beneath his dark brows were as Celtic as any Scottish Highlander's.

"I might ask you the same question," she said.

"Who are you and what are you doing here in our barn?"

"Lida," her brother began, lifting his finger to his mouth to signal her to be quiet. "He is here because I brought him here. Please . . . go back to the house."

"No," she said, clamping her lips together. "I will not go back to the house. Not until you tell me what is going on."

She saw the lift of the stranger's eyebrow, the glint of irritation and warning in his smoky eyes, and for a moment she took a step away from him.

No man had ever looked at her the way this arrogant intruder was looking at her. His gaze trailed slowly over her rain-soaked gown and caused her to become acutely aware of how the material clung to her and revealed her almost nude body underneath. Staring defiantly into his eyes, she pulled her cape closer.

"Are you the one responsible for my brother's absence night after night?" she demanded. "You are English, aren't you? Do you have any idea what will happen to him if he's found out? He will be shunned . . . he will be excommunicated from our church and—"

"Your brother is a grown man, Miss Rinehart," the cold-eyed stranger said. "Responsible, I presume for his own actions. Now, I suggest you go back to the house, as he suggested, and forget you ever saw me here tonight." His speech was different—slower and tinged, she thought, with the languid, honeyed lilt of the south.

How dare he stand there so coolly and tell her

to go to the house as if she were a child. She wouldn't do that and pretend nothing had happened. And how could he expect her to ever forget those cold stormy eyes? That proud, arrogant look, or the raven black hair that framed his face and gave him the look of a savage?

For some reason that she didn't fully understand, she felt breathless when she answered him.

"Not until I find out what you're doing here and why you have influenced my brother to leave his family and risk losing all he has ever known."

The man laughed then, a bitter sound that echoed softly in the barn. For a moment, his gray eyes wandered over the girl standing before him, noting the outline of her long legs through the wet material of her nightgown and cape, before moving up to her breasts that lifted with her agitated breathing.

He thought she looked like an avenging angel come to earth. A fair-haired angel with cornflower blue eyes that flashed and glimmered like sapphire beneath flickering candlelight.

"I doubt, miss, that you have ever known what it is to lose anything," he said softly, almost wistfully.

Lida stood staring at him, this man who had come like a thief in the night. A man cloaked in mystery with eyes that refused to reveal anything of himself. She glanced toward her brother, hoping for an answer, but she saw him turn away from her and she frowned. Ephraim had never behaved this way toward her—not in all their lives.

The storm was moving away to the north, and

the barn had grown quiet except for the occasional lowing sound of an animal and the quiet steady dripping of rain from the eaves of the building.

It was because of the quiet that she heard a sound and turned toward it, her eyes growing wide with disbelief. It was the sound of a child's crying that came from a corncrib at the back of the barn.

Lida pulled her cape around her and with a determined look at the stranger, she moved past him toward the sound.

"Lida . . . don't," she heard Ephraim say.

She didn't stop, but grasped the heavy wooden door of the corncrib and flung it open. She couldn't believe what she saw there in the glint of light that fell into the stall.

Four people stood staring at her—Negroes, a man and woman and two children, one of them only a baby that was held against its mother's breast. Staring back at them Lida thought she had never seen such fright in her life as she saw reflected in their dark shining eyes.

"Please, ma'am," the woman said, her voice full of fear. She took a step away from Lida, clutching her children to her.

"I won't hurt you," Lida said, her voice soft. "Please . . . come out . . . I promise no one will hurt you."

"What have you done?" Lida asked, turning back to her brother and the man who stood watching her, his hands at his hips. "What on earth have you done?" she repeated with alarm.

"Ephraim," the man said, not looking at her brother, but staring at Lida instead. "It's almost stopped raining. Do you think you can find your way on to the next station in the dark?"

"Yes . . . yes, of course I can. But what about you?"

Lida stared at Ephraim, amazed at the quick, proud way he had responded to the man. She realized that it was the first time she'd ever really seen him as a grown man instead of her little brother.

"I'll catch up with you . . . you take the family and go on ahead."

Without another word, Ephraim went to the family of Negroes and motioned them toward the door.

"Ephraim . . . wait," Lida said. "You mustn't do this. Do you know what will happen if papa finds out? What if the church discovers that you are involved in such deception and violence?"

"It's something I have to do, *Liebling*. I have to."

As the ragged runaways walked past Lida, the woman turned to look into her face. Her eyes were huge and dark and filled with a kind of pleading, silent request for understanding that tore at Lida's conscience.

Once Ephraim and his secret consignment were gone, Lida turned on the stranger with a vengeance, just the way he knew she would.

The man watched her for a moment, hardly able to take his eyes off her. Her hair, still wet from the rain, lay like spun gold over her shoulders and down her back. Inexplicably he felt his fingers clench into a fist with the need to touch it, to push it back away from her lovely face. It had been a long time since he'd been with a woman, and what seemed like a lifetime since he'd even allowed himself to come close to the wholesome, respectable kind like Lida Rinehart.

He wasn't sure what it was about her . . . the rain that shut them in, the closeness of her in the dimly lit barn, the scent of soap and rain that clung to her smooth peach-colored skin. Or perhaps it was those clear blue eyes, so innocent and yet filled with a quick intelligence that would challenge any man.

"Why have you done this?" she demanded. "Why have you recruited someone like my brother when you know he is Amish . . . when you know he is going against his church and his people?"

The stranger straightened then, pulling his eyes away from her and the alluring temptation of her face.

"I did not recruit your brother," he said, his voice infinitely patient for once.

Lida sensed that his show of patience was not genuine. She could see the real character of the man in his restless, impatient movements, in the haughty glances he threw at her from those cold gray eyes.

"You're lying," she said. "Ephraim wouldn't—"

"Why don't you open your eyes and ears, Miss Rinehart? Didn't you see the pride on your brother's face . . . hear it in his voice? He came to us of his own free will and he asked to join our cause. Believe me, I have no need to recruit the Amish. I have enough trouble as it is, getting these people through Ohio and into Canada."

Lida took a deep breath. She was getting nowhere with the man by being openly hostile. She would try another approach, a calmer, more diplomatic one.

"I appreciate your reasons for doing what you do," she said, deliberately softening her tone. "I'm sure it's a noble cause and a just one. You are to be commended for that, but—"

"Noble?" he murmured, turning to stare down into her eyes.

He stepped closer to her and she could hear the quiet jingle of his boot spurs. His face in the shadows looked menacing and dangerous and for a moment she held her breath, not sure of what he meant to do.

"I'm afraid you have misjudged me, Miss Rinehart," he said, his voice deceptively quiet.

He couldn't explain why he felt the need to dissuade her of his nobility or his goodness. Perhaps it was because he hadn't liked the warmth that spread through his chest at the sound of her softer, more cajoling words. Or maybe it was because he had learned this past year to live without forgiveness and understanding or even the expectation of it. He certainly didn't need this woman's understanding.

"My reason for doing this has nothing to do with nobility. It's money . . . pure and simple. Or else, I'd be back home in Tennessee in the safety and comfort of my own bed."

"Money . . . ?"

"Can you think of a better reason for risking one's life?"

"Why you're . . . you're nothing more than a mercenary," she whispered, staring at him as if she saw the devil himself. "A paid-for-hire gunman at best."

"At best," he said, unsmiling, his eyes cold with warning. "Now if you'll excuse me, I have to earn that money by seeing that this family is at a point several miles north of here before daybreak. And as for you, Miss Rinehart, I'd suggest you go back to bed and forget this night ever happened."

He turned to go, his rain slicker swinging out behind him, the jingle of boot spurs muffled in the rustle of hay as he strode toward the door.

"Wait . . . I . . . I don't even know your name in case . . . in case—"

"John," he said, not even hesitating in his march toward the door. "That's all you need to know . . . my name is John. Simple enough?"

Her gaze followed him until he disappeared into the darkness, until he walked out into the night and was swallowed up by it.

"Simple?" she whispered.

Somehow she thought there was nothing simple about this lean, hard-eyed stranger. He'd come like the storm to disturb her sleep and her senses and now disappeared into the darkness as if nothing had happened.

Oh no, there was nothing simple about him at all.

* * *

John Sexton cursed beneath his breath as he walked out of the barn and stood for a moment in the sultry rain scented darkness. He leaned his head back and gazed upward with a heavy sigh. The skies didn't seem to be clearing yet.

"Dammit," he muttered. It wasn't only the weather that bothered him. The appearance of Ephraim's sister troubled him, too. The more people who knew about the operation to spirit runaway slaves across Ohio and on to Canada, the greater chance there was that the authorities would find out who they were.

Despite President Lincoln's vow to free the slaves, the fact remained that there was still a Fugitive Slave Law in effect. It assured that anyone caught aiding the escape of a slave would be imprisoned.

And as John's friend Samuel Greenhow had warned when he recruited John for the underground operation, some officials were not so careful when arresting those breaking that law. John had learned that only too well this past year while guiding slaves through the dark Ohio countryside. Between the bounty hunters and the overzealous lawmen, some captured with the newly reactivated Underground Railroad hadn't lived long enough to see the inside of a prison.

"I'll just have to take my chances," John muttered.

It was the same response he'd given to Greenhow when he agreed to join the abolitionist's efforts.

John pushed through the wind and lingering rain toward a horse tied near the back of the barn.

He didn't know what had prompted him to tell the Rinehart girl he was in this work for the money. Maybe it had been that little hint of self-righteousness in the tone of her voice. Or maybe it was the glint of disapproval in those sparkling blue eyes.

Not that money hadn't been a consideration in his decision to join the cause. But he'd had every cent of it sent to a bank in Ohio where the money would be safe. When the war ended, he'd need it if he intended to go back to his family's farm in Tennessee.

As he pulled himself up onto his horse, John gave a low grunt of self-derision. *If* his father let him come back, he should have said.

But that was another problem he didn't need to think about at the moment—his relationship with his father and what this damnable war had done to their family.

As John rode away into the dark, misty night, he glanced back over his shoulder at the Amish barn.

Let the girl think what she would. It was just as well she thought he was a heartless, mercenary bastard. Maybe it was what he had become. And after all, it wasn't a much differing opinion than the one his own father had of him.

The war had cost him a great deal. His diploma

from West Point, his family, his home . . . and Katherine.

"Hell," he cursed, leaning into the wind. "What more do I have to lose?"

Two

Lida didn't bother going to bed after she got back to the house. She knew she wouldn't be able to sleep anyway. By five she was in the kitchen helping her mother with breakfast. She was so afraid that Ephraim wouldn't show up that she could feel a tightness gripping her chest as she kept glancing toward the doorway.

"Was ist los?" her mother asked. "What is it with you this morning, child? You're as skittish as one of the new colts. Did the storm keep you awake last night?"

"Yes, I guess so," Lida said, turning away from her mother to place a pitcher of milk on the table. "It . . . it didn't keep you and papa awake too, did it?"

"Nein," her mother said with a laugh. "You know nothing could wake your papa after a hard day of work, not even a thunderstorm."

"That's good." Lida glanced at her mother out of the corner of her eye. She felt only relief that her mother hadn't known about the rendezvous last night. She would be worried to death if she had any idea of what Ephraim was up to.

When her brother came walking into the

kitchen for breakfast, Lida breathed a sigh of relief. She felt almost giddy at seeing him, and it caused her to chatter all through breakfast until her mother looked at her oddly.

Lida caught Ephraim's gaze on her several times during the meal and she could sense that he wanted to talk. But it was almost noon before she had the kitchen cleaned and her other household duties done.

"Mama," she said, as soon as she had finished. "I'm going to take Ephraim a fresh drink of water. I'll be right back."

Her mother nodded from the table where she sat peeling potatoes.

Lida hurried out with the pail of water to the barn where Ephraim was working. He greeted her with a smile, took the bucket and set it down, then pulled her out of the barn to walk with him toward the orchards, where the tree branches were heavy with clusters of sweet fragrant blossoms.

She sensed that he could hardly contain his excitement.

"I'm glad you know," he said. "I'm glad someone finally knows and I can talk about it. I helped that family last night, Lida. I was actually the one to get them safely to . . ." he hesitated, knowing he couldn't reveal the next station, not even to his sister. ". . . to the next stop." He stopped, turning around in the deep grass and spreading his arms toward the sky.

"It was the most exciting adventure of my entire life," he shouted exuberantly.

"Ephraim," she began. "This is not good. Papa says excitement is not—"

"Papa says . . . papa says," he mimicked. "Papa has been stuck on this farm since he was a boy. He knows nothing of the real world, Lida . . . nothing! If he did, he wouldn't be so quick to judge what's right and what is not."

She didn't know what to say to him and she didn't know how to temper his excitement. His eyes sparkled with it, his cheeks were aglow because of it, and that frightened her more than she could say. He had the look of a young man bent on going *English* as the Amish would say. And that idea worried Lida.

"I don't know what's come over you," she whispered, staring at him.

"Life," he said. He took off his straw hat and tossed it toward one of the apple tree limbs. It hung for a moment before falling onto the ground, and he laughed. "Life!" he repeated. "I know how you feel now, Lida . . . remember how you used to say that our church restricted us . . . that it made you felt imprisoned."

"That was foolish talk," she said, frowning at her brother. "I was only a child when I said it."

"Admit it, sister," he said, taking her hands and staring down into her eyes. "You still feel that way. But you are trying to be a dutiful *Tochter* and you don't want to disappoint mama and papa, so you conform. Isn't that it?"

"No . . . no, that's not how it is."

"Are you going to stay here then . . . all your life? Marry Carl Miller or one of the Hostetler boys? Have a dozen babies? Milk cows and clean and cook every day, and then get up the next morning and start all over again?"

"I like the farm, Ephraim. I love the peace and contentment of it. That has never changed for me."

"You didn't answer my question . . . you can't marry any of them, Lida. You would be bored beyond words."

"Carl Miller is a fine man. What would be so wrong with my marrying a man like him?"

"Then why haven't you already done so?" he asked, taunting her with his smug look.

"I . . . I'm just not ready yet, that's all."

"Not ready—at *twenty,* when your friends and cousins are married at eighteen? No, I don't believe that's the reason."

"Oh," she said, crossing her arms and staring defiantly at him. "If you're so smart, why don't you tell me why I'm not married."

"Because you're more full of life than any of them, Lida. Your independence has always gotten you in trouble, and you know it. I hate seeing you repress it the way you do now. Last night in the barn, when you spoke to John, you were spirited . . . like your old self, and I think I understood you better than I ever have . . . it's the same way I feel."

"This man . . . John . . . he's the one who has made you think this way," she said, remembering the disturbing stranger. "Is that why you admire him—because he's different from us?"

"Who wouldn't admire a man like him?" he

asked. "He's daring and courageous and he isn't afraid of anything. They say he was wounded once, but that he kept going until he had delivered the people to safety. He didn't complain and he didn't tell anyone he was hurt. I've heard that he's risked his life time and again to help the slaves. They trust him with their lives . . . with their lives; everyone trusts him."

"Well, I don't trust him. He isn't brave, Ephraim," she said. "He's only doing this for money. Can't you see—?"

"Did he tell you that?"

"Yes, he told me that, and I believe it. You're blind to what he really is, Ephraim. He's only a mercenary. What he does, he does for money . . . nothing else. Don't confuse his actions with bravery and daring."

"You're wrong about him. You don't know him at all," Ephraim said. "Besides, I want to see the world, Lida," he said. His blue eyes grew clouded with his daydreams. "I want to take a train to Philadelphia, and to New York perhaps. Even across the western plains one day. I want to cross the ocean, go to Europe . . . to Switzerland where our grandparents lived. Don't you want that? What would be so terrible about that?"

"You know why. It's worldly," she said quietly. "We Amish don't need worldly things."

"Well, I need it," he said, his jaw clenched defiantly. "And I'm going to have it."

After that day, Lida worried constantly about Ephraim. There had been something in his eyes, a faraway longing that seemed to spark from his very soul. And she thought he would never be the same sweet innocent boy again.

And even though she begged him to stop what he was doing, she knew he hadn't. She would hear him slip out of his room at night, and she would stand by the window and watch him go toward the barn. Sometimes she thought he only met someone there, perhaps took them food and water. But other nights he would leave the farm and be gone all night.

He was young and headstrong and he wouldn't listen to a word she said. And although Lida kept his secret, she was afraid for him . . . terribly afraid.

In June the weather turned very cool, cool enough that Lida had to close her bedroom window before going to bed. One night she was so tired that she couldn't maintain her usual vigilance and fell asleep without waiting to see if Ephraim left the house. She snuggled down beneath her mother's handmade quilt and slept soundly for the first time in weeks.

Sometime in the night she woke suddenly, sitting up in bed, uncertain about what had wakened her. She blinked her eyes, trying to see into the darkened corners of her room. She had such an odd, disturbing feeling that she held her breath against it, hoping it would go away.

Then she heard a noise. It was here, in her room, and she was certain it was what had wakened her so suddenly.

"Ephraim?" she whispered. She reached out toward the lamp that sat beside her bed, and felt a tingle all the way up to her shoulder when a hand clamped around her wrist.

Her cry was a hoarse whisper before she felt the weight of a man's body on her bed, felt his hand touching her shoulder. She was so frightened she couldn't move.

"Shh," a voice said. "It's me . . . John."

Lida sat up even straighter in bed, afraid now for another reason. There was something odd about his voice. It was softer, as if he could hardly get the words past his throat.

"What are you doing here?" Her fear was not of him. She knew instinctively that he had not come to harm her. "What's wrong? Is it Ephraim?"

"Yes." His voice was so quiet, almost as if it were filled with pain. "I'm afraid your brother's . . . been hurt. He . . ." she heard his soft grunt in the darkness and when she reached forward to touch him, there was something warm and wet on his arm. He was shaking.

"Oh, God," she said, sliding quickly out of bed and fumbling in the dark to find her dressing gown. "Where is he? Is he hurt badly?"

He didn't answer at first and she wondered why he was still sitting on her bed.

She lit a lamp and turned toward where he sat slumped over on her bed. She drew in her breath when she saw the paleness of his skin and the glitter of pain in his gray eyes.

"In the barn," he managed to whisper. "Hurry."

Lida watched in horror and disbelief as he fell over onto her bed. She saw the blood on his shirt then, saw it seeping slowly onto her quilt. Her hand was trembling as she placed it on his chest. He was unconscious, but she could hear his quiet shallow breathing and the catch of it in his throat as if even in sleep he could not escape the pain.

With a quiet murmur of alarm, Lida took a folded towel from a nearby drawer and pressed it to his wound.

There was nothing to do but tell her parents. They had to know that Ephraim was hurt and she couldn't just leave this man alone here to die in her room.

Waking her parents, shc explained quickly what had happened.

"We have to hurry, Papa," shc said. "He said we should hurry."

"Mein Gott," her father muttered as he pulled his clothes on. "How has this happened? How in *Gott's* name has this happened?"

He hurried toward the stairs, glancing back once at his wife's ashen face as she stood in the doorway.

"You stay here, *Mutter,"* he said. "Help the English if you can. I will bring our boy back to the house so that you can see for yourself that he is all right. Come with me, Lida."

They found Ephraim sprawled in the hay at the back of the barn, a trail of blood leading to where he lay. The stranger had covered him with a blanket at least before coming for her. But as Lida fell to her knees beside her brother, she wasn't sure he was breathing.

"No," she cried, her voice frantic and desperate. "Ephraim, can you hear me? You're home now and we're going to help you. You'll be all right . . . do you hear? You have to be all right." She couldn't seem to stop crying.

The pain she saw on her father's face almost destroyed her, and she berated herself silently for not telling him a long time ago what Ephraim was involved in.

Her father quickly pulled a small wooden cart to where Ephraim lay and together they managed to lift him onto it. The cart was made to be pulled by a small animal, usually a goat, but it was still quite heavy. But with her father pulling and Lida behind pushing, they made it to the house in a matter of minutes.

They carried Ephraim into the living room downstairs where there was a small cot that her father sometimes used for resting during the day.

When Lida faced the realization that her brother wasn't breathing, her mind could not seem to conceive that he was dead. But in her heart she knew he probably had been dead even before they found him in the barn. After a moment her father knew it, too, and shook his head as he turned to face his wife.

"It's too late, *Mutter.* Our son is dead," he said, his voice catching with grief and pain.

Lida saw the tears flood her mother's eyes and she had to turn away. She felt as if she were in some horrible nightmare, as if any moment she might wake and find that this had all been just a crazy dream. She closed her eyes against the pain, opening them again quickly when she heard her mother's anguished cries.

"My son," her mother cried. "Oh, my *schön Sohn.*" Her voice rose at the end, a frail cry of despair and disbelief.

Her mother lay against Ephraim's lifeless body, her hands touching his face as if she might wake him.

Lida was shaking her head in disbelief as she watched her father gently cover Ephraim's face, then pull her mother away from him. She watched numbly as he took her in his arms and rocked her gently back and forth, holding her tightly against him, holding her away from the sight of her dead son.

"No," Lida whispered, moving forward as if in a dream. "No, this can't be."

She fell to her knees beside Ephraim, touching him, holding him, pleading with him to open his eyes. But she knew in her mind that he was gone, even if her battered heart refused to believe it. She knew her brother could not hear. He would never speak to her again, never look at her with such bright hope in those beautiful blue eyes. It had all happened so quickly. Yesterday he was alive—warm and happy and excited. And now, suddenly, he was gone, and she'd never be able to speak to him again.

The next few days were torturous ones for Lida and her family and for their friends and relatives. The funeral was solemn and sad, the grief so real and heavy that it seemed to weigh down upon the usually lively Amish people.

Lida thought that being a part of the sad procession to the cemetery was the most heartbreaking thing she'd ever witnessed. Seeing the long line of men dressed in black coats and black hats, the bonnets of black glistening beneath the summer sun, was something she thought she'd never forget.

But she only felt an odd sense of disbelief. She felt numb and cold even on such a warm summer day.

The man who had brought Ephraim home still lay unconscious in Lida's bedroom. He had been too badly wounded to risk moving, and for a while they expected that he would die, too.

Lida was not surprised, even after telling her papa everything and how the man named John was involved, that they chose to keep him in their house and tend to him. They were gentle, forgiving people, just as most of their Amish neighbors were. The main theme of their religious belief was in living their lives as examples to the rest of the world. And forgiveness was a major part of that example.

But Lida found that she couldn't forgive. She thought she actually hated the dark-haired man who lay so still and quiet on her bed. And even though she tended him each day, she was the only one who knew that she did it only for her mother's sake.

For besides forgiving the man, Anna Rinehart seemed to have transferred her tenderness and her motherly love from her dead son to this stranger. Their neighbors, who came every day to help, said it was natural, that it would help her heart to mend. And if it would do that, then Lida was more than willing to pretend that she cared about his healing, too.

She was curious though. She had sat with the man named John, watched the troubled expression on his face and heard his muttered, feverish ramblings. And she couldn't help wondering what they meant.

"Katherine," he'd said, as if calling out for someone. He'd gritted his teeth in anguish, and anger, too, Lida thought.

"Damn you," he growled. "Damn you all."

Lida was the only one with him the day he finally opened his eyes and glanced around the sunlit room. His gray eyes focused on the fluttering white curtains at the window before his gaze began to take in the entire room. He frowned before his gaze moved toward Lida.

"Do you know where you are?" she asked, rather dispassionately. She took a cool cloth and touched it to his forehead.

"Yes." His voice was hoarse from disuse, but his eyes were clear now and steady. "The Amish farm . . . Walnut Creek."

"That's right." Lida looked away from his questioning gaze. She clamped her lips together to keep from screaming out at him what he had done. Instead she took a glass of water and slid her hand beneath his neck to lift his head so that he could drink. She was surprised at the warmth of his skin and the healthy feel of strong muscles beneath her fingers.

During the days that they had tended him, Lida had seen him only as the one responsible for her brother's death. She hadn't seen him as a strong, attractive young man, so handsome that he would set any woman's heart aflutter. But the others who came, the Amish women who sat with him and took their turns nursing him, they had commented on his beautiful clean-shaven face, the glistening black hair that fell over his forehead. They had clucked around him sadly, sometimes giggling quietly about how handsome he was, about how strong and muscular his bare chest and shoulders were.

Lida had been enraged, wanting to scream at them and tell them that this was the man who had caused Ephraim's death. She had been able to contain herself only by leaving the room, by escaping the sight of him and running to the peacefulness of the orchard or the flower-strewn meadows.

But now, helping him to drink, touching his skin, she felt a bit of what the women had been talking about. It surprised her and disturbed her more than she could say. She felt as if her senses had betrayed her.

"You must be hungry," she said. "I'll go down to the kitchen and get you something to eat."

She stood up then, intending to leave the room, intending to escape all the questions in his dark, troubled eyes.

She felt his hand touch her wrist. His grasp, as he pulled back toward the bed, was amazingly strong considering how long he'd been abed and how badly he was hurt.

John stared at Lida, and at the blond hair he'd

thought so beautiful that night of the storm. It was different now than he remembered, twisted tightly back behind her head and covered with a white prayer cap that hid it from his seeking eyes. She had beautiful skin, pale and creamy with just a touch of sun on her cheeks, and the most incredible blue eyes he'd ever seen. But there was something else in their depths . . . some quiet hidden resentment in those blue eyes that he didn't quite understand.

"You're . . . you're Ephraim's sister," he said. "The one in the barn that night."

"Yes," she said. She was standing very still, making no effort to free her arm from his grasp. Her eyes were cool as she stared down at him.

"Your brother," he began. He took a deep breath, feeling an ache in his side that made him feel dizzy and weak. "Ephraim . . . he was hurt. How is he? Is he all right?"

She pulled away from him then, her eyes turning the color of a winter sky.

"Do you remember what you said to me that night in the barn?" she asked.

"I . . ." He shrugged, grunting softly at the pain in his shoulder when he moved. "I'm not—"

"You said you doubted I knew what it was like to really lose anything," she had to stop for a moment, biting her lips to keep them from trembling. But she couldn't stop the tears that filled her eyes and then spilled slowly down her face. "Well, I know now . . . because I've lost my only brother. Ephraim is dead."

She saw the regret fill his eyes, saw his lips move

as if he wanted to speak. Then he closed his eyes tightly, pushing his head back into the pillow as he made a soft groaning noise of protest.

When he opened his eyes again, she was gone.

Three

John lay very still, letting his troubled gaze move slowly to encompass the room where he lay. He barely remembered coming here. He had no idea how long he'd been here. And although he had known Ephraim was critically wounded when he left him in the barn, he had hoped against hope that he would live.

Could he blame the girl for the look of hatred in those flashing blue eyes?

Lida. Her name was Lida. It seemed to fit somehow with the look of her, from the long flaxen hair to her brilliant eyes. She was tall and, although she was slender, she had the look of a strong, healthy woman with no artifice and no need for the enhancement of powder or rouge on her beautiful sun-warmed skin.

John had dealt with the Amish before, had eaten in their homes many times. Not here, but in other communities. And he had been impressed by the warmth and natural wholesome beauty of the women. There was a glow to their skin, a strong lift in their walk, and although most of them were shy with the English, there was a certain lively look in their eyes. Even beneath their shyness and reserve, he had seen an open curiosity, almost a boldness, not often seen in the women of the *English* world as they called it. There seemed no need for artful pretense among them, no need for coy expressions and denials with these strong Amish women. John had admired that.

But he hadn't realized how much until he looked up a while ago to see every raw emotion of resentment exposed honestly in Lida Rinehart's beautiful, expressive eyes.

As he lay waiting, he touched his chest, feeling the wide neat bandaging that wound tightly around him and across his left shoulder. Gingerly he tried to move, drawing in his breath as the pain caught him in its powerful, surprising grip. It was a few seconds before he could breathe again. Gritting his teeth against the pain and dizziness, he forced himself upward in the bed, reaching behind him with his right hand and gasping as he tried to push the pillow behind his back.

A light sheen of perspiration appeared quickly across his forehead and he found his breathing growing hard and ragged.

Damn, but he was as weak as a newborn baby. He frowned impatiently, thinking he should probably be grateful to be alive after the ambush that lay waiting for him and Ephraim in nearby Tuscarawas County. But all he could think about was all the work he had left to do, about the people who were waiting, depending on him to see them through Ohio to safety. And about Ephraim. A young man with so much enthusiasm for life, and so much eagerness to touch and taste and feel it all.

John thought he had hardened his heart and soul the past months to all the ugliness of war and his part in it. But now, he felt an unaccustomed wrench of his heart at the thought of Ephraim's death.

He knew he couldn't blame Lida Rinehart for the hatred he saw on her lovely face.

"Dammit," he muttered with disgust, shaking his head as he tried again to test the strength of his arms by pushing himself further up in bed.

The door opened and John glanced toward it, surprised by the surge of expectation that ran through him. He'd like a chance to explain to the beautiful Amish girl, to let her know how deeply he regretted her brother's death. And his own inability to save him.

But it wasn't Lida who came into the room. It was instead an older woman, heavier and more rawboned, but one whose eyes were amazingly like Lida's. Except that there was warmth and tenderness in their quiet blue depths as she came toward the bed, carrying a tray of food. Like Lida, this woman wore a plain dark dress and a white organdy apron and Amish cap.

"*Guten Morgen!* It is good to see you are awake finally," she said, her voice carrying a heavy German accent. "Now, at last, we may know your name."

"John," he said, watching the woman closely. This was Lida and Ephraim's mother, he was sure of it. And yet there was no hatred, no resentment in her expression. All he saw was kindness and an infinite patience.

"John we know," she said, setting the tray beside the bed and standing with her hands on her wide hips. "What is your last name?"

"Sexton."

"Well, John Sexton. You have been a very sick man."

She handed him a small glass of some potent-smelling liquid and John frowned.

"What is it?"

"Cabbage juice. It is good you should drink it before eating your first meal. It will prepare the stomach." She smiled at him, still holding the glass toward him.

John shook his head and grunted as the movement caused an excruciating pain in his chest and shoulder. "I . . . I don't think so . . ." he managed.

"Ja," she said with a wise nod. "Drink. It will be good for you."

Finally, sensing she was going to stand there until he agreed, he took the glass and sipped the liquid. He was surprised by its cool, tangy taste. It wasn't bad at all. In fact, he could feel its cool pathway to his empty stomach and it did feel rather soothing.

"Ist gut, ja?" she asked, smiling and nodding.

John coughed and handed the glass back to her.

"Is good, yes," he said, smiling.

"Ah, you understand German?"

"Only a few words I'm afraid," he said.

"Is no worry," she said. "English I know, too. Now, I have brought you a container in which you might relieve yourself. And a wet cloth for your hands and face." Her face as she placed the container in the bed beside John was passive and unremarkable.

But John was hardly prepared for such plain speaking from a woman he'd just met. For a moment he only stared up at her.

"John Sexton, you do not look like a shy man to me," she said, teasing him in a quiet manner. "But of course, I shall leave the room . . . if you need no assistance."

"No," he managed, clearing his throat and frowning. "I think I can manage."

"I will wait outside the door."

Afterward when the woman came back inside, she proceeded to pull a chair beside the bed, obviously intending to feed John.

John felt exhausted and weak, and this time he made no protest as the woman assisted him and began to spoon broth into his mouth.

"Mmmm," he said, leaning his head back against the pillow after a few swallows.

"Is good?"

"Is very good," he said, opening his eyes and smiling at her.

She reminded him of his own mother—so protective and nurturing, and for a moment, he missed her and he missed his home in Tennessee more than he had in a long while. He needed to write and let her know he was all right. When she didn't hear from him she worried.

He hadn't seen her or his father since that terrible day more than a year ago when he'd been forced to leave West Point. After the first shots at Fort Sumter, the cadets had been asked to take an oath of allegiance to the Union. Most of the southerners, including John, had refused. As if that weren't a big enough blow, he'd told his father on arriving home that he had no intention of joining the war effort, either for the North or the South.

"You . . . what?" his father had gasped, seeming stunned. "What are you saying?"

"I'm saying that I have no intention of fighting for either side in this madness. I will serve in some other capacity, but I won't kill another man in a cause that I don't believe in."

His father had been enraged, reminding him vehemently of the sacrifices he'd made to send both him and his brother Nathan to West Point.

"It was Nathan's interest," John said. "Never mine. You know I never intended on a military career."

"By god it should be your interest, too. Sexton men are not cowards."

As always, his father's need to control everyone and everything caused him to see the situation with a completely stilted view. And as always that infuriated John.

"What does it take to please you?" John had shouted, his patience finally at an end. "My death? Nathan's? Would that make you proud? Make you feel that you had fathered heroes instead of cowards? Why don't you admit it, Father?

You couldn't be a soldier, so you want me and Nathan to do it for you."

His father's response had been one of choked disbelief. This was a subject they never discussed. But John had always believed that his father left the army as a young man, not because he was ill as he'd always said, but because he'd been afraid.

"Father . . ." John began with a heavy sigh. "I appreciate all you've done for me. I even began to appreciate West Point after a while. But you know it's not—"

"You will go into town this day and you will join the same company as your brother," his father said, his face red with anger. "And you will fight."

"No, Father . . . I will not."

"Then by God you will leave this house for good."

John's mother, standing near the door, had gasped aloud.

She'd tried to stop her husband, just as she'd tried through the years to stop the sometimes abusive language and treatment her husband heaped upon his sons. It would make them strong, he'd declared. Make them men.

John had turned on his heels that day and left the house in Tennessee, carrying all his possessions in a canvas bag and blanket roll. He had taken the sword he'd worn at West Point and a long-barreled Colt pistol tucked into the waistband of his trousers.

His father had never forgiven him. And probably never would.

John refocused his attention on the present and

the Amish woman who sat spooning broth into his mouth. He found he could only hold a few ounces of food, but the hearty taste and warmth of the broth left him feeling stronger and surprisingly sleepy.

"You rest now," the woman said, placing a soothing hand on his arm.

"Wait," John said, forcing his eyes to remain open for a moment longer. "Thank you," he whispered. "For everything you've done. I . . . I don't even know your name."

"I am Anna Rinehart," she said.

"You're Ephraim's mother."

"Yes." For the first time, a sadness sprang to her blue eyes and she turned away, busying herself with the dishes and tray.

"Mrs. Rinehart," John said, trying to see her face as he spoke. "I'm so sorry."

"No," she said, turning sharply and staring down at him. Her blue eyes were glittering with unshed tears. But she lifted her chin as she stepped closer to the bed. "It is not for you to feel sorry. Not in a guilty way at least. My husband and the rest of the church members would not approve of my saying so, but I will tell you that I am proud of what my son tried to do. And of you, John Sexton."

John hardly knew how to respond to her generosity.

"I cannot fault a man for trying to do what is right. The war is not of our making or of our world. And I hate the sorrow it brings to this good country. But it is here and there is nothing we can do about it. I do not blame you for what happened to my son," she said, her lips trembling. "I thank you for bringing him home to his family. You are a good man I think, John Sexton, and you are welcome here in this house and in this community, for as long as you wish to stay." Her last words were spoken in an almost shy way before she turned and quickly left the room.

John closed his eyes and slid wearily back down into bed. Her words, spoken in a guttural German accent, had soothed him. Yet they surprised him, too. Could anyone actually be so selfless and forgiving? Here was this woman who could forgive him so easily for any part he'd played in her son's death. And yet his own father couldn't forgive him for refusing to join the Confederate army.

Finally, as much as he wanted to stay awake, he found he could no longer fight his exhaustion and overwhelming need for sleep.

His dreams were troubled and restless. He thought he was awake and back in Tennessee and that he faced his fiancée Katherine, after having left his father's house. There was a strange, uneasy quality to what he saw in his mind's eye.

He saw her awkwardness and embarrassment all over again. The way she stammered and shrank away from him when he told her about his disagreement with his father.

"We can go ahead and be married now, if your parents agree," John had told her. "I have an offer to work with an abolitionist group in Ohio. We can move there—you'll be safe and—"

"An abolitionist group?" she had asked. Her

dark eyes had grown troubled and apprehensive. She had actually taken a step away from him. In his dream the words seemed to echo again and again through his mind.

"You mean you want to help *slaves?*" she asked, her voice filled with horror. "But, John, what will people think? What will they say if they know you're actually associating yourself with those people?"

"Those people?" he asked, puzzled for a moment.

She'd wrinkled her nose and looked away from him.

"Good heavens, John. Surely you don't expect me to be a part of such a . . . distasteful adventure." She stepped toward him, lifting her soft beautiful lips toward his, letting her dark hair swing away from her face for just the most flattering display of her beauty.

"Darling," she murmured, touching her fingers lightly to his chest. "Why don't you go back to your papa? Beg his forgiveness and tell him that you'll do as he says. After all it can't be for long. Why your own brother told me just yesterday that they'd run those long-legged Yankees back to Washington so quick—"

She stopped, removing her hand from his chest and stepping away when he made a noise of disgust.

John woke suddenly. He could feel the sweat on his face and neck, and he could still seem to hear Katherine's soft voice, here in this plain, simple room.

"Christ," he groaned, moving restlessly against the bed. All the feelings were back. The hurt and disbelief he'd felt seeing that look on her face. And how completely humiliated he'd felt when he realized that she was not the girl he had imagined her to be.

Katherine was so beautiful. He'd wanted to touch her, even as she sank her words of rejection like a knife into his heart. If the truth were known, he wanted her even now.

He had needed someone to understand. Someone to say honestly and without reservations that they agreed with his decision. And he had wanted that person to be Katherine.

He had hardly believed it when she turned her affections within a matter of days from John to his brother Nathan. But then Nathan was wearing a uniform, and that seemed to appeal greatly to Katherine.

John raked his hand over his face and closed his eyes again

He was surprised when he woke later to find the room dimmed by shadows. He could hardly believe he had slept away the whole long afternoon. He turned his head and glanced out the second-story window, seeing the pale golden glint of waning sunlight that tipped the tops of the trees. For a moment the swaying green leaves of the trees and the twitter of birds flying about in the limbs held his attention. It was a moment before he realized that he was not alone in the room.

He turned his head to see Lida Rinehart lighting a lamp near the bed. She looked so staid and proper in her dark dress and pristine white apron. Her blond hair was tucked sedately away from view, hidden by an accordion-pleated cap.

Once again John was conscious of an odd feeling of disappointment that he couldn't see her hair. He thought of the way she had looked that night in the barn, with her hair falling freely around her face, and strands of it clinging damply to her face and mouth. That memory caused John to take a long, slow steadying breath of air.

She heard him and turned.

"You are awake," she said, her voice cool, her eyes even cooler.

John wasn't sure if it was seeing this beautiful woman near his bed, so alive, so vibrant with health that made him feel the way he did. But suddenly he was impatient to be up, angry even with his inability to do the smallest things for himself. He hoped to God she hadn't come to help him "relieve himself" as her mother had so quaintly put it earlier.

Lida felt her cheeks growing warm as he continued staring at her without speaking. His eyes in the lamplight glittered as he studied her, and despite her vow that she would not let herself feel pity for the man, she frowned when she looked into those gray eyes. Was it sadness Lida saw there? Regret? Or was the dim light merely playing tricks?

Silently she handed him a warm washcloth.

"Shall I . . . ?" she began.

"No," he said, his voice harsher than he intended. Slowly he managed to reach and take the wet cloth from her fingers. "I can do it myself. I don't need a nursemaid."

"Indeed?" she asked with a lift of her brow. "If you ask me, Mr. Sexton, you look like a man who very much needs a nursemaid. In fact you look as if you need to be taken care of like a small, helpless baby." Her eyes glittered as she challenged him.

By God, she wasn't going to cut him any slack, was she? But then John thought she'd made that much clear from the beginning. He licked his dry lips as his eyes glinted dangerously at her. What the hell had he expected? It wasn't as if he wanted to become socially acquainted with the haughty Amish girl. His being here under her care was a mere inconvenience. One he would rectify just as soon as he could drag his battered body out of bed and away from this house.

If there was one thing he'd learned since his refusal to join the war and his fiancée's consequent rejection, it was to confine his attention to women of a decidedly different ilk than this one. And he had no intention of changing that course now, despite the enticement of full pink lips and the lure of silken hair so fine and soft that it practically begged for the touch of a man's hands.

Suddenly, using all the strength he possessed, John swung his legs around and toward the side of the bed, pushing himself into a sitting position with a quiet groan.

Lida moved toward him, her eyes growing wide with surprise as her hands flew to her mouth.

"What . . . what are you doing?" she exclaimed. "You can't possibly—"

John was breathing hard and he felt the unused muscles in his arms begin to tremble from the exertion. But he refused to give in to it. Instead, he slid even further until he was sitting on the side of the bed.

"I'm going to accommodate you, Miss Rinehart," he said, his voice rasping with fatigue. "By getting out of here."

"No," she whispered, her eyes gleaming with alarm. "No, you can't. You are too weak. For heaven's sake, you almost died," she added. For the first time, there was the slightest hint of concern in her eyes.

"Well, I . . . didn't die," he said, grunting from the pain of his movements.

"Please," she said, stepping toward him with an outstretched hand. "Don't—"

But John was already on his feet, swaying slightly. As he straightened, he felt the room spinning, felt his heart pounding hard against his ribs. And when he reached his hand up to his forehead, he saw a gray mist and then the glitter of bright lights flash before his eyes.

Lida saw the blood drain from the man's face, saw the glazed look in his eyes, and she knew he was going to faint. She stepped forward, quickly sliding her arms around his bare chest and waist and holding onto him with every ounce of strength she possessed.

But despite her height and strength, she could not hold him. He was a big man, well over six feet, and although he was lean and trim, he was built with solid, muscular strength.

All she could do was try to cushion his fall as both of them fell toward the bed.

Lida fell on top of him, hard against his chest, and as she pulled herself away, her hands went instinctively to the pulse in his neck. She had tended him before, but her entire body had never touched his in such a way, and for a moment she felt too stunned by the new sensation of it to move. The warmth of him, the firmness of his body and the evidence of his strong, steadily beating heart beneath her fingers was too enticing. Seeing that he was all right, she breathed a sigh of relief.

But now she was trembling and she actually felt grateful that he was unconscious so he could not see how disconcerted she was.

She scrambled away from him, alarmed by the stain of red that was beginning to spread across his bandage.

"Oh, dear," she murmured

Quickly she pulled his legs around into bed and brought a quilt up to his waist. Lying there, he looked so young and vulnerable, so different than he looked when he stared at her with those cold, defiant eyes. Her gaze turned for the briefest moment to his muscular chest and shoulders, to his strong chin and wide sensual mouth. His dark lashes lay against the paleness of his skin, and for a moment, Lida felt a deep, longing surge of grief inside her chest that made her want to cry. Grief for Ephraim, for herself and her family, and yes, even for this man and all he had suffered as well.

She shook the feeling away and took a deep breath as she bent to turn up the wick of the lamp. She began quickly to examine him to see what damage the fall had caused to his wound.

It was bleeding again and although there seemed to be a great amount of blood for a few moments, there was no new redness around the bullet hole and no extraordinary heat of infection when she placed her hand there.

Her mother would be so upset with her if she knew what Lida had done. Being so cold and indifferent to a seriously wounded man would be unforgivable in her eyes. And not only had she been cold, she had openly challenged and taunted him with her words. But she hadn't intended to make him so angry that he would reopen his wound.

Still, Lida couldn't help the way she felt; she couldn't help the resentment. Not when she saw this man alive and healthy, while her brother lay in the cold ground of the cemetery past their orchard.

From now on she would stay away from John Sexton. She would find excuses not to come here. There were, no doubt, plenty of other girls who couldn't wait for their turn to nurse the handsome dark-haired English stranger. Lida would just have to see that they did.

John stirred, groaning softly as his lashes fluttered, then lifted.

Lida found herself staring once again into those

riveting gray eyes, watching as they cleared, seeing the recognition in them, then the bitter defiance.

"You shouldn't have tried to get up so soon," she said quietly, as she dabbed the camphoric-smelling *Zeek Schmer* on the wound and finished placing a new bandage on his shoulder.

"Perhaps I should make one thing clear to you, Miss Rinehart," John said, his voice quiet and a bit weak. "I don't want to be here any more than you want me to be. As soon as I'm remotely able to ride, I'll be out of your life for good."

"Ride?" she said, not meeting his steady gaze. "I'm afraid that might take a while. You lost a great deal of blood and when you fell just now, the wound started to bleed again. It could take weeks to build back your strength."

"I don't have weeks," he muttered impatiently. "How did you manage to get me back into bed?" he asked, glancing to the spot where they'd stood.

Lida glanced up then, meeting his gaze. She didn't find the glint of amusement in those gray depths funny at all.

"I . . . you . . . we fell across the bed," she said, her voice hushed and hurried. "Or you might have been seriously injured."

"We?" he asked with a rakish twinkle in his eyes. "You mean, you and I? Together? The very prim and proper Amish Miss tumbled on this very bed with a dangerous English like me?" He smoothed his hand across the quilt toward Lida and she jumped up to stand glaring down at him.

"Oh my," he murmured. "Now I've frightened you," he drawled. His words might sound regretful, but there was not a hint of remorse in those gleaming gray eyes.

"No, you don't frighten me at all," she said coolly.

"You do have to admit it's an intriguing situation," he said, his voice mocking. "It's just a pity I was unconscious."

Lida pursed her lips together, looking like a disapproving schoolmistress as she glared at him.

"I don't find your jokes funny in the least," she said.

"Jokes?" he asked with mock innocence. His eyes changed then, becoming dark, the amusement almost gone. "I assure you, Miss Rinehart, I'm not joking. I can't think of anything more intriguing then the thought of you and I in the same bed. Of course I'd like to be awake the next time. And who knows, you might even enjoy it, too."

"I doubt that," she said with a huff, feeling her cheeks flame. She knew he was only trying to distract her and make her angry. She turned around and picked up the dirty bandages, determined that he would not accomplish his goal. "I'll have someone bring your supper up to you," she said, as she walked toward the door.

"Not you?" he asked, still mocking her.

"No, not me," she muttered, clenching her teeth together.

"Lida," he said, his voice deep and forceful.

She turned, not answering him, but waiting at the door.

"Whether you believe it or not, I am sorry about your brother."

She frowned, hating the lump that came to her throat and the unexpected tears that his quiet words brought to her eyes. She had no idea what to say.

"He was a fine young man . . . a strong, brave man. And one day before I leave—when you're ready—I'll tell you everything that happened."

Lida stared across the room at him, meeting his solemn gaze. Then she whirled around and ran out of the room.

Four

Lida's hurried footsteps rang hollowly in the confines of the narrow upstairs hallway. She was fighting back her emotions as she turned the corner toward the enclosed stairwell. She knew her mother was probably still in the kitchen, but she didn't expect anyone else to be about. When she saw her cousin and best friend, Christela Dietz, running up the stairs, she stopped and quickly wiped her eyes.

Christela stopped, looking up at Lida with wide eyes that were so dark they looked almost black.

"Lida?" she asked. "What has happened? You look as if the world itself is on your shoulders." Her voice lilted with the sound of her Swiss and German ancestry.

Lida stood at the top of the stairs, shoulders slumped, arms hanging at her sides. She shook her head and slowly stepped forward one step, then sank down, stretching her long, black-stockinged legs down the stairs.

"Oh Christela," she whispered, shaking her head. As was their habit when they spoke to another Amish, Lida now spoke German. "I don't know why he makes me feel this way. I know it isn't good to be this way with a stranger and an English at that. The deacons would probably call me to public confession if they knew how I behaved."

"How you behaved?" Christela came up and sat on one of the steps below Lida. Her dark eyes were wide with curiosity as she stared up at her cousin. "Exactly what do you mean? Did you and this handsome stranger upstairs in your bed . . . ?"

"Oh, for goodness sake," Lida said, huffing with quiet exasperation at the gleam in Christela's eyes. Knowing the girl's penchant for romanticizing everyone and everything—especially the English men—Lida should have explained herself better. "It's certainly nothing like that. I . . . I was awful to him . . . mean and uncharitable. Mother would be hurt if she knew. For some reason she's taken him under her wing like a motherless chick."

"My mother says he is taking Ephraim's place."

"He can never take Ephraim's place," Lida said. "Never!"

"I know . . . I know," Christela said, beginning to understand Lida's resentment. "I have watched you these last few days," she said. "And even though there's been little time for talking, I had a feeling when you spoke of what happened to Ephraim, that you blame this John Sexton somehow."

"I do blame him!" Lida came up from the stairs and bounded down, not waiting for her friend. "I hate him for what he's done."

Christela followed, finally managing to catch

Lida as they came out of the stairway enclosure into the farmhouse's main living room.

"Wait, Lida," Christela hissed. "Stop this running away. We must talk about it. You are not yourself lately."

"Of course I'm not myself," Lida snapped, focusing bright blue eyes upon the dark-haired girl. "And who would be? My brother is dead. My poor, sweet Ephraim who was so guileless, so trusting . . ." A sob caught in Lida's throat and she quickly disguised it by clamping her lips together tightly. Stubbornly she blinked away the tears that burned behind her lids.

"The members, they say that Ephraim had gone against the church and was working secretly with this man. Is it true?" Christela asked. "Was Ephraim actually helping slaves to escape from their masters in the south?"

Lida knew that Ephraim's secret would be safe with Christela, just as it was with all the members of the tight-knit community.

"Yes," Lida hissed, glancing about nonetheless as she admitted the words. "I blame myself, too. I knew several weeks ago what he was doing. I should have told papa then. He would have put a stop to it if I had."

"Lida," Christela said, her voice quiet and filled with a hint of pity. "Do you really think he could have stopped Ephraim when he set his mind to anything? He was as stubborn as you . . . stubborner, if that's possible," she added with an affectionate smile. "He would have *left* the plain people before he would have given up on something in which he believed. Perhaps in your heart you knew what would have happened if you told your father. Ephraim would have been lost to the church and to you."

"He's lost to me now!" Lida said, almost shouting. "But now he's lost forever. If he had been shunned, at least my eyes could still have seen him. I could have spoken with him. Now I have nothing of him left . . . nothing!"

"Oh, Lida," Christela said, reaching her arms forward. "I am so sorry."

The two girls embraced. Dusk had settled over the house and the living room had grown gray and shadowy.

Lida could hear the sounds of her mother's work in the kitchen near the back of the house. And as she pulled away from her friend's comforting embrace, she took a deep breath, acknowledging to herself the peace and the serenity that her home and her mother's presence always gave her.

"Besides being my favorite cousin, you're also a very good friend, Christela," Lida said, attempting a smile. "And you're right. I should talk about it. I'm afraid I've avoided everyone lately."

"It's all right," Christela said. "I am here, whenever you need me. You know that."

"I do. Now," Lida said with a rather sheepish look. "There is one thing I do need you to do. Would you mind taking supper up to Herr Sexton? I would prefer not seeing him at all, much less having to feed the man."

"Why . . . of course, I'd be happy to."

Lida was surprised at the light that appeared in Christela's dark eyes. She frowned at her as the girl fairly bolted from the room and back toward the kitchen.

For the rest of the week Lida managed to avoid actually seeing the man upstairs in her bedroom. She even managed to fend off her mother's questions about why she was so busy she couldn't tend John Sexton or take his meals up to him.

What she couldn't manage to do was avoid Christela's sighs and giggles when she spoke of John. Or any of the conversations that tended to drift toward him when the neighboring girls came to a quilting at the Rinehart house on Friday afternoon.

And she hadn't been able to get away from the deep rumble of his voice through the walls of the upstairs bedrooms. Or the sound of quiet conversation between him and the women tending him. What Lida couldn't understand was how everyone could find him so personable, when she herself could hardly stand him.

By Saturday evening she couldn't pretend any longer about her efforts to avoid John. At supper her mother quietly mentioned it as her father gazed across the table at his only daughter. His eyes were so much like Ephraim's. And for a moment, Lida wondered if he had ever been as carefree and spirited, as tempted to run and see the world as his only son had been.

"We are worried about you, daughter," her mother said. "It has been over two weeks since John Sexton brought your brother home to be buried. You know the church's feelings about the outside world. We are to try and bring healing and to witness about a higher way of life. Have you forgotten?"

"No, Mother," Lida said quietly, knowing exactly what her mother was leading to.

"We do not wish to change the world, or the English, but with our kindness we can perhaps help them see what is right and good. And what the plain people believe."

Lida's gaze rested on the tablecloth. She couldn't meet her mother's eyes or her father's. She merely sat meekly, forcing herself to listen and to acquiesce. She had quietly sworn to herself that she would not bring them any more sorrow than they'd already had. And if that meant pretending meekness and acquiesence, then so be it.

"You know it is an Amish father's wish to see his children remain *in the fold,* to show our spirit to the world. Do you think you are doing this, daughter?" her father asked. "Do you think you are witnessing to the world with your kindness and charitable love . . . to the English . . . and most of all to John Sexton?"

Lida's gaze flew up and she stared at his eyes in the lamplight. The house was so quiet; through the screen door there came the pleasant noises of frogs and crickets, and the faint whirring clack of the windmill out toward the barn. Inside the kitchen, a clock ticked loudly.

"I . . . yes," she said, knowing she was lying. Knowing they knew she was lying. "Yes, I think so."

"Nein, Liebling," her father said, shaking his

head. His eyes were kind. Lida had always thought her father had the kindest, calmest eyes of anyone she'd ever known. "You know very well what your mother and I mean." For a moment his gaze moved upward, as if toward the upstairs bedroom, and he nodded.

Suddenly Lida could contain herself no longer. She jumped up from the table, her fists clenched at her sides. Two spots of color appeared on her cheeks.

"He's responsible for Ephraim's death," she said, her voice breathless with agitation. "How can you sit here so calmly . . ." she turned from her father to her mother. "How can both of you behave as if nothing has happened? As if that man lying upstairs didn't lure him away from us . . . as if—"

"Enough," her father said. "You are wrong to blame him, daughter." There still was no anger in his eyes. Only a quiet sadness, a regret that only hinted at what he must be feeling inside. Ephraim was his beloved son—the one who should have inherited all of Jacob Rinehart's hopes and dreams. The one who would have carried on the highest Amish tradition of family and loyalty and good living.

Like water on a blazing fire, her father's look took away all of Lida's anger and made her feel ashamed.

"We have worked hard today, myself and the other women, cooking and cleaning," her mother said, intervening as she often did. "Church meeting will be held here tomorrow, and since I will be very busy, I will expect you to attend to John while we are in service."

"But—"

"No buts," her father said. He picked up his fork and began to eat again, dismissing Lida's protests. The conversation was ended as far as he was concerned.

Lida looked from her mother's quietly sympathetic eyes to her father's bent head. Then she turned from the table, forcing herself to walk from the kitchen with a calmness she didn't feel.

But once outside in the gathering dusk, her feigned patience left her and she leapt from the porch, running along the neatly laid flagstone path that ran from the house to the barn. Once out of sight of the house, she veered away from the path, racing across the green lawn and toward the orchard.

John Sexton stood at the upstairs bedroom window. Now that he was finally able to stand and walk a few steps, he had forced himself every hour or so to walk, and regain his strength. Every day he demanded more and more of his body. He was determined to leave the Rinehart's farm. Not because he didn't feel welcome. He had never felt more welcome anywhere in his life, not even in his own home. And not because of the girl. It had nothing to do with her. It had to do with all the things he needed to do.

The war had brought the Underground Railroad back to life as slaves feared what would happen in the south. And John's work as a conductor had become the most important thing in his life. It gave him purpose and meaning. And even though he had been deliberately misleading when he told Lida he did it for the money, that part was not entirely untrue. One day when the war was over, if he lived, he hoped to use that money to buy his own farm. Being here among the Amish, seeing the splendor and richness of their farms, he felt an eagerness to finish his work and for the war to end, so he could get on with his life.

Being here had decided one thing for him anyway. He would be finished with violence and wars and fighting. He realized now that he'd consented to a military career only to please his father. Now there was no need for that.

All he wanted was to work the land, to watch the crops grow in the green fertile Tennessee valley along the Nolichucky River. To see cattle and horses grow fat and healthy. Watching the Amish children play beneath his window, he had even considered the possibility of having sons and daughters of his own.

He shook his head, seeing an image of blond-haired, blue-eyed children. Seeing them held in the arms of Lida Rinehart.

He frowned and raked his hand across his eyes. How could he be having such thoughts about an Amish girl like Lida? She was forbidden as far as he and his life were concerned. He was tired, that was all. He needed to go back to bed.

It was then, out of the corner of his eye, that he saw a movement in the yard below. He moved closer to the window, holding his aching shoulder as he gazed hard into the growing darkness.

He knew who it was; he sensed it. It was Lida Rinehart who raced across the yard with her black skirts billowing, her black-stockinged legs reaching out in front of her like a carefree child's.

But he thought she seemed anything but carefree. She ran as if some very real, private demon chased her. He could see the anger, the frustration in every movement of her body. He watched in fascination as she reached up and raked her cap from her head, allowing her hair to fly free about her face and around her shoulders. It glimmered in the dusky shadows like something alive, its pale color fairly illuminating the darkness.

John didn't realize he was holding his breath until he felt the ache in his chest. Slowly he let the air out of his lungs, his eyes darkening as he continued watching the beautiful, but mystifying young woman.

Where was she going? And what was troubling her?

Even after Lida had disappeared into the darkness, John continued staring out the window, the vision of her still clear in his mind. It was only the trembling weakness of his overtired legs and his throbbing shoulder that forced him away finally and back to the bed.

But he lay in the darkness for what seemed like hours, seeing the visions of her again and again. Wondering what it would be like to touch that fall of silken hair. Imagining the texture and scent of her sun-drenched skin, the sweet taste of those full pink lips. He wondered what the feel of her strong healthy body would be like beneath his.

"Dear God," he muttered, moving restlessly in the bed. He surprised himself where this girl was concerned. His body had grown hard just thinking such forbidden thoughts about her, and he cursed himself for allowing his mind to drift in that direction.

John had heard that Amish girls were not falsely modest as far as men were concerned. They were both earthy and virginal, a practical breed of people raised in an open farm atmosphere where the everyday facts of animals breeding and giving birth could not be hidden. They considered it normal and healthy. And he knew that even though the church forbade any sort of promiscuity, it was also not unusual for the girls to begin courting early or to marry at sixteen or seventeen.

He'd wondered more than once about Lida. Did she have a young man who courted her? Had she been kissed and touched, perhaps already lain with a young, eager Amish lover? Always before when such thoughts came, John had made himself think of something else.

Tonight that was an impossibility. His body refused to cooperate.

Besides, nothing could ever come of what he was feeling for Lida Rinehart. Even if she were willing, which God knew she wasn't.

John could hardly pursue her, make love to her, then leave her to face the possible consequences of a child. And he certainly couldn't offer her anything else.

IF she were even willing, he reminded himself again.

Cursing, John turned over onto his right side, pushing the pillow beneath his head and taking a deep, strengthening breath of air.

"Sleep," he muttered, as if saying it aloud would make it happen.

He told himself she was probably running to meet a lover. Might even be in his arms now, allowing him to touch her full firm breasts, offering her mouth to him with all the sweet, hot delight of a young woman in love.

John groaned and kicked the quilt off his legs. Then he pushed himself upright in bed, feeling a sheen of perspiration on his body.

"Dammit," he muttered angrily, impatiently. He closed his eyes and raked his hand down his face.

It looked as if it was going to be a long, hot, miserable night.

Five

It was early Sunday morning when John heard the sound of horses and the rattle of carriage wheels near the house. He had been awake for a long time and now he walked to the window to watch the row of black buggies that came up the road and turned into the long driveway leading to the Rinehart farmhouse.

Children in their somber Amish dress and black shoes and stockings scattered from the buggies as some were parked beneath trees near the house. John watched as others drove past the house toward the barn.

He had sensed and heard a flurry of activity in the house long before dawn. And yesterday he had noticed the same thing. The house had been filled with women and the scent of baking bread and pies had filled the air around the big white farmhouse. From his window he had seen men whitewashing the long fence from the house to the barn, and trimming the lawn and the shrubbery.

Mrs. Rinehart had visited him for a while, telling him about the preparations for today's preaching. She had explained to him how the Amish used their homes or barns for church services every other Sunday.

"I guess I didn't realize that the Amish don't use churches," he'd said.

"The Lord dwelleth not in temples made with hands," she replied, as she busied herself about his room.

He wondered about the services now as he watched the children darting about on the emerald green lawn. The boys all wore broad-brimmed black hats and long-sleeved white shirts, some beneath black vests and others with long-sleeved black jackets.

John laughed as he watched them, thinking their playfulness and obvious enjoyment of the outdoors seemed a little incongruous with their somber-looking clothes.

Adult men and women greeted one another with warm handshakes and nods of welcome. The girls and young women, although still very primly attired, wore long, full dresses in lighter colors—blues and dark green, maroon and orchid. They also wore neat white aprons and white prayer caps.

John was still at the window watching the scene below when he heard the door open behind him.

He was surprised to see Lida, since he knew she'd been avoiding him the past few days. From the look in her eyes, she was just as surprised to see him up and about.

"Good morning," he murmured. He watched her expression closely, wondering if she still despised and resented him. And wondering wistfully what she would think if she had any idea of the miserable hours he'd spent last night on her behalf.

Lida muttered something not quite intelligible and went to set his breakfast tray beside the bed. Then she glanced up, meeting his gaze for a moment before she picked the tray back up and walked briskly to a table and chair on the other side of the room.

"I guess you don't have to eat in bed anymore," she said.

John noticed that Lida wasn't dressed the way the other young women in the yard were.

"Aren't you going to church?" he asked.

She turned to stare at him, her blue eyes cool and unreadable when she replied.

"Are you curious about the Amish ways?" she asked. She'd seen his gray eyes move over her with open interest . . . over her plain dress and pleated *Kapp*.

"I'm curious about *you.*"

His voice when he spoke was deep and warm. And there was an intimacy in the quietness of it that disturbed Lida. Against her will a tiny shiver raced down her spine.

Two worry lines appeared between her eyes as she glanced at him, then looked away. What in the world was happening to her? She busied herself with the dishes of food that she set on the small table.

"Please . . . eat," she said. She took the tray and wrapped her arms around it, holding it in front of her as if to hide herself from his probing eyes.

John turned and glanced out the window, nodding with his head before he walked slowly across the room.

"You hold your meeting in the barn?"

"Some do," she replied. "Some districts hold church inside their homes. But ours is a big district, and as you can see the families here have many children. Our living room will not hold them all."

John held his aching shoulder as he slowly lowered himself onto the chair. Lida didn't miss the pained expression on his face and the pinched look around his mouth as he settled himself. He was still very weak, but he seemed determined to do just as he had threatened over a week ago. To make himself well so that he could leave the Amish farm as quickly as possible.

"Shall I bring something for your pain?"

"No," he said quickly, with a stubborn shake of his head. But truthfully, his shoulder ached so badly this morning that it almost took his breath away. In fact the pain made him feel sick, and the sight of the hearty farm breakfast in front of him suddenly seemed unappetizing.

He forced himself to eat, knowing he needed it for strength and recuperation. And because he didn't want to offend Lida any more than he already had. He ate slowly, sipping a cool glass of milk and letting it soothe his stomach.

Through the open window came the sound of

singing from the barn, a slow chantlike sound with no musical accompaniment.

"I like it," he said, cocking his head toward the window.

"It is from the *Ausbund.*"

He grunted, having no idea what the *Ausbund* was, but assuming it was an Amish hymnbook of some kind. Lida's cool manner did not exactly encourage conversation.

John waved his fork toward the window, glancing up at Lida with a shrug of his broad shoulders.

"I don't expect you to stay here with me," he said. "If you want to go to the services—"

"I will remain here," she said with a slight lift of her chin. Her eyes were a clear, cerulean blue as she met his gaze.

"I thought only sick people could stay away from Amish services," he said. "I remember someone telling me that even tiny babies are required to go."

"I have been ordered to the house today," she replied, still standing stiffly and formally in front of him.

"Because of me."

"Because of you."

"Why do I feel as if I should apologize for that," he asked, his eyes glittering as he met her resentful gaze.

"Is there anything else you require?" she asked, ignoring his comment.

"Yes, as a matter of fact, there is," he said, leaning back in his chair. His gray eyes met and challenged hers. He put down his fork and shrugged his wounded shoulder slightly. "This bandage is too tight. Could you loosen it a bit?"

Lida clamped her lips together, then carefully placed the tray aside. She walked to him, conscious of his steady gaze, conscious of being alone with a man she hardly knew. A man whose presence troubled her and whose gaze was intense and more dangerous than any other she'd ever seen. She shivered, hesitating for a second as she stood before him, fingers outstretched toward the buttons of his shirt.

John held his breath, waiting for her touch, knowing he shouldn't be teasing her this way. Knowing he shouldn't be tempting himself.

But her arrogance intrigued him and some instinct made him want to shake her out of her smug complacency.

"Well?" he asked, his lips moving to the side with mock humor.

Lida knew he was taunting her, but she remembered her father's words last night and her vow not to cause her parents any more problems. She took a deep breath and quickly reached for the buttons. She caught the scent of soap and she couldn't help noticing his smooth, clean-shaven face, so different from the Amish men. For a second she closed her eyes against the strange, overpowering urge to touch his face, to test its warmth and smoothness with her fingers.

Her hands were trembling as she finally began to unbutton the shirt. It would have been easier if he had been standing. As it was she had to bend very near to him to undo the shirt, and it didn't help matters that his riveting gaze rested on her face all the while.

He was wearing one of Ephraim's shirt and she tried to concentrate on that. To force her mind to remember her brother and the resentment she should be feeling at this moment. But nothing seemed to work. Nothing seemed to penetrate her mind except this man's nearness, his blatant masculinity, and the hard feel of muscles beneath the material of his shirt.

With a quick little breath she unbuttoned the shirt enough to push it away from his bandaged shoulder. The bandage was knotted behind his shoulder, making it awkward to reach while he was sitting and she standing.

"I can't . . . it's . . ." Lida frowned, catching her lower lip between her teeth as she concentrated on untying the knot.

John couldn't seem to take his eyes off her mouth and when he saw the dart of her pink tongue and the way her even white teeth pulled at her full sensuous lip, he couldn't suppress a groan that came up from somewhere deep inside his chest.

"I'm sorry," Lida murmured, thinking she had hurt him. She barely glanced at him, but dropped to her knees, hardly aware in her engrossing task, of leaning against his leg, until she heard John curse quietly.

She glanced up then, seeing a look in his eyes that she'd never seen in any man's before. And yet instinctively she knew what it was and what it meant.

For a moment she stared into those eyes, caught by surprise and some deep unnamed primitive longing that she could not explain.

Suddenly she was all too aware of his skin beneath her fingers, of the whisper of his breath against her hair, and the touch of her breast against his knee. She pulled her hands away from his bandaged shoulder, holding them in midair as she continued staring into his stormy gray eyes. She couldn't speak, couldn't seem to make herself move.

John let his breath out with a quiet grunt, then closed his eyes. He swallowed hard, shaking his head before opening his eyes again.

It had been a mistake. Thinking he could tease and taunt her had been a very bad mistake. One with tormenting repercussions.

His hand shot forward, clamping around her fingers as he pulled himself and her upright. Once they were standing, he let go of her hand and stepped back away from her, careful not to look at her mouth or the puzzled look in those beautiful eyes.

"Never mind," he said, his voice sounding hoarse. "Just leave it."

"But I—"

"I said leave it," he snapped. He turned from her, stalking to the window and resting his healthy shoulder against the window frame as he gazed out at the spring sunshine and tried to slow his breathing.

He turned his head to look at her over his shoulder. She was standing very still in the middle of the room, her hands clasped at her waist as she stared at him with a troubled gaze. The look in her eyes was enough to make him want to walk back to her and pull her into his arms.

Almost.

"Well, go on," he said instead, frowning at her. "Get out of here. You obviously don't want to be here, so go on . . . leave."

Lida wasn't sure why tears sprang to her eyes. Except that it had been happening a lot since Ephraim's death. But this time there was a sudden, strange new ache that accompanied it in her heart. One she couldn't explain.

She didn't like the feeling, and she certainly didn't like the tone of John Sexton's voice when he spoke to her. Not to mention the disdainful look in those cool eyes. He probably thought she was just a stupid, clumsy farmgirl . . . someone he'd rather not have around.

She lowered her hands to her side with a quick, defiant motion, then turned to stride toward the door.

"You're right," she said over her shoulder. "I don't want to be here."

Lida was happy her mother was at service and not in the house. For she would surely ask why her daughter slammed the door so hard that the echo sounded throughout the house and rattled the upstairs windows.

She muttered beneath her breath, cursing in

German as she clamored down the stairs and hurried through the rest of the house.

If she couldn't attend services, at least she could sit outside and listen to the singing. She would be away from the hateful English upstairs and still be able to appease her mother's sense of duty and charity.

She wasn't going to let this man disturb her Sunday. She wasn't.

Six

John paced back and forth in the upstairs bedroom, his long legs reaching out restlessly as he walked. The exercise seemed to make his shoulder better. At least it was distracting.

He was impatient with himself. Weakness and inability was as foreign to him as another language. What he really wanted to do was go downstairs, find Lida, and talk to her, shake some sense into her if he had to. Make her listen to him for a change.

Kiss her. Hold her . . . release her long silken hair from that prim little cap.

"Stop it, dammit," he muttered, crashing his fist against a wall.

He had to get out of here. Somehow he had to find the strength to leave this place, and soon. Before he lost what little control he now possessed.

John decided that if he could pace the bedroom, he could certainly make it down the stairs. Perhaps being outdoors in the sunshine, walking in the green grass, smelling the fresh air and lovely flowers planted in the yard, was just what he needed to regain some perspective.

Downstairs it was very quiet. There was no one

in the house and the sound of singing from the barn had stopped. John stood for a while, resting against a door frame as he surveyed the room at the bottom of the stairs. It was a kind of sitting room—fully furnished, but plain. There were colorful hand-hooked rugs on the floor, two large rocking chairs near a fireplace. Above a backless settee that was against a far wall, there was a row of pegs on which hung several black coats. No doubt they belonged to Lida's father.

Mr. Rinehart had never come into the room where he was, and now John wondered if perhaps Ephraim's father was as resentful of his presence, of his being alive even, as his daughter seemed to be.

He stepped into the kitchen, nodding with approval at the clean spacious room. A colorful cloth covered the long kitchen table that sat four or five feet away from a huge black cookstove. Today the table was filled with cakes and pies and loaves of freshly baked bread. An oil lamp sat in the middle of the table and one hung suspended from a chain just above it. Long benches sat on either side of the table and at each end there were chairs. A large cabinet sat on the other side of the room. On it were several jars of canned vegetables and a covered wooden cheese box.

It was a very pleasant room, one that would serve not only as a kitchen and dining room, but would also welcome conversation or reading. John could imagine children playing in such a room while their mother cooked.

His stomach rumbled loudly and he realized he

was hungry. And feeling much better now that he had managed to distract the pain in his shoulder.

Stepping to the black cookstove, John peered into the warming shelf and found a loaf of bread. He pulled a large chunk of it loose and then walked to the open door, intending to go outside.

"What are you doing?"

Lida came up onto the porch, stopping in front of him with her hands on her hips.

John shrugged and took a bite of the bread. "Did you make this?"

"You shouldn't be downstairs," she scolded. "You are still too weak. What if you had fallen down the stairs. What if—"

"But I didn't," he said, amused by her quiet berating. "I'm fine, but a little tired of being cooped up in that room." He held up his hand. "The bread is good."

"Oh, you are so exasperating when you do that," she said, staring at him with bright eyes.

"Do what?"

"When you change the subject or pretend you don't hear. Do you ever pay attention to anything anyone tells you?"

"I try not to," he answered dryly.

"Well, at least sit down," she said, pushing her way past him into the kitchen. "Come in and sit down at the table while you finish the bread. My mother will be most upset with me if I let anything happen to you."

"Oh, and I thought all this concern for my well-being was personal." John stepped into the kitchen and sat at the table.

"No," she snapped. "I assure you it is not."

She poured a glass of milk from a blue stoneware pitcher and pushed it toward him.

"Drink this."

"My, but your hospitality is really quite endearing," he said sarcastically.

Lida didn't answer, but turned away from his amused eyes.

Both of them heard the sound of horses outside at the same moment. Lida went to the kitchen door and glanced out, then turned to John with a frown.

"It's the sheriff and two of his deputies," she said. "Do you think they could be looking for you? Perhaps you should go back upstairs."

John frowned. They probably were looking for him. He knew this sheriff, knew how he despised Negroes and how he delighted in catching those responsible for helping them escape through his territory. In fact he wouldn't be surprised if this particular man knew all about the ambush that had killed Ephraim Rinehart.

"I have no intention of leaving you here alone, Lida, if—"

"For goodness sake," she muttered, coming to the table and pulling at his shirtsleeves. "Don't be *verrückt*. I know these men—they are not going to harm a good Amish girl."

"Verrückt?" he asked, his eyes twinkling.

"Crazy," she said quickly, widening her eyes. "Now, please . . . go upstairs until they have gone." Her look for once was free of anger and resentment. It held only concern and just the slightest hint of fear.

For all his teasing, John didn't like seeing fear in those beautiful eyes. Without thinking, he reached forward, touching her cheek, feeling for only a moment the softness of her skin. And yet even that slightest touch sent a jolt through him that took him completely by surprise.

"All right," he said reluctantly, rising from the table.

"Go," she said, glancing toward the open door. "Go," she said more urgently.

John glanced over his shoulder, still not sure he should leave her alone to face the men who were walking toward the house. But from the weakness he felt, he had to admit that he would probably be of little help even if she did need him.

He waited just inside the stairway leading upstairs. He could tell from the sound of voices that Lida had stepped outside onto the porch to speak to the men, and although he could hear the rumble of male voices, he could not understand what was being said.

He was standing with his back against the wall, one foot propped on the first stair, when he heard Lida come into the living room and toward the stairs.

"They've gone," she said, her voice low-pitched and slightly breathless.

"What did they want?"

"They were looking for a man called the Sojourner, a man who helps runaway slaves move across Kentucky and Ohio." There was an odd knowing look in her eyes as she faced him.

John pursed his lips. She knew he was involved in the Underground Railroad and he wondered if she guessed that the capricious title belonged to him. He couldn't tell if she knew or not. Her eyes in the dimly lit stairway were grim and unreadable.

"I told them we did not know such a man." Lida stepped into the enclosure and stood with her back against the opposite wall, studying John's face as she spoke. "The sheriff asked how my brother died."

John pushed himself away from the wall. His hands shot forward to take her shoulders, his fingers digging with unthinking cruelty into her flesh.

"He's connected Ephraim to the Sojourner? What did he say exactly?"

"There's no need to worry. I told him Ephraim's death was an accident." Lida glanced away from John's penetrating gaze. "I told him that he fell from the top of the barn right here on our farm." There was only the slightest catch in her voice as she said the words.

John thought he'd never experienced anything like the anguish that ripped through him, hearing her softly spoken words. She had lied for him. This good, religious girl, who had probably never done a wrong thing in her life, had lied to protect him. Despite her opposition to the war and to his part in it. Despite the fact that she despised him for what had happened to her brother.

"God . . . Lida," he whispered. "I'm sorry . . ."

Acting purely on instinct and emotion, he pulled her forward into his arms, mindless of the ache in his shoulder. His fingers moved behind her head, seemingly of their own accord, touching the sleek, tightly wound hair, fingering its softness. The sweet strength of her body, the clean, fresh scent of her hit him like a bolt of lightning.

He was surprised that she offered no protest, that she came willingly, eagerly almost into his embrace. He held her, rocked her, and murmured quietly spoken words of regret against her ear.

John could feel his body stirring to life, just the way it had last night when he saw her racing across the yard and then upstairs this morning when she had touched him. Reluctantly he pulled away from her disturbing body, still holding her shoulders and gazing down into her eyes. Somehow he had to get it through his head that this woman was forbidden to him.

"I don't like being the one who causes you to lie," he said.

"A lie can be forgiven if it is made for the right reason," she said. There was a strange look in her eye when she spoke. "Father and the members had already decided what story we would tell about Ephraim if anything like this happened."

John took a deep breath and nodded.

"I see," he said.

How foolish of him to think that she might be protecting him, that the look in her eyes could actually be out of concern for him.

"What I have to do is find a way to get out of

here," he said. "If the sheriff comes back, or anyone else looking for me, I don't want this to happen again."

Lida had backed away from him. She seemed as disturbed by their embrace as he was, but John had a feeling it was for completely different reasons than his.

"Father says you are welcome to stay here as long as you wish. It is not our custom to turn anyone away who needs help."

John found her words sweet and soothing. He was not used to having her speak so softly and kindly to him. For a moment as he gazed at her in the darkness of the stairway, he felt the urge to reach for her again.

Lida saw the look in John's eye. That look she'd seen before upstairs in the bedroom.

"I . . . I have to go," she said. "To begin arrangements for our after church meal."

She couldn't explain the feeling she had when she looked in this man's eyes. It was a wild, tumultuous feeling, one she could only assume stemmed from her reluctance to be in his company. Still, it was disturbing. And she could not for the life of her explain why she had let him hold her just now. Or how she could possibly have enjoyed it.

She backed away into the living room.

"Why don't you rest now? And since you are able to be up and about, you are welcome to take your noon meal with us today. The others know about you, and they are curious and I'm sure eager to meet you."

John watched as Lida turned away and hurried toward the kitchen. The sway of her curvaceous hips beneath the plain material of her staid Amish dress made him smile against his will. And for a moment he wondered how she would look dressed in an elegant silk ball gown, with her beautiful blond hair fashionably styled atop her head. She deserved diamonds and rubies . . . sapphires to match those gorgeous eyes.

He sighed and turned to go back upstairs.

What a waste, to even be thinking such a thing. He doubted such daydreams ever entered Lida Rinehart's pretty head. Besides, who was he to change her or to wish that she were different than she was?

At the moment John couldn't think of any other woman he'd ever met who was more beautiful or more desirable. Just the way she was.

Seven

When John came back downstairs later, the kitchen was filled with women, who chattered quietly as they carried food outside to long tables set beneath the trees.

John stood at the door between the kitchen and living room for a moment, looking for Lida. But it was Mrs. Rinehart who saw him first and came toward him with a welcoming smile. Suddenly the kitchen grew quiet. Some of the women stared at him with open curiosity. Others smiled shyly and glanced away.

There were young women and older ones. Girls with slender figures and others more voluptuous, with round, rosy-cheeked faces. But like Lida, they all looked strong and healthy and used to work and outdoor activity.

Suddenly a small boy, who appeared to be about eight years old, came rushing across the kitchen to John.

"Is it true you are a soldier?" he cried. "Do you have a gun. And do you shoot other soldiers?" He stared up at John with blue eyes, grown wide with curiosity and animation.

One of the young women he recognized as having tended him came forward and took the tow-headed boy by the arm, pulling him away with an apologetic grin.

"Adam Frederick Dietz!" she exclaimed. "What a question to ask someone you don't even know. Where are your manners? Papa will be very upset with you. Now go outside and find yourself a place at the table."

John laughed and smiled at the dark haired girl.

"It's Christela, isn't it?"

"Yes," she said, obviously pleased that he had remembered her name.

"Is Adam Frederick your son or—"

"Oh no," she said, blushing. Christela touched the cap that covered her hair, turning with a frown when one of the older women cleared her throat in an obvious warning. The dark-haired girl ignored the woman and turned back to John. "The little *snickelfritz* is my brother. I . . . I am not yet married."

"Oh, I see," John said. "I didn't mean to embarrass you," he said, lowering his voice. "I guess I just assumed that someone as pretty as you would already be married."

"Christela." The voice from the doorway was stern and filled with impatience.

John looked to see Lida standing there staring at him and the dark-haired girl.

"Where have you been, cousin? The men are waiting for their bread."

"Oh," Christela said with a giggle. "I forgot." She turned away, then back toward John, grinning. Her movements were unsteady and she swung her arms in a childlike fashion. "Why don't you come with me, John Sexton? You must be hungry and I will introduce you to everyone."

"That sounds good," he said with a nod.

Christela hurried to get a large basket of bread and Lida barely stepped out of their way as they moved through the door. John thought, when he glanced down at her, that the gleam in her eyes reminded him of tiny sword points. Their brief, pleasant encounter earlier had obviously been forgotten. The resentment and anger were back in her eyes with a bitter vengeance.

As he followed Christela across the lawn, John shrugged his broad shoulders. It was just as well that Lida despised him. Nothing could ever come of his secret desires where the beautiful Amish girl was concerned. There was no point in hoping or wishing for anything else. Lida's undisguised dislike might keep him out of a whole lot of trouble.

John hadn't really known what to expect when he met the men of the community, especially Ephraim's father. But he couldn't have been more pleasantly surprised. If there was the tiniest bit of animosity or blame, he couldn't detect it, and he prided himself on his judgment of human behavior, it being a necessity in the work he did.

"Come, John Sexton," Jacob Rinehart said. "Sit here beside me. This is my brother-in-law, Levi Dietz. He is my wife Anna's brother."

John glanced at Christela and she met his eye and smiled.

"You must be Christela and Adam's father." John saw the young boy peeking around the man Jacob had just introduced. The boy's eyes were filled with a quiet mischief that refused to be restrained.

"Ja," the sober faced man said. "And three other children who are grown and married. We have the farm next," he said, nodding toward the west.

"How are you feeling?" Jacob Rinehart asked John. He didn't look at John, but instead continued eating.

"Fine, sir," John said. A plate was set in front of him and immediately everyone began passing food his way. The meal consisted of a hearty bean soup that was served in a long bowl set down the middle of the table and into which everyone dipped their bread. There were also platters of cold meats and cheeses, varieties of pickles, bowls of beets, and baskets and wooden trays of freshly baked bread. And later the women began to bring cakes and pies to the table.

"Snitz pie," Adam Frederick said, glancing with wide eyes around his father. "You like Snitz pie, English?"

"Well, I'm about to find out," John said, holding his plate forward for a piece.

Adam laughed, as did the other men seated along the table.

John saw Lida walking along the other side of the table. She met his eyes once, then looked away. Here in the dappled light beneath the trees, her skin caught the honey-colored light of the sun and the part of her hair that he could see beneath her cap gleamed a rich platinum gold.

John frowned, thinking it was a good thing he was better and that he would be leaving soon. Even knowing her animosity and how she felt about him, the girl was sorely a temptation. There was no doubt of that. If he stayed, he wasn't sure he'd be able to keep his hands to himself.

He glanced at Jacob Rinehart, feeling guilty. He'd already involved this man's son in something that ended up getting him killed. And now he couldn't seem to stop having lustful thoughts about the man's daughter, his only surviving child. What kind of man was he anyway?

For the rest of the day, he made himself keep his eyes away from Lida Rinehart's beautiful face and tantalizing figure.

It helped that he was the center of attention and the obvious object of curiosity. Adam Frederick and several of his cousins tagged along everywhere John went, asking questions and regaling him with tales of their boyhood. And from the corner of his eye, John couldn't help noticing that Christela and a few of the young women glanced at him and giggled, then huddled back together in hushed conversations.

It was late when the families began to pack baskets and boxes back into their buggies and wagons. The children were growing tired, some of the younger ones crying or hanging on to their mother's skirts.

Jacob Rinehart came to John. He had removed his split tail coat—which John had heard called a

Mutze—and now wore only black trousers and suspenders and a white shirt. He still wore the black broadbrim hat.

"I must see to the chores. Cows must be fed and milked even on Sunday. They don't know the difference." There was a wry smile on the man's face. A gentle humor, the same that John had noticed among the others.

"I'll go with you if you don't mind," John said. "I'd like to talk to you."

Jacob nodded, and there was only the slightest hint of curiosity in his faded blue eyes.

John felt more tired than he'd ever been in his life. But this conversation was one he needed to have. He'd just have to endure the pain in his shoulder and the weakness that plagued him as best he could.

He followed Mr. Rinehart as he milked the cows and poured the milk into huge copper containers.

"Mr. Rinehart, I've wanted to tell you how sorry I am about Ephraim. About—"

"Is no need for that," Jacob said, glancing briefly up from where he sat milking the last cow. "I can see the sorry in your eyes."

John smiled, bemused by the quaint language and the gentle ways of the Amish. It was something he didn't think he'd ever understand, although he had to admit it was pleasant to be in this atmosphere for a change. Instead of among men who wanted nothing more than to kill and maim and destroy life.

"Ephraim was a fine young man. I know that your church doesn't approve of involvement in wars, but I wanted to tell you that he was as brave and courageous a man as I ever met."

"*Ja,* he was. I know that."

"I just wish there was something I could do. Something—"

"There is nothing." Jacob stood up, bringing the bucket of milk with him. He was not as tall as John, but even at his age, he looked strong and fit. "It is not our way to condemn the world, even though we do not see a way to live in it. Ephraim was a grown man and it is too late for wishing, even though in my heart I wish he had not done what he did." Jacob clapped John on his healthy shoulder. "We do not blame you, John Sexton. Neither the boy's mother nor I."

John shook his head. Never in his life had he met anyone so devoid of bitterness. Most people would be seeking vengeance and here was this man, caring for him in his home, extending him every courtesy of a friend and neighbor. Welcoming him even.

"I don't know what to say. Even though I tried to defend Ephraim as best I could, I still feel responsible. Your attitude is very generous."

"We are plain people. Our songs say *Demut ist die schönste Tugend.* Humility is the most beautiful virtue. We are all sinners, John Sexton. And we all need help from *Gott.* I am no different from you." Jacob poured the milk in the container and turned to John with a smile that said the conversation was finished. "No more will be said about your guilt. That is between you and your own God. Now . . . come to the house. You must be tired after this long day. We will share a bottle of Anna's good homemade root beer."

"In a little while. I'd like to stay here for a minute if you don't mind. Oh, Mr. Rinehart—is there some way I can mail a letter?" He needed to let Greenhow know he wasn't dead and find out what his orders were once he was completely well.

"Mail? Of course. Someone will take it into the village tomorrow if you wish."

"That would be good. Thank you."

John nodded as he watched Jacob Rinehart walk through the wide doors of the barn and along the stone path toward the farmhouse. He had just turned to go back inside, intending to sit on a bail of hay and rest before going back to the house. He heard the rustle of a footstep in the hay behind him and whirled around, not knowing what he expected, but coming instinctively and from long experience to a stance of self-defense.

"Oh," Lida said, standing with her hands on her hips and staring at him with open defiance. "Are you to attack a woman now?"

"What are you doing here?" he asked, relaxing with a relieved burst of air from his lungs.

"It is my barn," she said, her look haughty and defensive.

"How long have you been here? Don't you have anything better to do than sneak around eavesdropping?" His gray eyes glittered at her.

"I was not sneaking," she said with a huff. Her cheeks flushed as she stared at him from across the wide expanse of hay. "I came here to gather eggs, and when I heard your conversation, I did not want to embarrass either of you by revealing my presence."

"How thoughtful of you," he said, his voice a soft growl.

"You are a sarcastic man, John Sexton. But your sarcasm does not bother me. My father and the others might be fooled by you, but I am not," she said. John could just make out her features in the gathering gloom of the barn. "Christela is young and naive and unfortunately easily flattered by men like you. And Adam Frederick is only a boy. But I do not understand my father's inability to see you for what you are."

"And that is?" John's voice was cold. It echoed through the barn, and for a moment, there was silence except for the quiet rustling of the cattle in their stalls.

"You've admitted it yourself. You're a mercenary. A man who cares for nothing else except money."

John knew that he had been the one to put that idea into her head. It was what he wanted her to think, wasn't it? Yet he couldn't explain why her accusations angered him so much. And why he found himself wanting to shake some sense into her.

He stepped closer, smiling when Lida took a step away from him.

"That's right," he whispered. "Run, *Liebling*. Get as far away from me as you can," he said, mocking her with her own language. "I'm a very dangerous man. And I don't much give a damn about anything or anyone.

John moved toward her, not taking his eyes off her face. He was so angry that he didn't care about the fear in her eyes now. In fact, he thought, perhaps a little fear was just what she needed. She was arrogant and bossy and just a bit too damned self-righteous for his taste.

And she was wrong. He did care. He cared too damned much.

He practically backed her against one of the stalls, silently stalking her with a cold glint in his eyes. When he took her shoulders and pulled her to him, he wasn't aware of the pain in his arm. He wasn't aware of anything except the nearness of her, the soft look of her parted lips, and the scent of clean sun-drenched hair and skin.

He heard her gasp just before his mouth covered hers in a kiss meant to punish. But instead he found himself drowning in that first sweet, forbidden taste of her, found that he was the one sent reeling. When he pulled away his muscles were shaking, and not entirely from the fatigue and pain.

Lida stared into his eyes as she lifted her hand and raked the back of it across her lips.

"You are evil," she hissed. "An evil English who has come to disrupt our household. And I hate you for it. I hate you for what you've done."

"Do you?" John asked, not moving to let her pass. He thought he had felt a response, thought she had touched his chest lightly as he kissed her. Just before she pushed him away.

Had he imagined that?

"Yes I do!" she said, trembling now with rage. "Now let me by."

Slowly John stepped aside, waving his arm with mock chivalry.

"If you despise me so much, then you'll be pleased to know that after tomorrow it's only a matter of days before I'll be out of your house, out of your bedroom, and out of your sight."

"Good!" she said, her eyes so pale they looked almost colorless in the shadowy interior of the barn. "That will suit me just fine. The sooner you are gone, the better off we all will be. I'll be glad, do you understand me? Glad!"

Lida ran past him and out of the barn.

John sighed and ran his fingers through his black hair, shaking his head with frustration as he dropped down onto one of the bales of hay.

"Dammit," he muttered, shaking his head again. He picked up a clump of dirt that had been carried into the barn on someone's boot. He stood up and threw it as hard as he could, wincing as pain ripped through his healing shoulder. He grunted and leaned back against a post, cursing beneath his breath and muttering quietly.

"It's what I want, too, you spiteful little vixen," he said through clenched teeth. "By God, it's what I want, too. And the sooner the better."

Eight

Lida ran back toward the house, but she didn't go inside. Instead she went around the side of the house that was more sheltered by trees. When she reached a huge willow tree where she'd gone all her life for solitude, she huddled down at the base of it.

She was trembling as she wrapped her arms around her body and tried to decide what it was exactly that she was feeling.

Fury. A white hot fury that made her want to rant and scream. To cry at the heavens for the unfairness of what had happened to her family.

But there was something else, too. Something mingled with the fury. Something just as powerful and just as disturbing. And she didn't know what it was.

All she knew was that it was connected to her turbulent, confusing emotions about John Sexton. She hated him, and yet when she'd seen him lying in her own bed, his chest bare and dark beneath the kerosene lamplight, she had felt an undeniable tingle of pleasure race through her body.

A pleasure that she had told no one about. It was something she hadn't even let herself think about, much less talk about to someone else. Not even Christela. Especially Christela, who seemed to be developing a growing affection for the arrogant English.

Lida touched her lips where he had kissed her. She had been kissed before. Carl Miller had kissed her, more than once.

But it was nothing like this. Never anything like what she felt when John kissed her.

How could she feel disgust and fear and this odd blending of pleasure all at the same time?

Maybe she should marry Carl. Maybe what she was feeling for this man was pure lust. A need for mating, like the farm animals in season. Like a healthy mature woman should feel at her age, when she was ready to marry and settle down to having babies. Still she blushed thinking about the possibilities.

She supposed that if there was one young man in the community with whom she was considered attached, it was Carl Miller. He had asked her to marry him—more than once, but she had always put him off . . . made some excuse. Lida had even used Ephraim's death as another reason for her not to discuss marriage with Carl.

But now, having such disturbing feelings for a man she barely knew—a man she should hate—Lida thought perhaps it was time to discuss marriage with her parents. And with Carl.

The next morning it was raining. John felt disappointed. He had enjoyed being outside on Sunday and the thought of being cooped up in the house all day was almost more than he could stand.

Mrs. Rinehart knocked at his door early, before daybreak. But he'd been awake for a long time.

"Guten Morgen. Do you feel up to having your breakfast downstairs this morning?" she'd asked, not bothering to come into the room.

"I'd like that. Thank you."

"It is good to see you're feeling better," she said quietly before closing the door.

John hadn't let himself think about how he would feel when he saw Lida again. He had spent much of the night not allowing himself to think about anything except getting back to work. He needed to immerse himself completely in the necessary physical task of escorting families across Ohio in all kinds of weather and circumstances. Numb his mind with the danger of it, let himself think only of the day he would go back home to Tennessee and begin his life over again.

But downstairs in the kitchen, watching Lida as she placed dishes on the table, John felt all those feelings return that he thought he'd managed to suppress during the night. He couldn't seem to take his eyes away from her mouth, that mouth that had been so sweet and soft when he kissed her. The intensity of his reaction shook him to the core.

John frowned at the feeling. Being taken by surprise always irritated him.

Lida glanced up, seeing the look of anger on John's face. She lifted her chin and glared at him, then whirled around and went to the cabinet to bring a pitcher of milk back to the table.

Mr. Rinehart sat at the head of the table and when Mrs. Rinehart took a seat at the other end, she motioned John and Lida toward the benches on either side.

John found himself facing Lida as she sat across the table. And even though he tried to see into those blue eyes, she would not look at him, not even when she was forced to pass food to him.

The meal was very quiet with only the clink of dishes and the sound of Mr. Rinehart's rhythmic chewing mingled with his intermittent sighs of pleasure. The hiss of fire in the big black stove and the sound of a clock ticking on a shelf were the only other sounds in the room.

When the clock struck six, John glanced up, thinking to start a conversation.

"It's a beautiful clock," he said, noticing the lace covering that sat beneath the clock and hung down over the wooden shelf. "And beautiful lace. Did you make it?" he asked, addressing his question to Mrs. Rinehart.

She smiled and glanced rather shyly at her husband.

"Yes," she said. "Even though the shelf does not need it. The lace is only for fancy."

"It's very pretty," John said, smiling. He found it rather endearing that she felt the need to apologize for having something impractical, something just for sheer enjoyment.

Again, the room grew quiet.

Finally Mr. Rinehart pushed back in his chair

and took up his cup of coffee. Now that he was finished, it seemed all right for him to converse with John.

"You said you have a letter for the mail?"

"Yes, I do," John said. He noticed the look of surprise on Lida's face as she stared at her father. "It's in my room. I'll go get it."

"Is no hurry," Mr. Rinehart said, glancing again at the clock. "Is too early. Chores first," he said, lifting his finger in the air as if he were addressing a group. "Then to town. Lida has errands. She will take you. Perhaps you will want to wear some of our clothes . . . and a hat, else there will be talk about an English being with one of the plain people." Mr. Rinehart hesitated, studying John's face as he did. "Maybe you should begin to grow a beard."

John glanced at Lida. He understood her look of exasperation now. Evidently her father had not told her until just now that he would be a passenger when she went into town on her errands today.

Mr. Rinehart rose from the table, put on his coat, and headed out the door.

"Here," Mrs. Rinehart said, pushing away from the table, too. She gathered a long black coat from a hook and went to the back door to hand it toward her husband. "Try not to get wet, Mr. Rinehart," she said, her voice taking on the universal nurturing sound of wife and mother.

John heard Mr. Rinehart grunt, but he reached for the coat, then nodded at his wife before trotting down the steps and out into the rain.

Mrs. Rinehart came back into the room and began clearing the dishes. She stopped, looking at her daughter who still sat at the table. Suddenly Lida's head came up and she looked with resentment at her mother.

"I won't do it," she said. "There's no reason he can't take the buggy himself," she said, glancing at John with fire in her eyes.

"Lida," her mother said. She practically whispered the words, her eyes darting toward John with an apologetic look. "This is not good to say. Of course you will do it—just as your father asks."

"No," Lida said, standing up from the table. "I won't. Please don't ask me to, Mother."

John could see the quick, agitated rise and fall of her breasts, the way she held her arms stiffly, her hands closed into fists at her side.

"It's all right," John said. "I don't mind taking the buggy into town alone."

"You are not yet strong enough for driving," Mrs. Rinehart said. She returned to gathering up the dishes. "Lida will do this, just as her papa asks. You will forgive my daughter. It is not like her to behave this way."

"Don't speak about me as if I'm not here, Mother. You, more than anyone, know how I feel about this man."

"Lida," her mother scolded, her voice filled with horror. Mrs. Rinehart pressed her lips tightly together in disapproval. "You will do this thing. It is not much your father asks of you. And if he knew of the things that lie in your heart since your brother's death, he would be much disappointed. You will not cause him worry, daughter. Not now."

Lida sighed and closed her eyes. Her mother had focused on the one thing that she could not deny either of her parents. Her protection and obedience. Her loyalty now that there was no one else except her.

"All right," she whispered. "All right, I'll go then. You don't have to say anything to papa about what I said."

"You are a good daughter, Lida," Mrs. Rinehart said. She walked to Lida and pulled her close, placing a kiss on her cheek. Then she left the kitchen.

Lida's gaze came up across the table to look straight into John Sexton's eyes.

"I'll bring some of Ephraim's clothes to your room for you to wear. I usually leave at eight."

Then she, too, whirled and left the room.

John sat for a moment, staring at the empty room, listening to the sound of songbirds just beginning to sing in the trees outside. Slowly, he pushed himself up from the table and went upstairs.

Lida took Ephraim's clothes from a trunk in his room. Lovingly she brushed her hands down the black collarless jacket. The barn door-style trousers with buttons in the front would be long enough for John Sexton. Ephraim had been as tall. But John was broader through the chest and shoulders, and she wasn't certain how the shirt and jacket would fit.

Still it would have to do, since her father insisted on continuing to help the man. She wondered if John had thought about the possibility of someone recognizing him in town.

She stepped quietly across the hall and tapped on the door. When John opened the door, she handed him the bundle of clothes, trying to remain calm as she did. Trying to avoid the touch of his hands, she practically shoved the clothes into his arms.

"I will bring the buggy to the house for you," she said.

"It's all right. I can walk to the barn."

"No, I—"

"Lida," he said with a heavy sigh. "Stop this. Just stop it. If I say halt, you say go. If I say no, you say yes. Believe me, I'm not trying to upset you. I had no idea that your father would expect you to take me into town when I mentioned the letter to him yesterday. I'll meet you at the barn at eight."

Lida took a deep breath, clamping her teeth together. Then, without a word, she turned and walked toward the stairs.

Why was the man so infuriatingly calm just when she expected to have an argument from him? Everything he said sounded reasonable and logical. And yet she found herself shaking with anger and frustration and dreading the time she would have to spend with him today.

Upstairs, John frowned at his image in the mirror, seeing himself dressed in Amish clothes. They were quaint, but actually quite comfortable. The shirt, which had no pockets, was roomy enough, although the sleeves were a bit short. But the black jacket strained across the shoulders and he couldn't bring the material across his chest to close the hook and eye fasteners.

He stood staring into the mirror. This wouldn't be a bad disguise for his work, except that he would never want to cause the authorities to come to the Amish community looking for him. The plain people had been too kind to him ever to take a chance on such a thing happening.

It had stopped raining, although the sky still looked dark and threatening. Lida and her father had the covered black buggy almost ready when John got to the barn. But he stepped in front of the horse and pulled the reins through, then tied them to one of the roof supports on the driver's side. He was surprised by the spirited horse. It was a beautiful bay with a shining coat and clean, well-bred lines. In the south, it would be considered a prime saddle horse.

"Beautiful horse," he murmured.

"*Ja.* We take pride in our animals," Mr. Rinehart said. "Keep them well fed and cared for and they will serve you well."

Lida let her eyes linger on John as he climbed into the buggy, noting the way the jacket fit his shoulders and smiling at the short sleeves. But he would do.

Neither of them said much for several miles, except for an occasional question or comment from John as he surveyed the land and the beautiful Amish farms.

"Do you intend going back to what you were doing?" Lida asked finally.

"Yes, I do." He touched the letter that lay on the seat between them. "That's the reason for the letter. I need to let someone know where I am."

"This money you are making . . . it must be very tempting indeed," she said with a slight tightening of her lips.

"Why do you say that?" His eyes were quiet and questioning.

"You almost died earning it," she said, glancing first at him, then back at the road. "I wouldn't take such a chance for mere money."

"You're not me."

"No," she said smugly. "I'm not." They drove for another minute or so. "And what do you plan to buy with all this money you're making, John Sexton? What is so important?"

John leaned back in the seat and stretched his legs out as far as he could in the small buggy. He crossed his arms over his chest and turned to watch her expression.

"Money can buy anything a man wants. Whiskey . . . expensive clothes . . . women."

Lida made a quiet sound of disgust and slapped the reins against the horse's back.

John laughed, knowing that would be her exact reaction.

"And what about you, Miss Lida Rinehart?" he asked. "Don't tell me you wouldn't like to wear a pretty red dress, all silk and satin with lace and ruffles. Or that you wouldn't like to wear jewels in that beautiful blond hair, uncover it for the world to see?" He glanced down at her feet, encased in broad, laced-up black shoes. "Maybe a pair of dainty red slippers?"

"Of course I would not," she snapped. "Why would I want to do such a foolish thing? I am Amish . . . of the plain people. It is against our beliefs."

"Sweetheart," he said, grinning as he saw the blush on her cheeks. "You might be Amish, but believe me, there's nothing plain about you."

"You shouldn't say such things to me."

"Why not? It's true. Don't you like it when men give you compliments? Wouldn't you like to wear a red satin dress just once and hear what men have to say about you?"

"Nein!" she said, slapping the reins again. "I would not."

Her action caused John to be thrown back against the seat. Then he laughed aloud and reached for the reins, taking them from her fingers and pulling the horse to a slower trot.

"You're lying," he said, leaning very close to her.

Lida had turned with surprise when he took the reins from her. She stared incredulously into gray eyes filled with warmth and mischief. Filled with something else that took her breath away.

"Actually I'd like to see you in a red dress." There was something in his manner, that arrogant knowing way of his, that infuriated her.

"That will never happen," she said, trying to regain her composure. "Never."

"Oh, don't be so sure. One never knows."

"We . . . we are almost in town," she said, her voice breathless. "Just around the next bend."

With a quiet smile, he placed the reins back in her hands, then settled back against the seat. But he didn't take his eyes away from her when he spoke.

"Too bad," he murmured. "The sight of you in a red dress, Miss Rinehart, is something I'd pay a great deal to see."

Nine

Lida refused to speak to John again until she had pulled the buggy into Walnut Creek's main street and parked near a store front reading "General Merchandise." Then she turned to him with a cool, polite look on her face.

"It might be best if you wait here. I'll take the letter in and mail it for you."

"Fine," John said, handing her the envelope. As much as he wished it, he could not make her meet his eyes again.

After the light rain that morning, the skies had begun to clear. By the time Lida stepped from the buggy, the sun was filtering through the trees and the lingering fog. She stopped and took a deep breath of air, determined that John Sexton would not spoil her day out. This regular journey into town was something she looked forward to all week.

When she made her weekly trip, she could look to her heart's content at all the colorful dress material in the store and run her hands lingeringly over the silks and satins that were forbidden to her. Sometimes she felt a twinge of guilt and stopped to glance about the store, wondering what someone would think if they saw an Amish girl look with such longing at something so worldly. But she told herself time and again that as long as she did nothing but look, there was no harm.

Today she wandered about the store, gathering items in her basket for her mother's list. There was always enough money for something special if she wanted it, but she rarely did. After all, what did a young woman her age usually want when she could buy something special for herself? Ribbons for her hair, baubles for her ears, a pin or flower for her dress. She'd watched the others, the English girls who also shopped in the store. And she had heard their laughter and squeals of delight over some new glittering hair comb or pin.

All of which were forbidden to Lida.

She placed the basket on the counter and went back to the threads and materials section. Perhaps today she would buy something for herself. Some new bolt of cotton, perhaps in a pastel color for summer. Maybe even a dress of crepe or shantung for Sunday.

Lida looked at the material, then sighed.

It was no use. No matter what she chose, the dress and its style were always the same. The apron was always the same, as was a woman's hairstyle and Kapp that covered it. She supposed if there was one thing she'd never understood as a little girl, it was why everyone had to look alike in the Amish community. One could hardly distinguish one from the other at a distance. The young men were like a flock of black crows with even less opportunity for being different. That was one of the reasons they were so diligent in their selection and care of their horses and buggies. It was the one way they could make a mark of individuality in the community.

She turned away and glanced out the window, startled when she saw Carl Miller talking to John. She had hoped to see Carl in town; he often made a point of being there on the same day as Lida. But she had not expected him to speak to John.

Quickly she paid for the items she'd bought and hurried outside.

"Carl," she said, glancing around him toward John. "It is nice seeing you today."

"Lida," Carl said, turning toward her as if he might embrace her. But quickly he lowered his arms and stood with his hands crossed as he smiled down at her.

Carl was very tall. Perhaps even taller than the man who sat watching her from the buggy. But he was slender and wiry. He had very pale blue eyes and pale skin and his thin, ruddy-colored beard was just a shade darker than his fair hair.

He was not an unattractive man. But now, seeing him beside John Sexton, Lida was acutely aware of his lack of vibrancy and ruggedness. He was as solemn as her papa and sometimes he treated her the same. As if he were her father instead of a potential lover and husband.

"Is good to see you, too, Lida," Carl said. He had a deep voice that seemed not to go with his tall, spare figure. "I have wanted to see you but we are busy with the planting."

"I understand," she said with a nod.

"I was just meeting your huh . . . cousin," he said, turning with a knowing smile toward John.

Lida breathed a heavy sigh of relief and placed her basket in the back of the buggy.

"When I saw you talking, I was afraid . . ." she said, glancing around at the crowded streets. She was also very aware of John's attentive gaze as she spoke and the way his eyes were hidden behind lazy, half-closed lids.

"Not to worry," Carl said, taking a step closer. "All the plain people know the story by now, even in other districts. Besides, you know I would do nothing to put you in danger."

There was such an intimacy in his voice that Lida glanced immediately at John and saw him grin and lift a questioning brow toward her.

"We should go," Lida said, starting around to the driver's side of the buggy. If she had wanted to speak to Carl about their personal life, she couldn't do it here, under the watchful, disturbing gaze of John Sexton.

"Wait," Carl said, touching her arm briefly. "I would like to see you now that your time of mourning is almost finished."

Lida nodded and this time she didn't glance at John.

"Saturday?" Carl said.

"Saturday will be fine," she said, going to get into the buggy.

As she drove down the main street and away from town, Lida could feel her cheeks burning as she sensed John's eyes upon her. They were in the country before John finally spoke again.

"Is Carl your sweetheart?"

"That's none of your business."

John laughed and settled back into the seat as if he were satisfied with himself.

"You know your mother packed a very fine lunch for us." He turned toward the back and pulled a covered basket up for Lida to see.

"I . . . I'm not hungry," she said, feeling a rising dread in her heart.

"Oh, but I am. In fact I'm feeling quite weak. And tired," he said.

She turned to glare at him, aware of the twinkle in his eye, yet knowing what her mother would say if she came home with the basket still filled with food.

"Oh, all right," she said, unable to hide her impatience. She pulled the reins to the right, guiding the horse off the main road beneath a large elm tree. Nearby ran a quietly flowing stream.

"All right. We are here. Eat," she said.

John made a little clucking noise with his tongue and shook his head.

"Miss Rinehart, you really must learn to relax and enjoy yourself more. Why even old Carl thinks you should have more fun."

"How would you know what Carl thinks," she said with a huff.

"He told me."

"You . . . you were talking about me?"

"Oh yes," he said, grinning. "In fact I learned

a great deal about you in those few minutes while you were shopping. Very interesting. About how you used to be the first to take off your clothes and jump into the creek on a hot summer day."

Lida rolled her eyes and jumped down from the buggy.

"How you used to wrestle with the boys. How you used to declare that you would never marry any of them, because none were as clever or as quick-witted as you were."

"Oh, he did not say that," she said, glaring at him with flashing eyes. "You only spoke for a few moments. And I do not believe that he immediately went into such a conversation about me."

John laughed and walked to the tree. He took a blanket and spread it on the ground, and placed the large picnic basket in the middle of the blanket. Then with a smile, he bowed and raked his arm forward to motion Lida to sit.

"This is foolish," she muttered.

"You should learn to do foolish things sometimes. Like when you were a little girl."

"I'm not a little girl," she snapped.

"No," he said, his look suddenly growing more serious. "You certainly are not." His gray eyes moved from her face, down over her breasts and slender waist, past her curvaceous hips. Then he looked back up into her startled eyes.

Lida felt she could barely breathe. How could she defend herself against this man? And how could she keep that little flutter from appearing in her chest every time he looked at her this way?

His looks and the way they made her feel frightened her to death.

"Is that what you told my brother?" she asked, her voice growing hard and cynical. Even as she lashed out at John, she knew it was her fear and confusion that made her do so. But she couldn't seem to stop herself. "Did you tell him that he should break free, do something foolish? Something adventurous?"

Her words hit their mark. She saw the pain flash immediately in his eyes. Saw the fun dissipate and the muscles of his jaw tighten convulsively.

"What do you want from us, John Sexton? For me to wear a red silk dress and break away from all that I've been taught? For my brother to have dreams of leaving our farmland to explore the sinful world? Isn't it enough that such things have taken him away from us forever. Now must you try to do the same with me?"

"That's not what I intended. And you know it," he said, his voice quiet. In his eyes was that cold, hard look that she'd seen the first night they met.

This was the real man, she told herself. This cold-eyed mercenary who cared little for anyone but himself. This was the man she needed to remember. Not the one with laughing eyes and sensuous smiling lips who tempted her beyond anything she ever had thought possible.

They stood staring at one another, she with upheld head and challenging eyes. He with a wounded, but stubborn glint in his.

"Excuse me," he said, turning away from her and walking toward the stream.

"Where are you going?" she asked, frowning with frustration at his unexpected actions.

"I need to walk. Go ahead and have your lunch, *Fraulein* Rinehart," he said, turning to speak to her over his shoulder. "I wouldn't want to spoil your appetite with my presence." With that he stalked away into the undergrowth.

Lida's head ached and she felt a sudden inexplicable urge to cry. Abruptly she raked her cap off her head and threw it to the ground, running her fingers impatiently through her tightly bound hair. Her trembling hands found the pins and she tore them out and threw them on the ground, too. Still she felt an overwhelming desire to lash out at someone or some thing and she kicked at the ground, sending dirt and pebbles scattering toward the stream to land with plunking sounds into the water.

"Damn you!" she muttered, kicking again. "Damn you, John Sexton!"

Finally, her fury spent, she turned about. But John was nowhere in sight. He had not come back from the canes and brush that pushed in along the creekbank.

There was nothing to do but wait.

For a while Lida threw pebbles into the water, then she settled down onto the blanket to wait for the stubborn English to return. Here in the quiet with the sun streaming through the limbs above her, she could hear the birds singing and the buzz of insects in the nearby grass. Her eyes grew heavy and lazy as she watched colorful butterflies flit about and heard the distant cawing of crows in the fields.

Finally she lay back on the blanket, her eyes half-closed as she watched the clouds moving past at a slow mesmerizing pace. She hadn't intended to sleep. Didn't even realize when her eyes closed slowly.

When John came back toward the buggy, he stopped, his gaze going immediately to the woman sleeping beneath the tree. She was curled up on her side with her hands beneath her cheeks. Her hair was loose and it fell in fine wispy strands across her face. She looked like a child, a sweet angelic child who had cried herself to sleep.

Had she? Had he caused her to cry . . . caused her to dredge up painful memories of her brother's death? He hoped not. Not when all he wanted to do was take the pain away from those beautiful eyes. See them sparkle with fun and pleasure. See forgiveness in their depths.

He took a deep, slow breath of air and walked toward her. His hand reached forward, tempted by the sheen of sunlight on her hair, moved by the sweet innocence of her, by her childlike ability to sleep beneath a tree on a warm summer day.

"Little Lida," he whispered, brushing a strand of hair away from her forehead.

Her eyes came open immediately and she sat up, frowning at him with a puzzled look. Self-consciously she brushed her hair back and began to look about for the scattered pins.

"No, don't," John said softly. He reached forward, taking her hands and pulling them away from her hair. "Leave it. Please. Just for today. As if there is no barrier between your world and mine. As if there is no war and we are just two people sharing lunch on a beautiful summer day."

There was such pain in his eyes. Such sadness and longing that Lida couldn't ignore it. And no matter how much her heart ached for her dead brother, her conscience wouldn't let her say another harsh, hurtful word to John.

She nodded, then brushed the hair that fell around her face back behind her ears in a slightly self-conscious gesture. No man outside of her family had ever seen her hair loose or unhidden except John. That stormy night in the barn and now. She found the knowledge of that a strangely moving and erotic sensation.

John began taking the food out of the basket, quietly placing it before them on the blanket. A squirrel ran partway down the elm tree, barking and chattering at them, as if he resented their intrusion into his private domain.

Lida looked up, smiling at the tiny chattering creature. And for a moment as she gazed back into John's eyes, there was an unspoken truce. A sharing of the peace and beauty that surrounded them. A respite from all both of them had suffered in the past month.

After they had eaten the lunch of cold ham and cheese and Mrs. Rinehart's hearty brown bread, they sat quietly drinking cider. Neither of them had spoken during the meal except to comment on the weather or some bit of nature that caught their attention

"I noticed the letter you mailed was to Cincinnati. Aren't you going to write your family? I remember you said they are in Tennessee. Don't you intend letting them know where you are and that you're well?"

"I don't have a family," John said, his expression immediately growing closed and wary.

"Oh, I'm sorry. I thought . . . I mean when you were ill and feverish, you mentioned your mother and I—"

"There's no reason to be sorry," he said coolly. "I do keep in touch with my mother. What I meant was that my mother and father are lost to me as a family, at least in all practicality. And my brother Nathan is serving with the Confederate Army. I have no idea if he's alive or dead."

"Oh," she said. Still she stared at him, as if waiting for him to explain further. Did his estrangement with his family have anything to do with his cynicism? His bitterness? "You also mentioned a girl's name," she said, her voice quietly cautious. "Someone named Katherine."

She saw John's mouth tighten, and if it were possible his gray eyes became even more distant than before.

"Since you seem to be so curious," he said rather curtly. "Katherine was my fiancée when the war began. But when I was drummed out of West Point just a few weeks short of graduation, it seems that she, as well as my father expected me to join the Confederate Army. Thinking, I suppose, that

I would show them and the world what a brave and honorable man I am. I refused."

"Forgive me if I seem a bit slow," she said, watching him carefully. "But since you chose a military career, why—"

"I didn't choose to fight against my own countrymen," he interrupted. "There's a difference."

"Yes, I suppose there is." She nodded her understanding. "But because you refused, your fiancée left you? And your father . . . he disowned you?"

"That's a good way of putting it," he said. "Kicked me out, disinherited me . . . turned his back. All good, worthy expressions. And yes, my fiancée asked out of our engagement."

Lida grimaced at the bitterness in his voice.

"That's terrible," she said. "You have questioned our Amish ways. At least we would never do such a thing. Here, families are everything."

"Really?" he said with a mocking glint in his eyes. "And what would you call the act of shunning, Miss Rinehart? It seems to me it's a form of banishment. Not much different than what my father did to me."

"Oh, no," she said. Then she shook her head in confusion. "Not really. Shunning is only done for a very good reason."

"Right," he said. "To make one person do as everyone else wishes. To insure that everyone in the church conforms."

"No," she said, frowning. "I mean, yes, but . . ." There was an odd expression in her eyes as she stared at him.

"Never mind," he said. "Perhaps we should talk about something else."

"Have you known Carl Miller all your life?" John asked, meaning to change the subject.

Lida sighed. She was actually as relieved as he to change the subject. But she was still just as curious about his past.

"Yes, most of it," she said. "He lives in another district on the other side of Walnut Creek, but in our world, there are few Amish that we do not know."

"And was he your childhood sweetheart?"

"No," she said, with a shake of her head and a wistful smile.

"But he's in love with you now." John waited, watching Lida, letting his gaze move over her beautiful hair, the warmth of sunlight on her skin.

"Love?" she said with a shaky laugh. "I'm not sure what love is, except for what I feel for my family and relatives."

I'd like to teach you, John wanted to say. God, how he would love to teach her about all the sweet pleasures of love. How he would love to be at this moment only a young man, courting a girl, far away from the thoughts of war. With no concern about his brother or his mother. With no thoughts of the frightened slaves who waited expectantly for someone to come and help them.

"Then what is your relationship with Carl?" he asked quietly. "If it's not too personal a question for me to ask a girl like you."

"I expect I'll marry him," she said with a slight lift of her chin. "Perhaps before the winter."

John pushed himself up straighter on the blanket and stared with a stunned expression into her eyes.

"Marry him? Even if you don't love him?"

"Love has little to do with it," she said calmly with a hint of her old defiance.

John frowned and took a deep breath. With a shake of his head, he began placing the food back into the basket.

"God," he muttered. "I can't believe you people."

Lida, too, began putting the food away, then she stood up when he did and quickly folded the blanket. She watched as he stalked to the buggy and practically threw the basket into the back.

"You're angry," she said. "Why are you so angry?"

"I'm not angry," he said, turning to her with an impatient gesture. "Here, get into the buggy. Your mother will be wondering where we are."

"You think I shouldn't marry Carl? Simply because I'm not in love with him? You must understand that here, we do what is expected. All our lives are dedicated to helping our parents and our relatives, to taking over the farm when they are too old to work and carrying on the Amish traditions into the next generation. You really shouldn't judge since you don't understand."

"I'm not judging, dammit," he muttered, coming around to her side of the buggy. Impatiently he took her arm, helping her up into the seat. "It's none of my business. As soon as I hear from my contact I'll be away from here and back doing what I know best."

"You're right it isn't any of your business," she said stiffly.

"It doesn't matter to me if you marry Carl Miller or not. In fact, Miss Rinehart, I don't give a damn what you do or who you do it with."

"Good," she said, with a stubborn glint in her eyes. She took the reins after he was in the buggy and flicked them against the horse's back.

"Because I don't need your approval, John Sexton. I don't need anything from you."

Ten

Lida thought it was the longest, most awkward drive she'd ever taken. She could hardly wait until they reached the house to climb out of the buggy and get away from John's brooding silence.

How could she ever have thought anything could change what was between them? Even if she could forgive him for what happened to Ephraim, they were far too different. From two completely opposing worlds. He seemed to have only quiet contempt for the way they lived their lives here in the rolling farmland of Ohio's countryside. While she could never fit into his world at all.

So what was the use of pretending? He was right. Soon he would be away from the Rinehart farm. She'd never see him again, and as far as she was concerned, it was good riddance.

From that day, Lida noticed that John seemed to throw himself into the farm chores. He insisted on helping her father, even herself at times, although he did the work with quiet determination and a minimum of conversation.

There were many times when she longed to speak to him. To ask what was wrong and why he had changed. Sometimes she would catch him watching her and there would be a quiet contemplation in his stormy eyes. And sometimes she would find herself staring at him and when she least expected it, he would glance up from his work and surprise her. Their glances would meet and catch and Lida would look away in embarrassment. Those moments frustrated Lida. She couldn't explain why her eyes wandered toward him so often, against her will even. Or why she found such secret pleasure in the look of his skin that the sun had darkened or the way muscles rippled beneath the material of his shirt when he worked.

Nor could she explain the dreams that she had begun having about him.

A few nights after their trip into Walnut Creek, Lida found herself so deeply involved in the first of those dreams that she thought it was real.

She dreamed about Carl. They were together at church meeting and for once there was a look in his eyes that pleased her. A look of admiration. A look that said he wanted her as a man wants a woman. She knew that look; she had seen it before. But where? When?

In the dream she looked up with a questioning frown into Carl's eyes again. But this time they were different.

Then she realized it wasn't Carl who looked at her that way. It was John. John with those stormy gray eyes. How could she have mistaken the two? John's face was smooth and clean-shaven—it urged a woman's hands forward against her will. To touch and explore.

John's hair was black and shining as a raven's wing. She could remember even now how it had glinted beneath the noonday sun that day as they picnicked by the stream.

How she'd longed to touch it, to place her face against it and catch the clean, sun-warmed smell.

No. From deep inside the word came again and again. But Lida ignored it and moved farther into the dream.

Slowly, expectantly she stepped into John's arms, her mouth reaching up hungrily for his. As if she'd known from the beginning how it would be between them. As if she couldn't wait to taste his kiss.

She wanted to feel his strong hands on her body. To have him hold her tightly as if he couldn't bear to let her go ever again. And God help her, she wanted to feel his body against hers. Wanted to savor every touch, every new sensation that he made her feel.

"I want to make love to you," she heard him whisper.

"Yes," she whispered in return. "Yes . . ."

She saw John smile and reach into his pocket. From it he brought out a bright red ribbon. He unfastened her cap and loosened her hair, then reaching behind her head, he began to tie the red ribbon around her hair. He was so close . . . so warm.

Lida closed her eyes as she felt her body responding, felt it trembling on the brink of some wild, forbidden discovery. She was smiling. Until she opened her eyes and saw her father standing behind John.

There was the most horrible look of disappointment in his eyes.

She looked again at John and saw the desire in his eyes.

"I can't," she said, pulling the ribbons from her hair.

The desire in his eyes changed to disbelief, then disappointment.

"Lida," he whispered.

"I can't," she said. "Please . . . I just can't do this."

Lida sat up in bed, pushing the heavy quilts away from her perspiring body. She was awake now. Fully, painfully awake and aware of every heartbeat, every tingling sensation that the dream had made her feel.

With a quiet cry of despair, she bent her head into her hands and took long deep gulps of air as she tried to compose herself. Tried to make the disturbing, erotic visions disappear that still lingered in her mind.

The mental picture of John's strong, muscular body . . . his steady, meaningful gaze . . . his mouth.

"Oh, God help me," she whispered, sliding her feet over the side of the bed and sitting there with a stunned expression.

How could her mind have betrayed her this way? How could she have dreamed something that was so totally wrong . . . so completely foreign to what she wanted.

But was it? a voice whispered.

"Yes," she cried. "It's Carl I will marry," she

said, her voice louder and stronger. She expected that hearing the words would bring reality back to her quickly. "It is Carl who will come to my bed. Not an English. *Never* John Sexton."

But she was trembling from the powerful images and feelings that the dream had brought.

How could she face him again, after this?

Lida was thankful that both of them were busy after that dream. But she was surprised that the visions of her dream still lingered long after that night.

The weather had been hot and sweltering all day. And now toward sunset dark, angry clouds gathered in the southwest, hanging ominously over the verdant pastures, making an eerie backdrop for the white barn and fence rows.

Lida felt a prickle of apprehension race along her spine. She was afraid of storms and she hoped desperately that this was merely a summer rain cloud that would pass quickly.

She had been helping her mother in the kitchen and now she stepped out onto the back porch and wiped her face with the bottom of her apron.

She saw her father hurrying in and out of the barn. John was with him. When her father looked toward the house and saw her, he waved and she heard him shouting for her to come help.

"Mama," she called back into the kitchen. "Papa needs me to help in the barn. There's a storm coming."

"Gehen sie" her mother said as she came to the screen door and glanced anxiously toward the sky.

"Go ahead, daughter. Tell your papa supper is almost ready. We will eat when the work is finished."

The wind gusted across the yard in front of Lida as she ran, blowing the dry earth into dust devils about her feet. It tugged at her hair and cap and pulled strands free around her face.

Lida's face still burned from working over the stove and yet the wind felt so hot against her skin that it offered little relief.

When she got to the barn, she saw her father and John struggling with a canvas as they tried to pull it over a mound of hay.

Quickly she ran to help, taking the side that billowed out in the wind. Once the canvas was secured, her father shouted something above the noise of the wind and pointed toward the barn.

"You and John close all the shutters and see that the back door of the barn is secure. I will go on to the storm cellar and make sure it's open in case we need it."

Lida nodded and hurried into the barn. The coolness inside brought an immediate relief from the fury of the approaching storm. Here it was eerily quiet and still. The barn was big and sturdy, and there was only an occasional flapping of tin high above on the roof to indicate that the wind was howling.

Lida didn't look at John, but went right to work, going into the stalls and pulling the shutters across the small square windows. When she had finished, she saw him coming from the back of the barn. She could barely make out the expression on his face now that all the shuttered windows and the closed back door left the interior dark. Lida was immediately struck by the feeling of intimacy that the enclosure brought.

The tension fairly crackled in the air between them, as powerful and dangerous as the lightning in the approaching storm.

For one brief moment she looked into his eyes. Then she turned and hurried toward the wide opening at the front of the barn.

Silently he helped her pull the long, heavy doors across the opening and secure the wooden latch. He was so close that she could smell the heat of his body. The wind blew long strands of her blond hair toward him, where it caught and mingled with his tousled black hair.

That odd blending captured her attention as nothing ever had and for a moment she stood mesmerized, her mind seeing the odd intermingling as a lover's dance. Intimate and seductive.

"Hurry," John said, glancing up toward the sky.

By the time they finished, it had begun to rain. Great heavy drops of rain plopped into the dust and pelted against the tin roof of the barn.

John grabbed her arm, pulling her with him as he began to run toward the house. The rain caught them from behind, coming in wave after wave of stinging assaults. By the time they reached the porch, they were both soaked through their clothes to their skin.

Her mother came out to meet them, bringing towels before hurrying back inside to tend her cooking. Through the screen door, Lida could see her going about lighting the coal oil lamps. Her father had probably gone upstairs to change his own wet clothes.

Lida pulled a towel up to her face and suddenly she was aware of John's gaze on her. She glanced down and saw where his gaze led. Her cotton dress clung to her body, emphasizing her breasts and hardened nipples, the wet material cleaving seductively to hips and thighs.

Her teeth were chattering as she met his gaze, then allowed her eyes to wander downward over his own wet clothing. His shirt had become partially unbuttoned in the wind, exposing smooth rain-slicked skin beneath.

Lida was aware of holding her breath. Aware of a heavy pounding in her chest and throat. She could actually feel the blood coursing through her body and into her legs that suddenly had become heavy and languid with heat.

She couldn't take her eyes away from him. She shook her head in confusion and glanced up toward his mouth, seeing it open slightly as if he, too, were having difficulty breathing.

Lida had never felt such a need in her entire life, as the overwhelming urge to move into his arms. To feel his wet, naked chest against her rain-soaked dress. To feel the heat of his skin next to hers . . . taste his beautiful rain-drenched mouth.

They stood transfixed, the storm raging all around them. Pounding against the ground and the house. The wind buffeted the huge trees with a roar that drowned out all other sound.

"Lida," she heard her mother shout from inside. "Come in. Both of you come in before lightning catches you."

"I . . . I have to go," Lida whispered, thinking that the words were foolish and unnecessary. Then she hurried into the house, away from those eyes, away from her own tumultuous feelings.

John closed his eyes after Lida went inside. With a quiet groan he leaned his head back against the side of the house, taking long deep breaths of air and letting it out slowly.

As he dried his hair, he could feel the muscles in his arms shaking. And he knew it wasn't from the work he'd done today.

"Damn," he muttered, flinging the wet towel aside.

A few moments ago as they'd looked into each other's eyes and the electricity surged between them, he had actually considered taking her hand and pulling her with him back out into the rain. Racing with her back to the privacy of the barn where they would be isolated from the house by the storm.

He'd been overwhelmed with the urgency to uncover those beautiful breasts that the rain had so plainly accentuated. To remove her staid cotton dress and run his hands down her waist and hips. To kiss her, hold her against him . . . lose himself in her if only for today . . . for this moment.

"Hell," he muttered again, amazed at the intensity of his feelings. He went to pick up the towel, telling himself that such wishes were an impossibility. Even a touch or an innocent kiss between them was impossible, and he knew it.

Thunder crashed nearby, making John realize how foolish he was to remain on the porch any longer.

But he could hardly go inside the Rinehart house like this. With his body hardened by desire for their daughter. Their innocent virginal daughter.

"John!" It was Mr. Rinehart who stood at the screen door now, glancing toward him with a concerned frown. "You must come in now."

John opened the door, going through the kitchen toward the stairs.

"I'm going to get a dry shirt," he muttered.

Later they ate supper in silence, even though the sound of the storm sometimes brought a murmur of worry from Mrs. Rinehart.

"Should we go to the storm cellar, Jacob?" she asked once when the wind seemed to actually shake the big farmhouse.

"The storm is passing to the south of us," Mr. Rinehart said with a calm nodding of his head. "It will be over before midnight."

John met Lida's eyes in the wavering light of the lantern. And what he saw in those blue depths made him catch his breath in silence.

The longing and confusion he saw there grabbed at his heart and his conscience.

And he knew he had to get away from this place. Away from her.

Before he did something he would regret for the rest of his life.

If Greenhow didn't get in touch with him soon, he would leave anyway. Go back to Cincinnati, get his instructions from someone else if necessary. He simply couldn't afford to stay here another day, not with this beautiful, innocent Amish girl looking at him the way she had today.

Not when he wanted her more than he'd ever wanted anyone or anything in his entire life.

Eleven

Jacob Rinehart was right. By midnight the storm had passed, leaving only the faint patter of rain on the roof and a whispering breeze in the trees.

The next morning the sky was bright and clear, as if the rain in its passing had cleansed the countryside. It was not long after daybreak that they began to hear the clatter of wagons passing on the road in front of the farmhouse. One of the wagons stopped at the back door and Lida saw Christela jump down and come to the house.

Levi Dietz walked toward the barn to find his brother-in-law.

"Christela," Lida said with a smile. She was glad to see her cousin and for a moment she thought perhaps the girl had come to spend the day. Then she saw the troubled look on her face.

"What's wrong?"

"Didn't the storm leave any damage here?" Christela asked, glancing about at the scattered green leaves and broken twigs in the yard.

"Nothing serious. Papa says the blades of the windmill and some tin on the barn roof will need replacing. Why . . . was your farm damaged?"

"No, not us. Haven't you heard?"

Lida shook her head and motioned the girl inside the kitchen.

"The Hostetlers lost their tobacco barn and the old Mr. Hostetler's *Grossdawdy.*"

"Mother," Lida called to her mother in the living room. "Did you hear? Christela says the Hostetler's grandfather house was destroyed in the storm last night." Turning to Christela, Lida asked, "Was Herr Hostetler or his wife hurt?"

"No. No one was injured. They were all in the storm cellar when the tornado struck."

"A tornado? Oh, I knew it was bad," Mrs. Rinehart said, coming into the kitchen. Her eyes were stricken and she wrung her hands out of concern for her neighbors.

"We saw the wagons passing by early this morning," Lida said. "Is that where everyone is going?"

"Yes. The men will clear away today and bring new lumber from the mill, then tomorrow we are to have a barn raising. It will be later before they rebuild Herr Hostetler's house. That is what we stopped to tell you. Papa has come to ask Uncle Jacob to go with him to the clearing today. I will go back home to help Mama with the cooking."

"Yes, there's much to do," Mrs. Rinehart said, tying her apron around her waist.

"I . . . I suppose the English will go with papa," Lida said.

"Yes dear," her mother said. "John is well now. It will be good for him to spend time with the men."

Behind Mrs. Rinehart's back, Christela caught Lida's attention. She wiggled her brows and grinned, and Lida knew that she was silently referring to her curiosity about the handsome stranger who still lived at the Rinehart farmhouse.

Lida shrugged, as if it didn't matter to her. And who could tell? Perhaps tomorrow, John and Christela would get acquainted and find that they liked one another. And perhaps she and Carl would speak of plans for their marriage.

All day wagons and carts drove past the house. Some carried lumber, while others were filled with people curious to see the storm damage. Some of the neighbors stopped at the Rineharts to visit and Lida and her mother were busy all day cooking and entertaining.

It was very late when Jacob Rinehart and John returned from clearing the storm debris at the Hostetler place. They had missed supper, because it was customary for them to eat with the host family. Lida knew that. But still, she couldn't help feeling strangely disappointed that she hadn't gotten to talk to them. She told herself that she was most interested in hearing about the damage at the Hostetler farm. Her wish to see them had nothing to do with John Sexton.

Lida and her mother were up long before daybreak the next morning, gathering food and supplies to take to the barn raising. John and Mr. Rinehart had already been to the barn and finished the chores before breakfast. Some chores, such as milking, could not be overlooked no matter what the disaster.

Lida felt especially happy that morning, knowing what fun they would have during a barn raising. She could hardly wait to see her cousins and friends.

"You must be careful today, John," her father was saying. "Just like yesterday, there will be English coming to see the storm damage and our work."

"Did something happen yesterday?" Lida asked, glancing from him to John.

"The sheriff's wife came with friends. She asked who John was."

"It doesn't matter," John said, taking a sip of coffee. "Even knowing my name, there is no way to prove that I'm the one they call the Sojourner. He's the one the bounty hunters are after. Besides, I won't be here much longer."

"It pays to be careful," Mr. Rinehart said with a wise nod.

"He's right," Mrs. Rinehart added.

"But surely they won't come back today," Lida said hopefully. She didn't want anything to spoil the day. "We will have a frolic no matter what."

John smiled at the expression on Lida's face. It was the first time he'd seen her this way and he liked seeing her happy and excited.

"Frolic?" he asked with a wry grin. "You call building a barn in one day a frolic?"

"It's just an expression," she said, smiling back at him across the breakfast table. "Besides, it is not all hard work. There will be a day of fellowship and laughter, not to mention the noonday gathering. Believe me, you will have a meal today that you will remember for a long time."

Her mother and father smiled and nodded and John found that he could not resist smiling back at them. Perhaps if he were lucky, this day would be the perfect ending to his stay in Amish country.

Later at the Hostetler farm, the sound of hammers rang out through the clear morning air. The stone foundation of the barn had been left standing, and before long the multitude of Amish men had the corner and supporting posts up. Workers swarmed over the structure like bees, some measuring, others sawing, still other men hammering. Several older men stood away from the barn, thoughtfully rubbing their beards as they spoke in quiet, nodding conversations.

Even the children helped. Little boys carried lumber and supplies to the men, while the girls helped their mothers with the long tables that were being set up beneath the trees that were left undamaged by the storm.

Lida and Christela and several other girls their age sat beneath one of the trees, separating eating utensils and dishes as they watched the workers.

"That English is a handsome man, Lida," one of the girls said with a sly wink.

"Yes, I suppose," Lida said. Still, she couldn't stop the blush that moved slowly over her skin. If her friends knew about some of the erotic dreams she'd had about him, they would be shocked.

"I'm going to ask him to sit with me at noon," Christela said. Her eyes had turned dreamy and languid and her gaze didn't leave the area where John worked.

The other girls giggled and nudged one another.

"That is, if you don't mind, cousin," Christela said, turning her attention to Lida.

"Why would I mind?" Lida asked, frowning at the dark-haired girl beside her.

"You don't fool me you know," Christela said, her look sly and teasing. "I've seen you looking at him, too. I never saw you look at Carl Miller that way."

"Oh, for goodness sake," Lida said. "You're imagining things. For your information, I'm planning on marrying Carl before winter."

Why on earth had she said that? Why had she put herself into a position that she couldn't get out of? She glanced toward the barn where John was working, and she knew the answer.

The other girls giggled and clapped their hands, causing some of the older women to glance their way with quiet, indulgent smiles.

"Oh, Lida," Christela said, reaching forward to embrace her cousin. "A wedding! I want to help. We'll all help," she said, glancing at the other girls with excitement.

"Shhh," Lida said. She couldn't resist smiling at Christela. Her cousin had always had more enthusiasm than anyone she knew. She could liven any gathering with her laughter, just as she was doing now, causing everyone to turn and look at them.

"I haven't told Carl yet . . . that I've decided."

Christela's dark eyes widened and then she laughed again and leaned toward Lida. "But he's asked several times. You know he will agree."

"Yes," Lida said, her voice becoming soft. "I think he will be pleased."

"Then you must tell him today," her other friends urged.

"Yes, tell him, Lida. Today at the barn raising would be the perfect time."

"I . . . I suppose I could. All right," she said, letting her gaze wander for only a moment toward John. "But none of you are to say a word until I've had a chance to speak with Carl."

By noon the workers had the heavy supporting beams in place across the top of the barn and had begun placing the rafters. Lida's father was one of the first to leave the barn and come to the table for a drink of water.

"The work is going well," he said with an approving nod.

"How is John doing?" Lida asked. She had been surprised herself that her eyes wandered so often toward the dark-haired man. And even more surprised that she felt a tug of worry for him, working so hard in the hot sun.

"Is good," Jacob nodded. "John Sexton is a strong man and a hard worker. I have told him to rest, but he insists on working as hard as the others." Her father clucked his tongue and shook his head. "The man is stubborn and proud. Like someone possessed. I will take him with me into town for more supplies after the meal. He will have to rest whether he wishes to or not."

"Good," she said quietly, watching with a catch of fear in her throat as John stood at the top of a ladder. Quickly she turned away, busying herself with the food. "It's so high," she muttered. "I can't watch."

Her father laughed and patted her on the back, then walked away.

The men working on the barn knew that it was almost meal time, and for the last few minutes they had become louder with their teasing and bantering.

Lida heard hearty male laughter and turned to see that one of the men had nailed someone's hat to the highest beam of the barn. It fluttered in the breeze and sat like a black crow waiting for its owner to claim it.

Lida's eyes scanned the workers and she saw only one who was not wearing a hat. His hair, uncovered, was black and shining.

Her breath caught in her throat. Did he understand that the men were playing a trick on him? And that they did it because they liked and respected him?

Knowing his temper, she couldn't be sure.

But she saw John begin his climb to the top to fetch his hat. The other men laughed and clapped. Some of them whistled and shouted encouragement. Lida found herself clenching her sweating palms tightly together. Unable to watch him and yet unable to turn away.

John retrieved the hat and waved it triumphantly in the air from his perch high atop the barn. As the men cheered, Lida closed her eyes and breathed a quiet sigh of relief.

"Men," she muttered, turning with a smile back to what she had been doing.

The men ate with great appetites after their hard morning of work. The meal of scrapple and chicken corn soup, along with an assortment of pickles and relishes and the usual collection of rich desserts, disappeared quickly. And if home meals were sometimes quiet and reserved, this one was marked by good-natured laughter and teasing. Several of the men commented on John's agile retrieval of his hat. Lida, standing just behind him with a pitcher of milk, leaned forward over his shoulder, murmuring quietly in his ear.

"They like you, you know. That's why they tease you."

He turned to Lida, smiling quietly. "I know," he said. The look in his eyes took her breath away. For once his eyes were free of pain and cynicism. They were happy and alive.

And more beautiful than any eyes she'd ever seen.

She couldn't help the feeling of disappointment that came over her later when she saw John and her father driving away in the wagon. It was a dark, sad feeling that she couldn't explain. She actually glanced up toward the sky once, thinking for a moment that the clouds had moved in to block the sun.

And yet the sky was as clear and bright as it had been all day.

Lida shook her head.

"What's wrong with you, *Fraulein?*" she chided herself. "You are becoming *ferhoodlt.*"

Twelve

It was late when the barn raising was finished. Mr. Hostetler walked among his Amish neighbors, shaking hands and thanking them. And after a prayer, the families began to gather their children into their wagons and buggies for the ride home.

Lida glanced about and saw her father and John talking and pointing with pride to the completed structure.

And she knew the time had come for her to speak to Carl. There had been little time for it all day. She even thought several times that if Christela and her friends hadn't kept at her all day, she might have changed her mind altogether about speaking to him of their marriage.

When she saw him carrying tools to a shed behind the new barn, she took a deep breath, gathering her courage. Then she hurried after him.

"Carl," she said, stepping just inside the door.

Carl straightened and turned. Even in the gloom, she could see the light that sprang to his pale eyes when he saw her there.

"Lida," he murmured. "I have wanted to speak to you all day."

"And I you," she said. It wasn't a lie, she told herself. This was something she had to do.

"You . . . you look beautiful today," he said, his voice quiet and shy.

"Carl," she said, moving farther into the shed. Should she touch him? Offer him her hand?

Carefully Lida placed her hand on his arm. When she saw the look of adoration in Carl's eyes as his gaze moved from her hand back up to her face, she almost changed her mind.

Why was this so difficult?

"Carl, I know I've been putting you off this past year . . . about our wedding. And when Ephraim died I—"

She stopped, unable to continue when she saw the look of joy that moved over his face.

"Yes?" he said. "Yes, Lida? Go on with what you wanted to say."

She shook her head. Was this really what she wanted? Was love really not important in a marriage, as the elders said?

"Maybe I shouldn't—"

Carl took her arms and pulled her toward him. His actions surprised her more than she would have thought. And the revulsion she felt surprised her even more.

Why didn't she feel all the heartstopping emotions with Carl that she felt when John Sexton touched her? When he looked into her eyes. She'd certainly never had erotic thoughts or dreams about Carl Miller.

"Then let me say it," he said, bending his head

as if to kiss her. "Lida Rinehart, would you do me the honor of becoming my wife?"

"Yes," she said quickly. Before she had time to think. Before she had time to change her mind.

She closed her eyes at the ache that appeared suddenly in her chest. And when she felt the brush of Carl's beard against her skin and then the light touch of his lips on hers, she opened her eyes.

"Oh, Lida," he murmured, gathering her closer in his arms. "This is all I've ever wanted. A good wife to bear my children, a farm . . . friends to gather close in our times of joy and times of sorrow."

"I know," she whispered, pulling away and looking into his eyes. "We will have a good life."

He was a good man. A decent, honorable man who would make her a fine husband. He would never cause her pain or worry. He was of her world and he understood everything about her.

Except how she felt about John Sexton.

And that was one thing she swore he would never know. That no one of her Amish family would ever know.

Carl started to kiss her again when they heard shouting outside.

"It is my father calling me," he said, stepping away with a sigh of regret. "I must go. But I am so proud you have agreed to be my wife, Lida. We will announce it at next church meeting, yes?"

"Yes," she said, feeling numb . . . feeling such fear that for a moment she almost called him back to tell him she had made a mistake.

She watched him hurry out the door before she wrapped her arms around her body and stood trembling in the middle of the darkened toolshed. She closed her eyes for only a moment. Then she heard a quiet voice in the shadows near the doorway.

"Well, for a young woman who's just become betrothed, you don't look at all happy." John stood just inside the door, leaned back against a wall, his arms folded over his chest.

"What . . . what are you doing here?"

He raised his arm, holding a leather pouch and a hammer in the air before tossing them onto a nearby shelf.

"You didn't answer me," he said, his voice deep and soft.

"What do you want me to say?"

"I want you to tell me that you're happy. That marrying Carl Miller is what you really want."

"I . . . I am happy," she said. But she couldn't meet his eyes and instead looked at the wall behind him.

"Little liar," he whispered.

"Oh, you are so arrogant," she said. She was trembling with anger and with some emotion that she couldn't explain. The same emotion she always felt when John was near . . . and when he looked at her with those piercing eyes. "What makes you think you know anything about me? Or about what I want? You come here, wounded and helpless, needing our help. And we have helped you. You involved my brother in something forbidden to our society and you don't even ask for forgiveness. And now you think you can tell me who I can marry. You are so—"

She heard his quiet laughter and she stopped, staring hard at him.

"It won't work this time, blue eyes," he said. He came closer, moving into a thin shaft of light that exposed the hard menacing look in his eyes. "You've done it before and I fell for it. But throwing what happened to Ephraim in my face won't turn me away this time."

Lida gritted her teeth and whirled around, marching to a tiny window that looked out over one of Mr. Hostetler's pastures. She put her hands on the windowsill, gripping it as if she might rip it out of the wall.

She heard him move toward her and she turned, positioning herself as if to fight.

"Don't," she said, trying to sound as if she meant it. "Don't come another step closer."

"Why? What are you afraid of?"

"I . . . I'm not."

"But you are, little one," he said, coming a step closer. Slowly, provocatively closing her in against the wall. "You're afraid of me and what's been happening between us."

"No."

"And you know what I think?" he asked quietly, standing only inches from her. "I think that's why you've run so quickly to Carl."

"No," she said again, her voice harsh with emotion. She put her hand up as if to ward him off, even though he made no other move toward her.

"You've agreed to marry him, thinking you'd

be safe from me. Thinking to substitute him for me." His eyes were steady and riveting.

She opened her mouth to protest again, but no words would come. She was too angry. Too insulted. Too breathless.

"Ist lächerlich," she finally managed to whisper.

"Ridiculous?" he asked. "Or are you cursing me again in high German?"

"I have to go. Get out of my way."

"Run then, *Liebling,*" he taunted. "Because you'll never be safe as long as you're within arm's reach of me."

A slow smile crossed his face, and for a moment she thought he would not let her pass. Then he took one step to the side, motioning with his arm for her to go.

But when Lida stepped forward, he caught her in his arms and dragged her against him, holding her and forcing her to look up into his face.

"You look me in the eye, Lida Rinehart. And you tell me that what I've said is not the truth."

"It isn't," she said, clamping her lips together. "It isn't the truth," she cried softly.

"Do you know how long I've wanted to hold you?" he asked, his breathing ragged, his voice rasping with emotion. "How long I've wanted to kiss you?"

"Don't do this," she said. Lida closed her eyes against the onslaught of unbridled emotions that his touch, his voice, his heated looks made her feel.

"I have to," he whispered, pulling her closer. "God, just once before I leave . . . I have to."

He took her mouth in a kiss that was hungry and wild. As passionate and tumultuous as all the emotion they'd tried to suppress these past few weeks. And as soon as his lips touched hers, Lida was lost, despite all her denials. She encircled her arms around his neck and savored the taste and heated male scent of him. Returned his kiss with all the wild desperation and desire that she'd been feeling for so long.

Never in her life had she been kissed like this. And yet her wild response to him came as naturally as breathing. She felt his tongue and she opened her mouth. Accepting him, wanting him . . . needing him more than she'd ever needed anything. She heard . . . felt his quiet groan of desire as he imprisoned her against the wall with his body.

His hands were unrelenting, going to her breasts to touch and explore and making her gasp with wild, unexpected pleasure.

"John . . . no," she gasped, knowing she should leave. Knowing she should deny him this, for Carl's sake. For her parents. For her own sanity and salvation.

"Yes," he growled. His hands moved upward, enclosing her face as he pulled her forward to taste her mouth again.

Lida was aware of what went on between a man and a woman. But where the senses and emotions were involved, she was completely innocent. And if any man had ever felt sexual desire for her, it had been hidden and unknown to her.

But John made no attempt to hide it, or deny

what he was feeling. Made no murmured apology in an attempt to shield her from his desires. His hands moved downward, past her waist to the curve of her hips. He pulled her against him, letting her feel his arousal, as his mouth devoured hers, letting her know just how much he wanted her. His kissed moved hotly down her neck and she arched her head, giving him free access, shivering when he began to whisper sexual, forbidden words against her ear.

With quiet whimpers of surrender and a feminine instinct she didn't even know she possessed, Lida found herself moving against him. Touching, savoring, giving herself to him as completely as if they were actually making love.

The feeling for Lida was exhilarating. And frightening.

She was gasping desperately for breath and for sanity when she finally made herself pull away from him.

Her breasts rose and fell rapidly as she stared into his eyes, as she saw the desire and felt it surging hotly between them.

She never imagined in her wildest dreams that anything like this was possible between a man and a woman. She had thought only of her duty toward a husband. Of a quiet friendship as she bore children and they raised them together. No one had ever told her about feelings like this, or that a man like John Sexton even existed.

"This is wrong," she whispered, her eyes stricken as she watched disappointment move into his eyes.

"It isn't wrong," he said, his voice husky.

"I . . . I have to go."

"Don't marry him, Lida. You don't have to do that. Not because of me. I won't be a threat to you anymore, once I'm gone."

No threat? How could he say he was no threat when every inch of her body urged her to lie shamelessly with him right here and now? To make love to him the way they both wanted. With wild abandonment that couldn't be stopped. Uncaring of who might step inside that door. Uncaring of what this would do to her parents and her status in the church.

He was a threat to her heart and mind. To her very soul.

She looked deep into his eyes, wavering for long moments. Then with a quiet murmur, she turned and ran toward the door.

She wasn't certain when she ran outside if the heavy sigh of regret she heard was her own. Or if it came from the room she had just fled.

That night long after they had arrived home, Lida could hear sounds from John's room. She heard him walking about and she knew he was awake and just as restless as she was. After the house was quiet and the meadows around them echoed with night crickets, Lida paced the floor in her own room.

What was she to do? How on earth could she deny these desires any longer after today? When her every waking moment was filled with him, consumed by him. When all she could think about was how it would feel to kiss him forever, to feel his hands touch her body . . . to lie in bed with him, unclothed . . .

"Stop it," she whispered, clenching her fists as she paced. "I can't . . . I shouldn't feel this way. I can't sleep with an English and I certainly can never marry one. What I'm feeling is wrong . . . it's sinful. My decision to marry Carl is what is right for me. Not John," she added, almost prayerfully.

Then why did saying those words of renunciation hurt so much? And why did the thought of denying John and all that she felt for him make her heart ache so painfully?

"God," she whispered, moving to the window. She gazed up at the clear sky and the stars that hung glittering above the earth. "Help me. Please . . . you have to help me."

Thirteen

Lida lay awake that night for the longest time, listening to the familiar night sounds of the house and its surrounding land. Thinking about today and John. Remembering. Envisioning every word, every touch between them.

No matter how hard she prayed, she found no relief from the pain and confusion. And no matter how many times she told herself it was wrong, she couldn't seem to make those disturbing visions go away. She couldn't stop thinking about John and wondering what she was to do about him.

But there *was* nothing more she could do. He was leaving, and that was probably the only thing that would save her from making the biggest mistake of her life.

What she hadn't counted on was her father's announcement at breakfast the next morning.

"John received a letter yesterday when we went into Walnut Creek. He's been advised to stay here another week at least." Her father barely looked up from his food, but Lida could see by his expression that he was pleased.

"Der gut," Anna Rinehart said with an approving nod. "Good," she repeated in English.

Lida looked across the table, directly into John's eyes. If the questioning look she saw in his eyes meant he sought her approval, then he was going to be disappointed. No matter how joyously her heart sang at hearing the words, she knew her entire soul was in jeopardy if he stayed.

How could he even expect such a thing? Did he have any idea of the battle that raged within her when he was near? When he merely looked at her?

"What has happened?" she asked, trying to keep her voice calm and dispassionate.

"According to the letter, there are bounty hunters looking for me. They were probably with the sheriff that day he came here to the farm. My friends want me to stay here until a small group of men arrive to escort me back to Kentucky. They seem to think this is the safest place at the moment."

"Regardless of the danger you put us all in?" she asked with a cold glitter in her eyes.

"Lida!" her father exclaimed. It was one of the few times she'd ever heard her father raise his voice. "You will not speak to a guest at my table in such an accusatory manner."

"But, Father, you know it's true," she said, making sure to keep her voice low and calm. "You said yourself that the sheriff's wife was asking about him. What if they find out that John Sexton is actually the Sojourner? And that he is staying here with us? Do you know what they will do to all of us . . . to this farm? He is not a friend, Papa. He's an enemy to all of us . . . and our friends and relatives."

"If thine enemy hunger, feed him," Jacob said firmly, quoting the Bible. "There will be no more talk of this, daughter. I don't know what's come over you these last few weeks. If the brethren knew of your ungracious behavior, I fear you would be called before them for a public confession."

I *need* to confess, Lida wanted to shout. I need to confess to the whole world about all the forbidden thoughts I have for this man. And I need to confess that if he stays, my soul is in danger of being lost.

She glanced across the table at John and she thought he could actually read her thoughts. That he knew somehow exactly what she was thinking and feeling. And she could have sworn he was enjoying it.

With a quiet murmur of protest, Lida excused herself from the table.

On Sunday, after church services held at the Dietz farm, Carl announced their marriage plans to the congregation.

There were quiet murmurs of delight and congratulations. Then the girls gathered around Lida, teasing her and giggling with excitement. The young men who came to Carl offered their best wishes and made jokes. But the teasing was good natured and affectionate, and for a while Lida actually felt a glimmer of happiness.

Then they all went outside to the tables set for

their noon meal. And she saw John leaning against the trunk of a large tree as he waited for services to be over. Even from this distance she knew he was watching *her.* Accusing her somehow.

Lida wanted to run. She wanted to pull her hand from Carl's and just run as fast as she could. Away from John's looks, and her mother's pleased expression . . . away from everyone's congratulations. Away from the falseness that lay in her own heart.

But she couldn't. She had to stay and face it all. Now that the announcement had been made, Lida knew there was no turning back.

Somehow, for the rest of the week, she managed to avoid John. But the looks between them, the way she would catch him watching her, played on her nerves. She found herself feeling breathless with anxiety. Some evenings she would slip out of the house and run across the fields to relieve some of the tension she felt. And during the days she worked herself into total exhaustion.

Her mother had planned a husking bee for Saturday, where the neighbors would come to sweep and clean the barn in preparation for the gathering and husking of the corn crop. And as always when the faithful were together, there would be food and socializing. And Lida knew she could not avoid John on that day.

But the men who would escort him to Kentucky would arrive on Sunday. Only one more day. If Lida could make it until then. If she could only manage to stay away from him.

But as much as she wanted him to go . . . *needed*

him to go, there was an ache in her heart when she thought of his leaving. And that was what frightened her the most.

Saturday was a good day. The sun was bright overhead, but a slight breeze rustled the leaves of the trees and kept the summer heat from being unbearable.

Lida worked with the other women, and after their meal they sat beneath the trees watching the children run and play corner ball. Some of the girls sat in the shade using complicated hand and foot rhythms as they sang fast-paced folk songs.

Carl was pitching horseshoes when Lida saw John walking toward her. He came and stood directly in front of her until she was forced to look up at him. Christela and the other girls sitting around her were completely silent, glancing with sly looks between John and Lida.

"Could I speak with you a moment, Lida?" he asked. He held his hand down toward her, as if to help her up. As if he actually expected her to place her hand in his here in front of her friends. "Alone?" he added, seeing her hesitancy.

"Well, I . . . we . . ."

"Go on," the others urged.

"Yes, go," Christela said, nudging Lida. Even though there was a hurt, disappointed look in her cousin's dark eyes, she urged Lida to go with him.

"I have to help Mother and the others with—"

"This won't take long," John said, his gray gaze steady. "We won't be out of sight."

Normally Lida would have taken his last sentence as a challenge or as some kind of mockery.

But when she looked up into his eyes now, she saw no teasing or mischief. Only a quiet, solemn look.

Lida came to her feet, brushing past him and ignoring his hand. She heard Christela's and the others' whispered comments as John fell into step beside her and they walked across the lawn.

He pointed past the vegetable garden where a path led to a spring and a springhouse. Here in the open, rolling countryside of Ohio, they would be seen no matter which direction they chose.

"I wanted to tell you about Ephraim before I leave. I didn't think I'd have a chance after today."

Lida stopped, staring up at him, frowning at the ache that sprang to her heart.

"I . . . I'm not sure I want to hear it."

"You need to hear it, Lida. I would like for you to understand. And not just for my sake."

Lida lifted her chin and began walking again. But John didn't say anything else until they had reached the spring.

Lida took a deep breath and sat on a low rock wall that had been built around the spring and springhouse.

John rubbed his chin, his eyes focused on the ground as he began to speak.

"That night, Ephraim met me at Sugar Creek. My orders were to proceed to Strasburg to pick up two slaves—a young man and his wife—and escort them to a station in Wayne County. I was told that the woman was expecting a child and that she wanted desperately for it to be born in

Canada. She and her husband were concerned that if they remained in Mississippi, their child might be sold at some future time."

Lida made a quiet noise and when John turned to look at her, she was staring at him with wounded eyes.

"Is that true?" she asked. "Can they really take someone's children and sell them?"

"Yes, it's true," he said quietly. "Some owners are more compassionate and try to keep the family united . . . sometimes for a lifetime. But with many, it's simply a business. Selling a slave's child means no more to them than the selling of a horse or a cow."

"Did you help this young couple?" Lida had forgotten why he was telling the story. All she could think of was the young expectant mother and what anxiety she must have been feeling for her unborn child.

John looked away from her intense gaze. He couldn't bear looking into those clear, honest blue eyes when he told her the rest.

"There were no lights in the house. I knew something was wrong from the beginning," he said. "It's something you begin to feel in your bones after a while. I told Ephraim to wait, to remain in the trees near the house while I went to see." John walked to a nearby tree and reached up to break off a limb as he gazed off into the distance. His back was turned to Lida now, and his voice was so low that she could barely make out what he was saying.

Instinctively she got up from the rock wall and walked closer. She held her breath as she listened.

"I heard someone in the barn. It was a woman, crying. When I crept closer and looked, I saw it was a black woman. Then I saw her husband." John hesitated a moment, then clenched his jaw and continued. "They'd strung him up by his wrists . . . beaten him unconscious. Not dead," John said with a rising note of fury in his voice. "He was too valuable to kill," he added cynically. "I don't know if they made his wife watch or if they simply didn't give a damn that she was there. But she'd seen it all and now she lay in the straw, crying and clutching her stomach as if to protect—" John stopped and looked at Lida. The anguish in his eyes was painful to see.

"Well," he said, releasing the air in his lungs. His teeth chewed at his lower lip and he shook his head. "I didn't behave rationally. I didn't take all the precautions I would normally take . . . had been trained to take. I simply reacted . . . and your brother paid for my mistake."

This wasn't what she'd expected. Even though she had accused him, blamed him, she never thought to hear him actually admit that he felt responsible for Ephraim's death. Oddly enough, now that he had said it, all she wanted to do was go to him, put her arms around him, and hold him.

"There were two of them in the barn—bounty hunters. I made the mistake of thinking that they had simply found the slaves, beaten him, and planned on taking them back to Mississippi. I had no idea that the whole scene was planned . . . that they'd been waiting, or that they were using the slaves to get to me."

"You?" she whispered.

"The Sojourner," he said with a wry twist of his lips. "Notoriety is not always a good thing. Once I was inside the barn, two others came in behind me. I shot one of them, not thinking that Ephraim would hear and come . . ." His voice trailed away and he glanced at Lida, his eyes sad and lost. "But he did. Even though he refused to carry a weapon, he came rushing into the barn like an avenging angel, with no thought for himself or his own safety. One of the bounty hunters used the moment to pull a gun from his holster. And then all hell broke loose."

John walked away from Lida, shrugging his shoulders and staring across the endless expanse of farmland.

"When it was over, Ephraim and I both had been shot. Two of the bounty hunters lay dead, and the other two wounded. At this point I suppose they were only interested in getting their bounty out of there and heading back toward Mississippi. So they left us for dead." He turned now and looked straight into Lida's eyes. "After they'd gone I managed to drag myself and Ephraim onto a horse. You know the rest."

Lida was aware of a terrible ache in her heart. And the pain in John's eyes.

"I'm sorry," he whispered. "All I wanted to say before I go is that I'm sorry. If I could go back . . . if I could change what happened, even if I could take Ephraim's place, I would." Their gazes met across the space that separated them, but neither of them moved.

"That's not something I would have said a few months ago," he said, his voice quiet now and so soft that Lida could barely hear it. "But that was before I met you."

His confession caused a sob to escape past Lida's lips, and without thinking she crossed the distance that separated them. She began to cry, tears flowing unchecked down her face. Her lips trembled as she looked up into his eyes. She stopped without touching him, aware of where they were and that everyone could see them.

They stood no more than a foot apart, staring into each other's eyes, not touching or moving.

John had hoped for Lida's forgiveness, but he had not expected it. And he hadn't expected to see in her eyes what he was seeing now. His eyes darkened and he shook his head, uncertain if his mind and heart were playing tricks on him.

"Lida," he whispered, still not moving, not wanting to believe what he saw on her beautiful face. And knowing he shouldn't want what was happening between them.

"I don't want you to go." Her voice was a mere whisper, her words a confession more than anything.

"You don't . . . ? Lida, what are you saying? That you've forgiven me. That you—"

"Forgiveness . . ." she murmured with a little shake of her head. "Oh, I think I forgave you long ago. You see, I knew Ephraim better than anyone. I knew how stubborn and contrary he was. There wasn't anything anyone could have said to keep him from doing what he did. Not even you, John. And if the truth is known, I admire him for what he did. For taking a stand about something that was so important."

John took a deep shuddering breath. There was nothing in the world he wanted more than her forgiveness. Except to pull her into his arms right now. To kiss that soft sweet mouth. Feel the length of her warm body against his.

"All the things I've said to you since you came," she whispered. "All the accusations, the ugly words . . . I didn't mean them. I was just hurt and afraid . . . confused about all the things you made me feel."

"Lida . . . don't," he said, his voice carrying a quiet warning.

"I don't want you to go, John," she said, ignoring his words and reaching forward as if to touch him. "I don't know what I'm saying, or what I mean. I'm not even sure of what it is I feel or why I do. God, John . . . all I know at this moment is that I can't bear for you to go. I can't."

"Don't do this, Lida," he said. His eyes had turned a stormy silver now. Troubled and tender. "Dammit, don't do this. Not now when I have to go. I have to."

"You don't," she whispered, her voice hurried with desperation and pleading. "You can stay here. Mama and Papa love you already . . . like a son. There is no one else to inherit the farm . . . the land, except me and the husband I choose."

"Lida," he said again, shaking his head and staring at her with disbelief in his eyes. "What about Carl . . . your marriage plans?"

"I don't love Carl. You know that . . . you've known it all along."

Seeing him frown, she laughed nervously. "Here I am, making a fool of myself in front of an English like you, John Sexton. But all I want is for you to stay. You can join the church . . . forget the war and stay here with the plain people, where you will be safe."

"I can't," he whispered. He closed his eyes for a moment, and when he opened them, he looked at her with regret and tenderness.

"It is permitted," she said, ignoring the quiet look of concern in his eyes. She went on, hurriedly as if she hadn't even heard him. "An English may join us. They ask only that you meet the Christian requirements and—"

"No, angel," he said. He took her shoulders and pulled her with him to the shelter of the large tree. At this point he didn't care who saw them or what the others would say. "Don't do this. God, don't make it any harder for me to go than it already is."

She closed her eyes and shook her head hard, causing fresh tears to spill down her cheeks.

"I can't forget the war, Lida. Don't you see? What I'm doing is important to me," he said, tapping his chest for emphasis. "Not being an officer for one side or the other. Not leading a company of young men into battle, knowing that most of them will die. I'm *saving* lives," he whispered emphatically. "And as much as I'd love to stay here with you, safe and secure from all the ugliness . . . I can't. I can't."

"You can," she whispered, shaking her head against the pain in her heart.

"Sweetheart, you know there's no future for either of us. I'm not Amish. No matter how hard I might want to try and do it for you, I'll never truly be Amish. And you can't be anything else."

"But I love you," she whispered, looking through her tearstained lashes up into his eyes.

John groaned and leaned his head back against the tree.

"Don't even say such a thing," he said through clenched teeth. "Don't love me. I can't stay. I'm not worth what you would have to give up, blue eyes," he said, reaching out to brush the tears from her face. "Don't love me," he whispered fiercely. His eyes were tortured as he brushed a wisp of silken hair from her face.

Then he released her and turned away, walking back toward the others, leaving Lida staring after him.

She thought she would die as she watched him go. She actually thought she would die from the ache in her heart.

Fourteen

Going back to the festivities, Lida avoided Christela and the other girls. She didn't want them to see her red, swollen eyes, and she didn't have the heart to tell them a lie about her conversation with John.

When everyone had left for home, Jacob and John went to the barn to attend to chores. And since John would probably leave during the middle of the night, Lida was sure that her father also wanted to be alone with him, to say his goodbyes and wish him a safe journey.

But Lida thought she couldn't bear another goodbye. She refused supper on the pretense of being tired and that she wanted to go to bed early.

Then she went to her room and sat by a window, moving back and forth in a rocking chair as she watched the shadows of evening move slowly across the countryside and into the corners of her room.

Later, she heard her parents come up the stairs and go to their room. Then John, who seemed to hesitate for a moment in the hallway outside her door before going past.

Tonight Lida had no desire to leave the house

and race through the cool green grass. No energy to spend herself in a relentless flight from something she didn't even understand. Tonight she felt lifeless, numb with grief and despair.

What if John died, too, like Ephraim. She wouldn't even know. She would merely be left here to marry Carl and raise his children. And she would never know what it was to love and be loved in the wild, passionate way her heart told her it could be.

She finally went to bed, even though she knew she'd never be able to sleep. She lay staring at the shadows, seeing the sparkle of stars out her window as she waited to hear John leave the farmhouse for good. She didn't know what time it was when she heard a noise at her door and sat up in bed.

She turned her head, as if in a slow moving dream. And she saw him standing there, a dark silhouette in the unlit house. But she knew it was him. Knew it in her heart and her soul.

"John," she said, her voice choked.

He closed the door and stepped into the room, walking silently to her bed.

Lida could feel her heart tripping against her ribs, hammering out a rhythm that kept time with the rush of blood through her veins.

She slid out of bed and went to him as if he had commanded it aloud, putting her arms around his waist and resting her head against his chest. His arms enclosed quickly around her and she heard him groan before he took her face in his hands and pulled her up for his kiss.

Lida's heart was singing when the kiss ended. She heard John take a deep breath, as if he sought control. She found herself trembling wildly, expectantly. She was acutely aware of her nakedness beneath her prim white gown as she moved her hands up from his taut stomach and over his chest. She heard his swift intake of air before he caught her up against him and took her mouth in a hard, searching kiss that left both of them breathless.

John paused, wishing there was a light so that he could see her. He couldn't take a chance on waking her parents and having them find him here.

But the darkness seemed to enhance his sensitivity. Every quiet sigh, every movement told him what she was feeling. He could feel her body trembling in his arms, hear her quiet murmurs of pleasure as she snuggled against him.

When he moved his hands to her breasts, he could feel their fullness, and the way her nipples tightened beneath his fingers. That quick, minute, instinctive response of her body made him groan with pleasure.

When John traced his hand down her stomach, Lida moved against him involuntarily, her body wanting more, seeking some primitive fulfillment that she had never felt before. Yet knowing it existed.

She was burning up. Hot . . . tense. Needing something more. Trying to push herself closer and closer against him and yet unable to express to him what it was she wanted. It was unbearable . . . and irresistible.

Suddenly frightened, she pushed away from him, backing away a few steps and trying to see his face . . . his eyes. She could hear his harsh breathing in the quiet of the room, as she felt her heart pounding at her throat. And yet, despite the hot rhythm of her own blood, she was afraid.

Did he want to make love to her? Here . . . tonight, in the room just down the hall from her parents?

"Lida," John whispered. He stepped closer, pulling her against him again, his mouth going to the soft area at her neck.

Lida shivered. She felt weak, unable to resist. The pleasure of his mouth and his hands was like a slow, insidious drug, turning her resistance to smoke, seducing her until she thought she might actually scream from the sheer glory of it.

When John pushed her to the bed, she didn't resist. And when she felt him unbuttoning his shirt, her hands went automatically to help. She pushed the material aside with quiet little gasps, and with an impatience she didn't even know she possessed. When his skin was naked beneath her hands, she sighed and buried her face against him, tasting, exploring, her teeth nipping at him until both of them were wild with desire.

John could feel her body quivering beneath his. Her fragrance, her primal response to his kisses and his caresses, drove him on against his better judgment. He knew, as a man knows, that what she wanted and needed more than anything was a man's lovemaking.

His lovemaking.

And even though he had promised himself that he wouldn't let this happen, that he intended only to say goodbye, he felt his resolve melting away beneath her sweet, sensual assault. And he knew he was lost. That both of them were lost.

He moved his hand lower, feeling the heat of her, feeling the ancient instinctive rhythm that urged him on. He pushed her gown out of the way, and when he touched her, a quiet little cry burst from her lungs as she moved against his hand.

The need to take her then and there was almost unbearable. And John knew that she would accept him now, despite her lack of knowledge about what was happening. Despite her innocence, she was as hot and as desperate as he was.

Her hands clutched at his shoulders, as she arched against him, making desperate little noises against his neck. Her teeth bit at him, sought his mouth, urged him without words to make love to her.

John gritted his teeth, resisting his own wants and using his hands and fingers to give her pleasure. To teach her about what would happen and to make sure she was ready.

She cried out at his explorations, moved wildly against him. She was pleading quietly now . . . desperately, her blond hair becoming a tangle as she thrashed back and forth against the bed, seeking fulfillment without knowing how or why.

John's instinct and need to bury himself in her was overwhelming. His body urged him to do it and have done with it once and for all. To finally release all the pent-up feelings and emotions that had existed between them almost from that first night they met.

But feeling the heat of her body and her nearness to release, he fought his own instincts.

"John," she whispered, her voice pleading . . . desperate. "John!" she cried, clutching at him as her body shook with a wild, untamed furor. "Love me," she whispered even as her frenzy began to recede. "Love me."

It was what he wanted, too. To make love to her. *All* he wanted.

It took every ounce of strength he possessed to pull away from her then, away from the warmth of her arms and her lips. The soft sensuality of her body was ready for him in every way.

He pulled himself away, breathing raggedly as he sat on the side of the bed.

"Jesus," he muttered, pushing himself up from the bed and grabbing his shirt from the floor.

"John," she protested. She pushed herself up on her elbows, staring at his shadow in the darkness, unable to believe he would leave her. Not now.

"I came to say goodbye," he said, his voice hoarse.

She could see him pushing his shirt into his trousers, his movements quick and impatient. She felt the knowledge of what he was doing wash over her in one quick, violent sense of regret. He *couldn't* leave her now! Not after what had just happened between them. After what she wanted to happen now. He wanted it, too. No matter how much he denied it, she knew now without a doubt that it was what he wanted, too.

"I didn't intend for any of this to happen," he said, his voice harsh with recrimination. "I only wanted to say goodbye. To kiss you one last time . . . and hold you. God," he muttered, walking to the window and taking long, deep breaths of air.

John was angry with himself. Furious and disgusted that he had let his own needs bring them both to this. Thank God he'd had enough self-control to stop it before he made the mistake of his life.

But his body still ached for her. And he feared that any touch, any sweet, caressing word from those lips would undo his resolve and make him go to her despite his vow that he wouldn't.

He couldn't take a chance on leaving her with a child. Hell, he had no idea when or if he'd ever be back here again. If he'd ever see her again. If he'd even be alive this time next year. And he wasn't the kind of man to dismiss his responsibilities so carelessly. Especially with a woman like Lida Rinehart.

Lida slipped from the bed and walked tentatively toward him. John turned with an almost violent motion.

"Don't," he warned. "God, this is difficult enough already."

"I was sure you had come to tell me you'd stay. That you loved me and wanted to stay."

"I can't stay," he said. He raked his hands through his hair and walked away from her, keeping his footsteps soft and quiet on the wooden floors. "You know that. You know—"

"And you don't love me," she said. She had to hear it. Had to make him tell her once and for all that he didn't feel the same way she did. And that he never could. There was a tightness in her voice now. The tenderness and pleading was gone as she realized that he still intended leaving, despite her feelings. Despite her urging him to stay. "Say it, John. Tell me you don't, that you never can love me."

"I can't love any woman," he said rigidly. "Not now. Not when what I'm doing is so dangerous and uncertain."

"So . . ." she said, her voice flat and resolved. "You've made your choice."

"Lida . . . dammit," he snapped. "There is no choice. That isn't the question. Don't you see? Can't you—?"

From somewhere outside the farmhouse came a long, low whistle. And now through the open window, they could hear the whinnying of horses.

John stepped to the window. In the dim light of the quarter moon, he could barely make out the riders that sat astride their horses in the yard below. He saw the quick flash of a light, the signal he'd been told to watch for.

"I have to go," he said. "If I know your father, he's already heard the horses and the whistle. I can't let him find me here in your room."

"Then it's over," she said, her voice quiet and anguished. "You're going. And I'll probably never see you again."

"It's over," he said, his voice quiet. "It has to be."

She nodded, although he couldn't see her in the darkness. She walked quickly to the table beside her bed and struck a match, lighting a lamp despite his quietly muttered warning.

She ignored him. Didn't he know how desperately she longed to see him this one last time? To look into those gray eyes and see the desire she'd seen there before? To see the same heat that had surged between them that day in the rain and the storm?

She turned, her eyes glittering with tears, and she stared at him across the room.

"Lida . . ." he whispered, his voice soft and husky. "Lida, sweetheart . . . I never meant to hurt you or cause you even the smallest amount of pain. I don't fit into your life. And I can't ask you to fit into mine."

"I won't beg you," she said, standing with her fists clutched at her side.

John thought she looked like an angel there in the lamplight in her soft white gown. He heard another low whistle from the riders in the yard. But before he turned to go, he allowed himself this one last moment. To let his eyes take in every inch of her. From the soft blond hair that lay tangled against her face and shoulders, to the heated flush on her cheeks.

She stood straight and proud, letting him have his fill of looking at her, with no false modesty about her body. He could see the outline of her lush curves through the thin material of her gown. Could plainly see her firm round breasts and taut nipples.

But it was the pain in her eyes that almost stopped him from going. He shook it off with an impatient shrug.

"I'm doing you a favor, Lida," he whispered. "You might not think so now, but believe me, blue eyes . . . I'm doing you a favor. I should have left long ago," he said, his voice raw and filled with emotion. "I knew what was happening and I should have gone then."

He walked quickly across the room and took her shoulders, pulling her close for one last kiss.

Her mouth clung to his . . . sweetly, desperately, belying the anger and frustration he saw in her blue eyes when he pulled away and looked down at her.

He took one step away from her. "Marry Carl," he murmured as he turned to walk to the door. "Forget you ever met me, Lida. Marry Carl Miller and be happy."

Then he was gone and Lida was left standing in the empty room, feeling a deep sense of despair like nothing else she'd ever felt.

Marry Carl? Now . . . after John had come to her room, after he had made her feel an ecstasy such as she'd never felt before? After he had made certain that she could never marry anyone or love anyone except him, for as long as she lived?

How could he be so cruel? How could he ever expect her to do such a thing?

She heard the sound of the horses riding away.

She went to the window and dropped down to her knees, leaning her arms against the window-sill and propping her chin against her arms.

She couldn't even cry. She felt so empty . . . so heartbroken that she couldn't cry.

"Forget you?" she said softly to the darkness. "*Nein,*" she whispered. "It is not so easy as that, my love."

Fifteen

Lida woke sometime in the early morning, still sitting at the window with her head nestled against her arms. She stretched, feeling stiff and cold, and finally pushed herself up wearily from the hard floor.

Shivering, she went to the bed to get warm, if only for a short while. She'd heard the clock striking in the hallway—that must have been what woke her—and she knew it was time to go downstairs and help her mother with breakfast.

Her mind was filled with thoughts of John. With the wild, tumultuous way he'd made her feel. Lying in bed, she ran her hands down over her breasts and stomach, remembering his hands . . . remembering every sweet torturous thing he had done to her.

She blushed thinking about it.

A quiet sob escaped her lips when she remembered his leaving. The pain this morning was just as strong, just as real as it had been then.

She should be angry. This man . . . this English stranger had come into her life and turned it upside down. If he hadn't come, she could have gone on living the quiet peaceful farmlife that was expected of her, just the way she had resigned herself long ago to do. She would have married Carl. She could even have been happy if John hadn't come. If only because she simply never would have known the difference.

But that was before John made her feel these forbidden things . . . before he forced her, body and soul, to see how it could be between a man and a woman.

Yet he had dismissed her last night as easily as if she'd been a child. Telling her he was doing her a favor indeed!

Lida sat up in bed and flung the covers back away from her. Her eyes sparkled with blue fire as she quickly dressed.

"No more of this," she muttered as she made the bed. "No more mooning over a man who does not want me and has made it plain that he could never love someone like me."

She walked to the window and glanced out at the beauty of her native farmland. This land . . . this quiet simple life, should be more than enough to please a woman. It should be enough for her.

"It is," she vowed fiercely. She gritted her teeth and turned from the window, determined that John Sexton was not going to ruin her life.

Love him, she did. But she was wise enough to know that a woman could not make a man love her in return, no matter how badly she wanted it.

Even now he was probably thinking about the life he had left. Looking forward to going back to it. He probably couldn't wait to wear real English clothes and dance with English women. Make love to a woman who wore expensive jewels and perfumes and roses in her hair. A woman of his own world—one he could be proud of.

"Stop it," she said to herself. She could feel the tears and the despair threatening. "See what you've done," she muttered, berating herself as she whirled around from the window.

She saw her mother standing at the door. She was watching Lida with an odd expression.

"Lida? *Was ist los?* Have you taken to talking to yourself now?"

Lida's laugh was forced as she hurried toward her mother.

"Nein," Lida said, placing her arm around her mother's waist.

"Eilen," her mother said, still watching Lida's face with a curious look. "We must hurry. We have all overslept this morning. Did you hear John leave, too? I don't think your papa slept another wink after that."

"Yes, I heard," Lida said, not turning to meet her mother's eyes.

While they were having breakfast, Lida's Uncle Levi stopped by. She could tell by the way he looked down at the floor as he held his hat in his hands that something troubled him.

"Met some men on the road this morning," he said, seating himself at the table.

Lida's heart skipped a beat and she was immediately alert.

"Bounty hunters, I think," he continued.

Jacob Rinehart nodded thoughtfully, but said nothing.

Lida knew her father was worried, not only about John, but about all their families as well. The war was coming closer every day, and no matter how many times the Amish declared themselves neutral, they couldn't pretend it didn't exist. And they couldn't pretend they didn't care that their fellow countrymen were dying in large numbers, in the North as well as in the South.

"The papers say it doesn't look good for the South," Levi said. "There were heavy blows struck there in the spring. Some say the war could end this summer."

"Let's pray it does." Jacob said.

"I don't know," Levi said, shaking his head. "They say President Lincoln is not pleased with McClellan, that he urges him to move more energetically. If he does not—" Levi Dietz spread his hands in a questioning gesture. "Who knows?"

"What about the slaves?" Lida asked. "Are many of them leaving the south and coming north?"

Lida's father gave her a long, solemn look. He knew exactly why she was asking. Not that John's identity was any secret from her Uncle Levi. Or any of the Amish for that matter. Jacob Rinehart simply didn't like war discussions at his table, or even in his house.

Still, Lida knew that he was as curious and as concerned as she was.

"They say we are on the main escape route,"

Levi said, nodding wisely. "That's why the bounty hunters roam this area night and day. It's dangerous . . . growing more dangerous every day to help them escape. President Lincoln should do something. It is his duty."

"He will," Jacob said. "Some say he will act soon to free the slaves. Then there will be no need for this escaping . . . this hunting and chasing them across our farms like animals."

Her father's words brought John's story back to Lida. About the night that he and Ephraim were ambushed. She had thought about the young pregnant slave and her husband more than once since then. And every time, remembering it brought a little ache to her heart. She hadn't been able to put a name to that little ache before. But now she could.

Guilt.

She felt guilty that she did nothing and that her family did nothing. That the Amish people were expected to sit back and watch objectively as the war raged around them. It wasn't the way she would have chosen if she weren't Amish.

For the first time, she was really beginning to see why Ephraim had become involved.

By July, the war had changed sharply. The string of Northern victories had ended. And Lida had heard that while the South was still being held at bay, there was now renewed hope among the Confederates.

She was disappointed and frightened. She had

hoped, like her uncle said, that the war might end this summer. That John would be free of his responsibilities. That he might even come back to her.

Now, that all seemed unlikely.

When Lida drove into town for her weekly shopping, the war was all that anyone talked about. Old men and crippled veterans who'd been sent home from the war stood in the shade beneath the store awnings, or on the street beneath the spreading elms. They talked almost exclusively of the war.

Lida paused as she looked through vegetable barrels on the front porch of the general store. Her family had all the vegetables they could eat, but she used the opportunity to listen.

"That General Lee," she heard one say. "Now, there's a soldier. McClellan should take some advice from him."

"Luck," another said. "Pure luck. Lee might be pushing McClellan back from Richmond now, but he's outmanned. Can't keep it up for long."

"What about Vicksburg?" The man posing the question had only one arm and he still wore a blue Union cap, although he was dressed in civilian clothes. "Farragut should have taken Vicksburg by now. Chattanooga hasn't fallen either, they say."

"That's right. Why, this time last month, none of this seemed possible. We thought it was over."

"Lida."

Lida turned at the sound of her name. She forced herself to smile when she saw Carl coming toward her. She had managed to avoid him since

John left, although she'd known she'd probably see him today as she usually did. She had no idea what she was to do about him, or how she could humiliate him by telling him that she couldn't marry him. But now, seeing the light in his eyes as he walked toward her, she felt a deepening sense of guilt.

"Hello, Carl."

"What are you doing looking at vegetables?" he said with a laugh. "Did you let your summer garden go to seed?" he teased. "Do I need to give my wife-to-be a lesson in gardening?"

"No," she said, managing a laugh. "Our garden is flourishing, thank you. Even in this sweltering heat." She leaned toward him and whispered. "I was only pretending. So that I could hear the men talking about the war."

"Ah," he said, frowning down at her. "A pretty young woman does not need to hear such things. When we are married, I will demand that you do nothing except cook and clean. And a little gardening," he added with a grin. "You are much too beautiful to trouble yourself with such worries."

Lida frowned. Carl's talk was mostly light and teasing. But still, it troubled her. One of the things she had liked most about John when they sat talking after supper was that he never spoke to her or her mother with condescension. He treated Lida as if she had a mind, as if he was as interested in her opinions as he was his own, or those of other men.

She shook her head. She had been trying her

best to forget him. To forget anything good about him. He had left her. Abandoned her. And she shouldn't be wasting her time thinking about him. Certainly not thinking good things about him.

"I have to go," she said, gathering her basket and other things she had bought.

"Wait," Carl said. He touched her arm only slightly before pulling away. He was so gentle, so eager to please.

So why couldn't she love him? Why didn't he excite her? Make her feel all the wild, tumultuous feelings that . . .

Stop it, she told herself. Stop thinking about a man who doesn't want you and doesn't need you. She told herself that her feelings for John were superficial—not the kind of thing that would last a lifetime. Not the kind of secure love a woman needed.

"Yes?" she said, forcing herself to stand still and face Carl.

"We still haven't decided about the wedding. My mother is anxious to make plans. Could we sit down together Sunday? Talk about what we want to do?"

"I . . ." She needed to tell him. Now, before Sunday came. Before any further plans were made.

"Good," he said, reaching to take her hand and squeeze it. "I will tell my mother." With a smile and a polite nod, Carl hurried toward his buggy. He turned and waved and Lida managed a weak wave back.

Driving out of Walnut Creek, Lida had gone no more than two miles when she saw a group of people moving slowly on the road toward her. She squinted against the sunlight, wondering if it might be soldiers. But when she drew nearer and she saw who they were, her heart began to pound erratically.

In front were several men seated on horseback. Rough, unkempt men, well armed, with hard, dangerous-looking eyes. Some had ropes tied to their saddles. The ropes reached back to several young black men who struggled to stay on their feet as the horses pulled them along. Behind the captured men was a wagon with a driver seated up front, a rifle across his lap.

"Get on there," he called to the men who were walking in front of his wagon.

When Lida pulled up even with them, the riders tipped their hat, and although their grins and looks were leering, they said nothing. Lida supposed she could thank her manner of dress for that. Most people would not harm the Amish, even the most dangerous men who moved across the Ohio farm country.

As they passed she could see that the young slaves were covered with scratches and dirt where they had fallen and been dragged. Their wrists were bloodied where the ropes dug into their flesh.

But it was their eyes that captured her full attention. They were filled with a quiet anguish. A despair that she had seen only once before—on the faces of the family that night in the barn. The first night she saw John.

"Wait," she called, turning around in the seat

of the buggy. She was afraid to get down and even now, confronting such men, she felt fear weakening the muscles of her legs.

The entourage stopped and the riders turned around, staring at her.

One of them moved away from the front and rode around to her buggy. He was the cleanest of the lot and not an ugly man. Until he smiled, a leering, ugly smile that showed tobacco-stained teeth.

"What can we do for you, miss?" he asked.

Lida heard the other men laugh quietly. They were all watching her with the same look in their eyes as their leader. For a moment, she felt her hands tighten on the reins. All she wanted was to get away from them, from the stench of this man's unwashed body.

Then she looked into the black men's frightened eyes again and straightened her shoulders. She turned to the horseman with all the defiance she could muster.

"Where are you going with these men?"

"Why, honey, that ain't your concern. Why you askin' anyway?" The man leaned forward in the saddle, staring down into Lida's face as he continued his leering grin.

"I beg your pardon," she said, trying to keep her voice calm and polite. "But it is my concern. Can't you at least let them ride in the wagon? Just look at them—they're hurt and tired. They—"

The man beside her buggy threw back his head and laughed aloud.

"Tired are they? Now, ain't that a shame? Maybe

next time they take a notion to run away from their masters, they'll think about how tirin' it is bein' free." The man wasn't smiling now. His face was as hard and embittered as his eyes.

"Please," she said. "These men are human beings. They deserve—"

"Human?" the man said with a sneering laugh. "You hear that, boys? This pretty little Amish girl says these boys is human. Shore can't tell it by lookin' at 'em, can you?"

The others laughed, some slapping their thighs as if it the funniest joke they'd ever heard.

The man beside the buggy tipped his hat and tugged at his reins.

"I'll be sure and tell that to their masters down south, honey, when we get 'em there."

The riders moved forward then, pulling the black men with them.

Lida felt sick. Actually physically sick, knowing she couldn't help. Knowing that these three young men probably would never make it back to the south.

She slapped her reins across the horse's rump, causing the carriage to jump forward. Her sick anger was quickly turning to rage and frustration. She wished she were a man. She wished she had a gun and that she wasn't bound by her church's rules of passiveness. And for the first time in her life, she truly wished she weren't Amish.

Sixteen

Lida drove the buggy past the farmhouse and toward the barn so fast that it sent a billowing cloud of dust into the air. When she pulled the buggy to a stop, the horse whinnied loudly and the wheels made a scraping noise as it slid to a halt.

Her father came rushing out of the barn. He took off his hat and wiped the sleeve of his shirt across his brow before walking toward her with a worried frown. Lida saw her mother hurrying around the barn with a basketful of eggs.

"*Gott in Himmel,*" her father shouted. "What is wrong? Why are you driving so fast and abusing this poor animal?"

"Papa, we have to do something. I just saw men taking slaves back to the south. They were bound with ropes, being forced to walk behind the horses." Lida's words all ran together as she leapt from the buggy and ran to her father.

"Calm down . . . calm down," her father said. "Come. We will go into the house. Your face is red and you are too excited. *Mutter,*" he shouted over his shoulder. "To the house we go. The girl needs something cool for drinking."

"I don't need anything to drink," Lida protested, looking from her father to her mother.

"Come, dear," her mother said, taking her by the arm. "Let your papa unhitch the buggy. You and I will go to the house. Then you can tell us everything that has happened."

Once her father joined them, Lida found that she couldn't stop talking. The vision of those men . . . the look in their eyes. It would not leave her.

"And what do you think we can do?" her papa asked, after she'd told him everything.

"Surely there must be some law—"

"There is a law that says these people are to be returned to their owners," he said with a sad shake of his head. "And although I do not agree, it is not our way to interfere with the laws of the world."

"I'm not saying we should interfere. But there must be some way we can make them treat these people decently."

"This war," Jacob said with a shake of his head. "It is becoming too dangerous, even for the plain people. I should not have let you go into Walnut Creek alone today. I'm afraid, until the war is over, that you must not do so again, daughter."

"Papa—" she protested.

But seeing the stubborn look on his face, she didn't pursue that point further.

"I must ask you something," she said, her voice growing quiet.

"Ask anything," he said.

"I want to know what you think, Papa. Tell me,

here in the privacy of our own home . . . what you really think about the church's views about the war."

"The church's views are my own," he said, frowning at her question. "We do not participate in wars. They are nothing to us."

"But this one is," she said, leaning toward him with emphasis. "I know you were not born in this country, Papa," she said. "But I was. I am an American. These soldiers who are being killed, both in the north and south—*they* are Americans. So, how can you say it is nothing to us? I want to help, Papa. I need to do something to help."

Jacob Rinehart's mouth was set in a hard line and he wouldn't look his daughter in the eye.

"Is not your place to question the ministers of the church." His voice had actually risen, something Lida and her mother were not used to. "Is it not enough that this war has taken your brother? Do you expect me to give my permission for losing you as well? *Nein!* I will not. Now . . . there will be no more talk of this war, or of your helping." Mr. Rinehart rose from the table, took his hat from the peg on the wall, and walked out the door.

"Mother," Lida said, looking with stricken eyes at her mother.

"He is right," she said. "There is nothing you can do, *Liebling.* Nothing any woman can do. It is for the men and the soldiers."

"But—"

"Is no more discussion," she said, lifting her hand.

"Well, if you ask me, the men and soldiers are

doing a pretty damned sorry job of it." Lida got up from the table and stormed out of the room toward the stairs. She didn't even bother to look back at her mother, standing in the doorway. She knew if she did, she'd see shock and dismay on her plain sweet face. And that was the last thing Lida intended.

It was only two days later that they found the bodies of two black men, hardly a mile from where Lida had encountered the sullen-eyed men on the road.

When she heard, Lida was inconsolable. Despite her father's attempt to soothe her, she ran away from him. Away from the terrible things the neighbors had said about the dead men.

It reminded her of the couple John had told her about. Had the same thing happened to them? She sat for hours in the orchard, praying for guidance. She could no longer run away from her conscience. She asked God time and again, why such things happened, hoping that he would give her some sign of what she should do.

But in her heart, Lida already knew. She thought she'd known from the day she and Ephraim had walked here and he had spoken with such intensity about what he wanted in life.

Lida had felt the first stirring then. The first half hidden wish that she could be so brave . . . so determined, as her brother was.

And now she could be. Somehow, she had to find a way to help those whose lives had been shattered. She had to do everything she could to help herself forget those young Negro men she'd seen and not helped. All of the slaves with their dark, beseeching eyes.

After a long, sleepless night, she knew what she would do. And as it turned out, it was easier than she'd ever have dreamed.

"Mama . . . Papa," she said at breakfast. "I'd like to get away from the farm for a while. If it's all right, I'd like to visit Aunt and Uncle Kaufman in Cincinnati."

Her parents exchanged glances, and Lida thought she saw a pleading look in her mother's eyes directed toward her husband.

"It won't be for long. I'll come back before the corn husking. And Christela can go with me. We'll take the train. We'll be safe on the train."

Her father lowered his head. Anna Rinehart reached across the table and placed her hand on his arm. She didn't have to say anything. Her actions let her husband know what she was feeling.

Jacob sighed.

"I know it has been hard for you," he said. "Losing your brother. Having to care for John Sexton and tend his wounds, even though you felt the way you did about him."

You have no idea, Lida thought. No idea how it was or how I feel about John Sexton.

"Sometimes is good for a young woman to have her freedom," he said, nodding.

Lida could hardly believe it. He was going to let her go! He was actually going to let her go to Cincinnati where John was.

"When you come back, it will be time for working . . . *ja* . . . we work hard and get ready for winter. And for your wedding."

Lida's heart jumped. Carl. She hadn't even thought about him. Had not considered him at all in her decision to go.

She'd leave a letter for him. That was the only thing she could do.

The next day on the train, she settled down into her seat and turned to Christela.

"This is unbelievable," Christela said. "It all happened so quickly. But I'm happy you asked me to come with you."

"Christela . . . there's something I must tell you before we reach Cincinnati. I might need your help."

"I knew it," Christela said, her eyes sparkling. "I knew you were up to something the moment I saw you today."

Lida quickly explained about what she'd seen on the road. And she tried to relate about her guilty feelings.

"I suppose it's all tied up with Ephraim's death, and the fact that I refused to listen or understand how he felt. But this is something I need to do. Something my own heart tells me is right."

"What do you want me to do?"

"I wouldn't ask you to become involved," Lida said quickly, seeing the doubt in her cousin's eyes. "But I will need you to cover for me if I can arrange a meeting with this Mr. Greenhow. You know I won't be allowed to go anywhere alone, but you and I together . . ."

Christela nodded.

"All right, of course I'll do it," she said. "Oh, this is so exciting," she added, clasping her hands together.

The next day, after they had settled in at their aunt and uncle's house, Lida set about finding Samuel Greenhow. And although their cousin Seth went with them into the city that first day, she used his offer of a tour to find the address that she remembered from John's letter. When they drove past the building and she saw a sign reading Samuel Greenhow, Attorney at Law, she turned and looked into Christela's eyes and winked.

The next morning, she and Christela were on their way alone into the city. Luckily, her aunt and uncle, although Amish, were more liberal in their beliefs than her family. And much more lenient with their freedoms.

Lida and Christela walked to the front of the building and stood for a moment. Lida took a deep breath.

"What if he isn't the one? And if he is, what if he refuses my offer of help? What if he isn't even here?"

"We'll know in a few minutes," Christela said with a grin, as she pushed Lida toward the stairs.

There was a young man seated at a desk. He looked at the two Amish girls with a mixture of curiosity and doubt.

"May I help you?" he asked, looking over his wire-rimmed glasses.

"Yes, I'd like to speak with Mr. Greenhow, please," Lida said.

"Is he expecting you?"

"No but—"

"I'm sorry," the man said with a look of smug satisfaction. "Mr. Greenhow is a very busy man. I could make an appointment for you for in two weeks if you'd like to come back."

"Oh, no," Lida said. "That will be too late. I . . . I'll be back home by then."

"I'm sorry," the man said with a shrug. He turned away and began rifling through papers as if Lida and Christela weren't even there anymore.

"Please," Lida said. "I must see him. If only for a few moments."

"I'm sorry," he repeated, using a stronger, sterner voice.

Just then a door opened and a man stepped out. He was studying some papers and when he looked up, his eyes moved over Lida and Christela. She knew it had to be Samuel Greenhow and she was surprised.

He was a young man, tall and well built beneath his somber business suit. His brown eyes sparkled with intelligence and his beard was neat and closely trimmed. His gaze moved over Lida's face with curiosity.

"What is it, Horace?" he asked, without looking at his young assistant. "Is there a problem?"

"I didn't mean to disturb you, Mr. Greenhow," Horace said. "But this young woman insists on—"

"Mr. Greenhow?" Lida asked, looking at the tall man with renewed interest. "Please," she said. "I won't take but a few moments of your time. This is very important."

"Come in," he said, stepping aside and motioning her through his doorway.

Lida turned to Christela. "I won't be long."

Inside his office, with the door closed, Samuel Greenhow stepped behind his desk, but he didn't sit. He stood with his fingers hooked into his vest pocket, as his gaze moved over Lida's distinctive Amish clothing.

"Are you Lida?" he asked. "Lida Rinehart?"

Lida's eyes grew wide and she felt an odd tingle race through her body.

"How . . . how did you know?"

"John Sexton described you quite accurately, I think." Sam's dark eyes twinkled as he motioned for Lida to take a seat in one of the large leather chairs in front of his desk.

"Allow me to offer my condolences about your brother. He was of great service to many people."

"Thank you," she murmured.

"We're all grateful to you and your family. John Sexton probably wouldn't be alive now if it weren't for you. He's become a very good friend and I'm grateful."

Lida nodded. She thought he seemed almost shy when he spoke about John. Did he know about her feelings for his friend? Had John told him?

"Now . . . Miss Rinehart, what can I do for you?"

Lida leaned forward in her chair. Quickly she told him about the bounty hunters she'd seen and about the two dead men that had been found on a nearby farm.

Sam frowned. He brought his hands together in a prayerful clasp, with his fingers against his mouth. He was staring at Lida, but she had a feeling he was not really seeing her.

"I want to help," she said.

Sam seemed surprised and this time his eyes focused on her face.

"Help? You mean—"

"I won't be able to leave the farm often and any thought of deceiving my parents is abhorrent to me. But I feel I have to do something. There is a house on our property—what we call a Grossdawdy, or Grandfather's house. But my grandparents are no longer living, and the house has been empty now for several years. It's far enough away from the house that my parents wouldn't notice any activity." Lida looked with pleading eyes at Greenhow as she hurried through her words. "It could be used as a resting place. I could feed them. Whatever is needed." She stopped staring into his eyes, feeling almost breathless with nervous excitement.

Sam leaned back in his chair. His brows were knitted together and he watched her as he seemed to mull her offer over in his mind.

"Under normal circumstances, I would turn you down flat, Miss Rinehart," he said quietly, coming forward in his seat.

"But—"

"However . . ." he said. "We are in desperate circumstances right now. Especially in your area of Ohio. Since your brother was killed, there have been over a dozen slaves captured by bounty hunters in that area alone and returned to the south. Some unfortunately, like the men you told me about, never made it out of Ohio alive." He stared hard at Lida. "Even so, if we do take your offer of help, for your sake and your parents, I must insist that you be involved in a very limited capacity."

"That's fine," she said, her eyes coming to life. "Whatever you say will be fine." Her face grew more serious. "I just want to do something."

"How long will you be here in the city?"

"Two weeks," she said.

"Good. That will be ample time to make arrangements. Before you return home, Miss Rinehart, you will meet your contacts, you will have been briefed. And you will know exactly what your duties will be."

She felt her heart actually skip a beat. She had not allowed herself to actually think about this moment. But now, she felt a mixture of hope and fear.

"But for now . . ." Sam Greenhow stood up and walked to a window behind his desk. When he turned back to face her, there was the oddest expression on his solemn face. "I think we might use your help here in the city, that is if you're agreeable. We might even call it a little test . . . to see if this is really what you want to do."

"Of course," she said, sitting forward in her chair. "Whatever you say."

He laughed then and lifted his brows as his gaze took in her staid Amish dress and cap.

"Do you have any objections to wearing a disguise?"

"A disguise?"

"Let me explain. We have a small dilemma. John is being held for questioning—right here in Cincinnati."

Lida's breath caught at his words and her eyes grew bright.

"What we need is a young, beautiful woman to go to the authorities and present an alibi for John. Preferably a woman that no one in the city knows. The disguise is necessary since naturally, they would hardly believe that John was involved with an Amish woman."

"Naturally," she said, blushing.

"Well then," he said. "Do you have any objections to wearing English clothes . . . posing as a wealthy, sophisticated woman who has had a liaison with John Sexton?"

Lida was speechless. Being involved with John was not a problem. But pretending to be a wealthy, sophisticated English was something else indeed.

"I . . . I don't know," she murmured. "What would I say? How would I act?"

"We'll take care of all of that. Before we let you go, you will know every detail of what you are to say."

"But the clothes . . . where will I get such clothes?"

"We will take care of that as well," he said, grinning at her.

Lida blushed and shook her head. Suddenly, she wasn't so certain this was a good idea. But the thought of seeing John, and of actually helping him made her heart beat a little faster. And she knew she could not abandon him. Not now when he needed her and when she was so close.

She stood up with a determined nod.

"I'll do it," she said.

"Good," he said with a wide grin. "Somehow I thought you would." Sam was still grinning as he walked her toward the door.

"Oh, and Mr. Greenhow," she said, turning to face him. Her blue eyes glittered and there was a wistful little smile on her lips.

"Yes?"

"The disguise . . . could you make it a red dress?" she asked. "A bright red silk dress . . . with yards of lace."

She turned with an energetic bounce and went out the door, leaving Sam Greenhow to stare after her with a bemused little grin on his face.

"John Sexton . . . you lucky dog." Sam chuckled quietly as he closed the door. "Help is on the way."

Seventeen

Lida had never seen such a dress in her entire life. And she'd certainly never thought to wear one like it.

The driver that Sam Greenhow had sent for her in the middle of the night had taken her to a small, abandoned house somewhere on the edge of town. The first thing Lida saw when she stepped inside the bedroom was the red dress.

"I'll be waitin' outside when you're ready, miss," the driver said.

Lida took a deep breath, gazing nervously around the room before turning back to the red dress spread across the bed. A small envelope lay on the dress. It contained a card which read: "I took the privilege of picking a color that I considered flattering to your complexion. Rather than scarlet, I chose rose red. I look forward, with great pleasure, to seeing you in it." It was signed only SG.

Lida smiled and shook her head, thinking that Sam was right. The elegant, understated rose color would be much more flattering to her fair skin than scarlet.

When she was dressed, she turned to the long

mirror on the other side of the room. She could hardly believe it was her image she saw reflected there.

The imported red silk dress was a perfect fit. It revealed her throat and the tops of her rounded breasts in a way that made Lida blush. The tight bodice wrapped around her back and joined at the front with concealed hooks. Elegant ecru lace dripped from the elbow-length sleeves. Rows of matching lace encircled the bottom of the wide bell-shaped skirt. There was even a matching small cap which Lida knew from the fashion books at the general store was called a *frontange.*

She turned about, making sure she could properly handle the huge skirt. And she certainly was not used to the matching leather high-heeled slippers that she would have to wear.

Finally, with a deep breath, she stepped out of the house and walked toward the waiting carriage. She gasped as the driver opened the door and revealed a gentleman seated inside.

"Good evening, my dear," the older man said. "Don't be alarmed. I am to pose as your father for the evening. A young lady of breeding would never be allowed to go out alone at night."

Lida climbed into the carriage and with a rustle of silk, settled herself into the seat across from the older, very elegantly dressed gentleman.

"You look lovely," he said with an approving nod.

Lida didn't ask who he was. And she didn't ask where they were going. She tried to remember all that she had to say and hoped that she wouldn't make a mistake, or trip over the yards of silk material in her dress.

The building where the jail was housed was isolated. Inside, the rooms were poorly lit and there was a decided dampness in the air. Lida felt a tug of fear as she and her "father" were escorted down a long corridor and into a small room.

Lida could hardly contain herself when the door opened a few moments later and she saw John's tall form and the gleam of light on his dark hair. He was looking down at the floor, but stepping into the room, his head came up and he looked straight into her eyes.

Lida saw shock and disbelief there, and she realized with a jolt that although John might have known the plan, he had no idea that she would be the woman posing as his lover. With a quick frown, he managed to hide his surprise as the sheriff and deputy pushed him into the room.

The gentleman who posed as Lida's father stood straight with an air of authority before the law officers.

"My boy, how are you? Are they treating you well? This young man has done nothing," he said. "And since you would not believe him, my daughter and I have come to see that justice is done."

"Yeah?" the sheriff said. "And who the heck are you anyway?"

With a haughty look, the man whisked a card from his vest and handed it to the sheriff.

Lida glanced at John and saw the look in his eyes. His gaze moved quickly over her, down the red dress and back up to her partially exposed breasts. He looked stunned. When he met her eyes, she smiled, but it elicited no response from him. Finally he shook his head as if to clear his thoughts, then looked away.

"Oliver G. Cromwell, at your service," the older gentleman said. "I am the owner of Cromwell Mines," he said rather proudly.

"Oh, that Cromwell," the sheriff said. But there was a bit more respect in his eyes when he handed the card back to the man. "You ain't from hereabouts, I guess."

"New York, my dear sir," the impostor said with an impervious manner. "We are here visiting relatives . . . the Strattons? I'm sure you know them."

"H.G. Stratton?" the sheriff asked, his eyes wide with appreciation. "Yeah . . . yeah, everybody in this town knows Mr. H.G. Stratton." The sheriff frowned. "You say you know this man here? And Mr. Stratton knows him, too?"

"Of course he does. This is my daughter, Penelope. She and this gentleman are very close friends. They have an agreement, you understand. We could hardly believe it when we learned that you were holding him for some ridiculous charge."

"Helpin' runaways," the sheriff said. "There was a big meetin' here last week and we suspect Mr. Sexton of bein' one of the biggest backers of this effort. The Liberty Line some calls it—kind of like the old Underground Railroad."

"Runaways?"

"Slaves . . . runnin' away from the south."

"Oh, my dear man," he said with a laugh. "You

have made a dreadful mistake. Tell him Penelope."

Lida stepped forward, her heart pounding so hard she could feel it shaking her.

"Father is right," she said with just a hint of feigned amusement in her voice. She tossed her head as she'd seen the English girls in Walnut Creek do. "John and I have been together every day since my arrival in Cincinnati over two weeks ago. Why, he's hardly been out of my sight. What night was this meeting, Sheriff?" she asked.

The sheriff stared at Lida as if he had just now seen her. His eyes roamed down over her full bosom and small waist, then back up to her flirtatious blue eyes.

"Huh, meeting . . . the uh, meeting was last Saturday night, miss."

"Well, you see?" she said with a breathless little laugh. "Then John couldn't possibly have been involved. He was with me that night, Sheriff. Until very, very late." She arched her brows and lifted a fan that hung from a ribbon at her wrist. Spreading the fan, she used it to teasingly hide her smile from the sheriff. Then she tapped him on the arm with it. "I'm afraid you've made a mistake and I must insist that you let him go. We'll take him home with us. Isn't that right, Papa?" she said, turning to the impostor.

"By all means," he said, clearing his throat and looking down at the sheriff. "By all means. Unless you would like to have Mr. Stratton stop by and confirm what we've already told you."

"I guess that won't be necessary." The sheriff

and deputy exchanged glances. Almost together, they reached to unlock the chains on John's wrists, then stepped aside, and allowed him to move toward the door.

Lida thought her legs would not hold her as she followed John. She could hardly believe he was here before her—tall and handsome and real. She stared at his back and broad shoulders, wanting nothing more than to touch him, to lay her head against his chest and feel his strong arms around her.

"Hurry," the man posing as her father said as she reached the buggy. "Before they figure out we're not who we say we are."

Inside the buggy as they hurried through the deserted streets, John stared at Lida. This was the moment she'd been waiting for, and she felt breathless as she looked back into his eyes.

But he was angry. She could see it in the tight flexing of his jaws and the way his eyes sparkled in the dimly lit coach.

"What the hell do you think you're doing?" he asked, his voice an impatient whisper. Then he turned his wrath to the gentleman sitting beside him. "Who the devil's responsible for this? How did you find me?" he asked, turning back to Lida with disbelief.

"One question at a time, John," the faux Cromwell replied with an amused drollness. "One question at a time."

"This little charade has Greenhow written all over it. He likes nothing better than playing games. Where the hell is he anyhow?"

"You'll see him in just a moment." Cromwell turned and opened a flap over the window, glancing back behind them to make sure no one was following. Then he tapped with his cane on the window of the carriage.

"All's clear, laddie," he shouted. "Continue on with the plan."

John kept staring at Lida, although he didn't say a word. Rather than being pleased at seeing her in the red dress, he seemed to grow angrier as each minute passed.

It was a relief to Lida when they arrived back at the small house where she had changed clothes.

"I'll say farewell for now," said the man who posed as her father. He reached for Lida's hand and brought it to his lips. "If you ever need a job on the stage, my dear, you've only to let Greenhow know."

"Why . . . you're an actor," Lida said, staring at the older man with wonder.

"Ah, yes," he replied. "And you? You are not?"

"No . . . no, I'm not," she said with a quiet laugh.

She stepped out of the carriage and turned back to the gentleman inside.

"You played your part well," he said with a bow before closing the door.

"Get inside," John said. He took hold of her arm in the darkness and Lida felt a shiver travel down her spine.

She pulled away from him and stopped, facing him beneath a dim streetlight.

"Why are you so angry?" she said. "Would you prefer staying in jail rather than accept my help?"

"Angry is hardly adequate to describe what I'm feeling right now." He reached out and flicked a finger beneath the lace trim on her dress. "What the hell do you mean . . . wearing such a dress? Have you completely lost your mind?"

Lida's mouth flew open and she stared up at him. Had he forgotten that conversation when he taunted her about a red dress? Or had he ever meant it in the first place?

"You were the one who wanted to see me in a red dress, John Sexton. As I recall, I believe you said you'd pay a great sum of money for that privilege. Don't you like it?" she asked, staring at him with a defiant glint in her eyes.

"Yes, I like it," he growled reluctantly. "I like it too damned much. What do you want from me, Lida?"

"A small thank you would be nice," she replied tartly.

"If you involved yourself in this danger for a mere thank you, I'm afraid you're going to be terribly disappointed. Now, let's go inside. If I can't get a sensible answer out of you, Samuel Greenhow is going to explain to me exactly what the hell you're doing here." Abruptly, John turned and walked to the house. He opened the door and waited for Lida.

Finally, with a sigh of exasperation, Lida picked up the skirt of the red dress and hurried past him, barely glancing at him from beneath her lashes.

This was not the glorious reunion she had anticipated.

Sam sat in a chair in the tiny living room. There was only one lamp burning and the room was gloomy. In the shadows they could see the orange glow of the tip of his cigar.

He stood up, ignoring John and walking directly to Lida.

"Well," he said, as his gaze moved over her. "This was certainly worth waiting for. You look exquisite."

"All right, Greenhow," John said, his voice deceptively quiet. "Do you want to tell me exactly what's going on here?"

"John, it wasn't his fault," Lida interrupted. "I . . . I came to him to—"

"You—?" John took a deep breath, his hands at his hips. He paced the room before turning back to Lida with a spark of anger still burning in his eyes. "Why, Lida? Why would you do such a thing? After the way you felt about Ephraim's involvement in all this?"

"Lida," Sam said. "Why don't you go ahead and change your clothes. John and I have some talking to do."

Lida could hardly believe what she was hearing. The two of them. How alike they were. Both stubborn, both thinking they were right, and neither giving an inch. And both of them intent on leaving her out of the decision entirely.

Lida clenched her teeth together and ripped the lacy frontange from her hair, throwing it hard on the floor. Then, with a huff of exasperation, she crossed her arms and stood facing the two men, who were now looking at her with obvious surprise.

"I will not! Do you think I'm some little puppy that you can pat on the head and send on its way? I'm involved in this now, and I will not be sent to the other room like a wayward child. Whatever you have to say, I insist on hearing."

Both of the men stared at her for a moment. Then Sam shook his head and laughed aloud.

"What the hell does that mean?" John asked, his voice dangerously low. "Tell her she has to go."

"Wait," Sam said when Lida stepped forward, intending to continue defending her position. "She's right, John. I apologize, Lida," he said with a slight deferring bow. He took another puff of his cigar, squinting through the smoke at John's angry face.

"You remember the conversation we had recently . . . about finding another connection near Walnut Creek?"

John turned his head slightly and his eyes narrowed as he looked with dawning disbelief between Sam and Lida.

"No," he said with a stubborn shake of his head. "Oh, hell no."

"John . . . listen to me, man," Sam said. "I know everything you're going to say. And I understand your reasons for thinking this won't work. But—"

"No, Sam . . . you have no idea why I *know* this won't work," John said through clenched teeth.

His eyes met Lida's and for an instant, there was a sharing . . . a remembering of every touch, every moment they'd spent alone together. The intensity of that look made her knees grow suddenly very weak.

John shook his head, as if denying that he felt it, too. Then he turned on Lida with a vengeance.

"Go change your clothes, Lida. Put on your sweet, demure little Amish dress and your serviceable shoes. And don't forget the prim apron and cap." His voice was hard . . . sarcastic as he stared at her through narrowed eyes. Suddenly he frowned. "Where are you staying anyhow?" Then with a shake of his head, "Never mind. Wherever it is, I'm taking you there. Just as soon as Sam and I have settled this thing."

"Oh," Lida said, turning on him with fire in her blue eyes. She was like a cornered wildcat as she came at him. "You!" she hissed. "You self-centered, arrogant . . . man! You will not tell me what to do and you will not take me anywhere! I came here to help you, you selfish boor. And you don't even appreciate it. You don't appreciate anything." She was breathless with anger and bright spots of red appeared on her cheeks. "Did it ever occur to you that I want to help these runaways because it's the right thing to do? That someone is needed desperately in Walnut Creek or more and more innocent people are going to die? No, of course you didn't. All you can think about, like most men, is what you want and what you think."

"Lida," John murmured, his eyes glittering dangerously. "I'm warning you—"

"Dammit, you two," Sam said, stepping between them. He turned his head, looking from one to the other. Then his eyebrows lifted and he smiled. "Let me remind both of you that I'm in charge here. The money to fund this project comes from myself and my friends," he said, patting his chest. "So I suggest that both of you cool off and let's sit down and discuss this."

"There will be no discussion," John said, gritting his teeth. "She goes."

"I'm staying."

Sam looked toward the ceiling and rolled his eyes.

"Give me strength," he muttered. "Lida . . . sweetheart, you're the sensible one in this room. Please . . . would you make us some coffee or tea . . . whatever you can find in the kitchen. I promise that John and I won't make one decision without you here."

Lida lifted her chin, glaring stubbornly past Sam into John's eyes. Then, with a quiet huff of exasperation, she turned, red skirts flouncing.

"Oh, all right," she muttered as she left the room.

Eighteen

"Quite a woman," Sam murmured as he watched Lida leave the room.

"You have a lot of explaining to do, my friend," John snapped.

"Wait a minute. Lida came to *me.* How was I to know that there was anything between the two of you?"

"Anything between—?" John cursed and stalked across the room before smashing his hand down against a table. "There is nothing between us. There can never be anything between us. Lida Rinehart is Amish. Or hadn't you noticed? Her people are the salt of the earth. They've already lost their only son. Lida is all they have left."

"God, you're even more self-righteous than I thought. Do you think I don't know that? Do you think I didn't consider it when she came to me? I made it clear to her that her involvement would be limited. Nothing more dangerous than bringing food to a house on the Rinehart property. Hell, she won't even have to be there when the conductor and his passengers arrive."

"I don't want to see her. I don't want to be involved with her. Can you understand that?"

John said, raking his hand through his hair. "And I don't want to involve the Amish in this. They were good to me—more decent than I deserved—and I'll be damned if I'll see them hurt."

"Developing a conscience on me, old friend?"

"Hardly," John snapped, turning a furious stare at Sam.

"No? Then why did you send a message through the Underground that you want to see your brother Nathan?" Sam's unexpected reference to Nathan stunned John for a moment.

"How did you know about that?" John asked, glaring at Sam.

Sam shrugged and gave a mysterious little grin. "Do you intend making up with him? I hear that he and Katherine became very close once you were out of the scene."

John gritted his teeth, still glaring at Sam.

"It's a good thing I consider you a friend," he muttered through half-clenched teeth. "Or else you'd be on the floor at this moment."

Sam actually laughed.

"You can't fool me," he said. "Admit it—Katherine is not the woman for you and she never was. She's too timid . . . too conforming. She'd turn you into a stuffy old man who did nothing more than sit by the fire at night and play with the dog. Now that you're away from the situation, you can see that."

"You could be right," John said grudgingly. "So?"

"So . . . you're going to meet with him? What is that all about? You want to tell me?"

"Let's just say I've changed my way of thinking in some matters. Life's too short to hold grudges."

"I agree," Sam said. This time the mischief was gone from his eyes. He nodded his head approvingly and stepped forward to slap John on the shoulder. "Do it. Then write your father and do the same with him."

John shook his head. He bit his lip as he looked thoughtfully down at the floor. "I don't know if I'd go that far."

Sam puffed on his cigar, studying John through narrowed, suspicious eyes. As long as he'd known this man, he was still an enigma. He kept his own counsel and rarely shared his thoughts or his problems with anyone. And Sam knew where to stop.

"All right. Back to the subject at hand. Why exactly don't you want to work with Lida, John? Can't stand the temptation? Too much woman for you?"

John cursed beneath his breath and glared across the room at Sam.

"Believe me," Sam said. "There are plenty of men who'd be glad to take her off your hands."

"Including you?"

"Including me," Sam admitted with cool eyes and a quiet smile.

"Dammit, Sam, this is not a sack of flour we're talking about here. She's a grown woman—an Amish woman. Does that mean anything to you? And you heard her. She's as stubborn as a mule, and willful to boot. She'd too damned intelligent to ever consider sitting in the background. She won't listen to anyone when she thinks she's right and—"

"Doesn't exactly sound like the typical Amish believer to me."

"She isn't typical," John admitted grudgingly. "Believe me, she isn't like anyone I've ever met—Amish or not."

"You realize you've just given the perfect argument for making her my choice," Sam said.

"All right," John said. "Let's just drop the pretenses, shall we? The bottom line here is this—I don't want her involved. And you need me, Greenhow. So it looks as if you're going to have to make a choice. Which will it be, boss?" he asked sarcastically. "Lida or me?"

"You're not serious." The laughter immediately left Sam's eyes as he stared at his friend and cohort.

"I'm dead serious."

"John," Sam warned. "Don't ask me to make that decision, because I can't. I need both of you. This operation is the same as lost if I don't have you. But we can't continue running these people across Ohio without a safe house in Holmes County."

"Then find another one."

"There's no time for that. At this very moment there are at least a dozen people waiting in Kentucky to cross Ohio. The longer they wait, the more danger they're in. These damned bounty hunters are everywhere. I shouldn't have to tell you that."

The two men stared into each other's eyes.

Then finally John took a deep breath of air and let it out loudly in the silence of the room.

He was still muttering as he paced back and forth across the living room.

Just then Lida stepped into the room with a tray containing cups and a teapot. She saw Sam's troubled look and heard John's muttered curses as he stalked the floors.

Lowering her eyes, she set the tray down. Spreading her rose red skirts, she sat on a worn settee and demurely began pouring steaming tea into the cups.

"Gentlemen," she said with a sweet innocence, as if they were doing nothing more important than having afternoon tea. "Sugar . . . cream?"

Sam looked at John with an amused lift of his brows. Finally John shook his head and, with a grunt of laughter, raked his hand down over his face before walking to a nearby chair.

He took a cup of tea and stretched his long legs out, crossing his booted feet at the ankles as he stared at Lida.

"I have to admit, you did a good job at the jail," he said begrudgingly. "The sheriff was completely captivated by your genteel charm."

"Why, thank you, sir," Lida said with just the slightest hint of a southern drawl.

John shook his head at her, but he couldn't help the grudging smile that flickered on his lips.

Damn, in that red dress she was the most exquisite thing he'd ever seen. If Sam Greenhow weren't present, he'd be tempted to sweep her into his arms and make love to her right here and now. The way both of them wanted. The way *she* had wanted to be loved that night he left the farmhouse. Be damned with their differences. And be damned with what happened afterward.

Thank God for Samuel Greenhow's presence.

"Well?" Lida asked, looking from one of the men to the other. "Have you made a decision about whether I can help or not?"

"Yes," Sam said.

"No," John muttered at the same time.

"John," Sam warned in a soft voice. "Think about what you're doing. You know we need her."

"I don't like it."

"You don't have to like it," Sam said.

"I'll be careful," Lida said, looking straight into John's troubled gray eyes. "I'll do everything just as you say. I won't give you any reason to worry about me."

"If that's a promise . . ."

"It is," she said quickly, her eyes filled with hope. "It's a promise."

Sam changed the subject to something trivial, insuring that there were no more disagreements for the remainder of their stay in the small isolated house.

"My horse is tied out back," Sam said finally. "I had the carriage driver wait, if you'd like to take Lida back to where she's staying?"

John nodded. But there still was a troubled look on his handsome face.

"I'll go change," Lida said.

"Go easy on her," Sam said after Lida had left

the room. "She cares a great deal about this . . . and about you, I think."

"Look," John said with a glint of warning in his eye. "I realize you Yanks are used to running everything. But just leave Lida to me. I know her better than you ever will."

"Ah," Sam said with a grin. "And aren't you rebels given to boasting a great deal? Sometimes with nothing but sticks to back yourselves up."

"Well, you know what they say," John drawled. "A reb with a stick can whip ten armed Yanks any day."

Both of them grinned. Sam shook John's hand and slapped him on the shoulder.

"Lay low, John. Be careful and remember what I said about Nathan and your father. We'll meet here again tomorrow night and brief Lida on everything she's going to need to know."

Moments later Lida stepped back into the living room. The red dress was gone and once again she looked like a very sweet and wholesome Amish girl. Now that she and John were alone, there was an awkwardness between them. It seemed to hang in the air like a tangible object—tense and vibrating.

"Are you ready?" John asked.

"Yes." She turned slightly toward the bedroom. "The red dress . . . I . . . I didn't know what to do with it." Wasn't he going to say anything else about the red dress? About how she looked wearing it?

"Leave it."

Outside, he helped her up into the carriage,

being careful not to touch her anymore than necessary. He seated himself across from her, rather than beside her.

They drove for long silent minutes until finally Lida couldn't stand another moment of his brooding.

"I know you don't like this," she said.

"It's done," John murmured, turning to gaze out the window. "There's no need discussing it any further."

"Don't you even want to know why I came to Sam? Why I asked to help?"

He turned to stare at her and there was a knowing look in his eyes.

She laughed quietly, not knowing whether to be flattered or angry.

"You think I did it because of you," she said.

"Didn't you?"

"I hate to deflate your male ego, John Sexton, but no, I didn't. Not entirely anyway."

John wondered as he sat staring at her in the dim coachlight, if he would ever stop wanting her. If he would ever be able to convince himself that she was out of his reach . . . forbidden to him forever.

"I should haul you across that seat and put you over my knee. You need to be spanked like the willful child you are."

"Well, Mr. John Sexton, I've never been spanked by anyone and I should tell you I don't intend starting now."

"Perhaps if you had, you wouldn't be so damned stubborn."

They stared defiantly at one another across the coach. There was only the sound of their quiet breathing, and the tension that never seemed to leave when they were together.

Finally, Lida began to tell about the bounty hunters she'd seen. More to change the subject than anything. And to explain why she'd gone to Sam Greenhow. But she hadn't counted on his reaction.

At first he shook his head in disbelief and concern. Then suddenly he leaned forward and grasped her arms, pulling her toward him until she almost slid onto the floor. She would have if he hadn't been there to hold her.

"Did they hurt you? Or insult you? God," he spat. "If they did, I swear I'll track the bastards down and—"

"John," she murmured, reaching up to place her fingers over his mouth. "Your swearing has become even worse since you left us. And no, they didn't hurt me."

She was in his arms now, cradled awkwardly half across his chest and the lower part of his body. She could feel his male arousal against her hip and she smiled with a sense of wonder.

Until this moment she'd been afraid that what happened between them at the farm meant nothing to him. That he had only used her. That any woman would do. And that the emotion she felt that night in her room didn't mean the same thing to him as it had to her.

But now she knew that wasn't true. It wasn't just his body's response that proved it. It was the look in his eyes. That look of half-tenderness, combined with a fierce determination to protect her. Even if it meant pushing her away from him forever.

Lida had never known what it was to be bold with a man. But now, she leaned forward, disregarding the warning look in his eyes. She leaned her head over until her mouth lay at the point where his neck and shoulder met. Then deliberately she pushed his shirt away. She felt John's entire body tense as she slowly, slowly lowered her mouth to his shoulder.

She sighed when she tasted his skin and breathed in the heady male scent of him. It was a scent that was his alone and so achingly familiar that she shuddered as she opened her mouth and tested the texture of his skin with her tongue.

"God . . . Lida," he groaned. "What are you doing?"

But despite his protests, she felt his arms tighten around her, felt him pulling her up until she was sitting astraddle him. Her arms went around his neck as both of them sought each other's mouth. His hands moved quickly from her waist up beneath her arms where he could feel the fullness of her breasts pressing against his palms.

That first kiss, after such a long wait, was like an explosion. A white hot explosion that sent convulsive shudders through Lida's body and made John groan with the needs that he could no longer deny. The reality of having her in his arms, so close, so willing, shook him to the core.

Lida could feel the hardness of him through

the thin material of her dress. Her movements against him were unconscious, instinctive. She only knew that she wanted . . . needed, and that this man was the only one who could stop the relentless hunger that threatened to drive her insane.

Suddenly the coach stopped, causing Lida to fall even harder against him.

With a quietly muttered expletive, John encircled Lida's waist with his hands and pushed her up and away from him.

Lida made a small cry of protest when she found herself sitting across from him again, stunned, and staring into his expressive gray eyes.

"We're here, sir," they heard the driver call.

"Dammit it, Lida," John said. "You're playing with fire."

"I know what I'm doing," she whispered.

"No, you don't," he said with a humorless grunt. "You have no idea what you're doing, or what you're pushing me to do. I swore this would never happen again. When I left your house, I promised myself I'd never come for you, and never let myself ruin your life." He looked at her with a quiet despair. "Why in hell did you have to come here?"

"Why are you so determined not to love me?"

"This can't be. You know it as well as I do. You're an unmarried Amish girl. And I—"

"You . . . are the man I want." She reached across and touched his face, pleased when he held her hand there and turned his mouth to kiss her palm. "Do you think the Amish are so pure that this never happens to them?" she asked gently. "Do you think they never make love? Evidently you haven't noticed all the children clamoring about over the Ohio countryside," she added in an attempt to lighten his mood.

"For someone like you, it happens with an Amish man—the man they marry."

"It could never be like this with any Amish man I've ever known," she murmured, still touching his face. "Never like you."

His eyes were so stormy, so troubled that she could hardly bear it.

"Marriage is the only option with a girl like you. And I can't marry you. You know that as well as I do. I might not be the most honorable man in the world, but I'll be damned if I will let myself make love to you without marriage. Do you want to be left with an illegitimate child to raise alone? So your church and your family could shun you and the child for the rest of your lives? I can't take a chance on that happening, Lida. As much as I want you, dammit, I can't. *We* can't. You have to forget this."

"Never. I'll never forget it. Or you, John Sexton."

John closed his eyes in defeat and leaned his head back against the seat.

"Please . . ." he said, his voice husky. "Just go in the house before someone hears us and comes out to investigate. I'll see you tomorrow night."

"You are the only man I want, John. The man I will always want. And nothing is ever going to change that."

Silently she slipped out of the coach and ran toward the house.

John opened his eyes just in time to watch her disappear into the darkness. With a shake of his head, he tapped on the roof of the coach.

"Get us out of here, driver."

John muttered beneath his breath. "Before I go after her and do something really, really foolish."

Nineteen

Early the next morning John kept his appointment with Nathan. He'd known that his brother's regiment was bivouacked near the Kentucky/Ohio border. And he'd shamelessly used his influence with a Union general, a West Point comrade, to obtain a meeting with his brother.

As he waited in a thicket near a place called Licking Creek, John could hear sporadic shooting in the distance. He could hardly believe that he might actually see his younger brother in such a situation, until he heard a horse moving through the brush and then saw the soldier in a stained and ragged gray uniform.

John got down from his horse and waited for Nathan to join him. They met each other warily, neither moving forward for a handshake. Nathan eyed his brother with open suspicion and John took in Nathan's appearance with disbelief.

"God, Nathan, you look like hell."

Nathan looked as if he hadn't shaved in days. His hair, dark like John's, hung limply in his eyes and down past his frayed collar in back.

"Thanks for cheerin' me up," Nathan drawled. He made a slight, amused grimace that was so reminiscent of the boy he'd once been that John had to laugh.

"Sorry. I just didn't expect—"

"Hey," Nathan said, lifting his hand. "Don't. I know what you mean. Believe me I know how I look. At least if it's anywhere close to how I feel."

He was weary, John could see that in the slump of his shoulders and the redness of his eyes.

"Well, I see you've made Major already," John said, nodding his head toward the insignia on his brother's faded jacket.

"Yeah. In this war, it seems whoever lives longest gets the promotion."

"Here," John said, motioning toward a nearby tree. "Sit a while. I have food and water in the saddlebags if . . ."

Only months ago, Nathan not only would have refused John's offer, but he probably would have thrown it in his face. They had parted with bitter words about their differences in the way they viewed the war. John had been cynical and distrustful. And Nathan had been filled with the high purpose of the South's cause and the nobility of his service in that effort. The fact that Katherine had turned so quickly from John to his brother hadn't helped ease the strain.

Nathan took the food, quickly consuming part of it and placing the rest in his own saddlebags. As he settled himself on the ground, his eyes met John's, and there was a wry look of awkwardness on his lean, handsome face.

"Katherine told me you were working with an

abolitionist group in Ohio. But I hardly expected to see you here."

John's eyebrows lifted and for a moment he seemed uneasy.

"Don't worry," Nathan said. "I haven't told anyone and neither has she."

"You shouldn't have to tell me that, but under the circumstances . . ." John watched Nathan carefully. Besides his brother's obvious exhaustion, he seemed different somehow.

"Hell, don't apologize," Nathan said, looking directly into his brother's eyes. "I can hardly blame you for being distrustful."

John nodded and picked up a leaf, turning it over and over between his fingers until it fell into shreds on the ground beside him.

"How is Katherine?" he asked quietly.

"She's fine, far as I know," Nathan said. "I don't hear from her much anymore." He sat up straighter and cleared his throat.

"John . . . about Katherine. There's nothing between us. There might have been once, I'll admit that." His gray eyes, so much like the ones he stared into, were solemn and apologetic. "I couldn't see anything except that beautiful face. And I felt so lucky to have her lean on me . . . need me." Nathan shook his head slowly, as he were shaking off a dream. "Hell, I'd no sooner left town than she took up with another man. Senator Greeson's son—you know him. He bought his way out of service and plans on taking his father's seat in the Senate once the war's over."

"If there is a senate," John said.

"Yeah."

"Don't worry about it," John said. "It's not something I even think about anymore."

They sat for a while in silence, letting the warm breeze brush against them, listening to the shooting in the distance.

"I was a fool," Nathan said suddenly, looking at John with a troubled gaze.

"Hell, we both were. But Katherine's not the only woman in the world."

"It's not just Katherine, John," Nathan said. "It's everything. The war—the Confederacy. I had this noble idea that I was defending my home. I thought we'd fight a few skirmishes, then someone would declare a truce. I figured we'd all be home by Christmas. Instead it just gets meaner and uglier by the day." Nathan shook his head and looked through the trees into the distance. His eyes glittered with some remembered scene.

"I've seen so many good men die," he said, his voice choked. "So goddamned many."

John knew the feeling. He'd seen it, too, and been sickened by it.

"You were right about the war," Nathan said. "And I'm glad you found me, so I finally had the chance to say it to you in person. I wasn't sure I'd ever get to."

"Hey," John said, leaning closer. He took his brother's arm and shook him a bit. "Don't you feel bad about a thing. Not a damned thing, you hear me? You did what you thought was right and I admire you for that. Actually I came here to apologize to you. Guess I've learned a few things, too."

"You? Apologize?"

"Hard to believe, huh?" John asked, grinning.

Nathan rubbed his hand across his eyes and grinned, too.

"You know what I want, big brother?" he asked.

"No, what?"

"Well, I want this damned war to end—that goes without saying. But when it does and if I live through it, all I want is to go back to that beautiful green valley in Tennessee. Find myself a nice sweet woman who doesn't put on airs. A woman who loves me just the way I am." He lifted his brows toward his brother and John nodded his understanding. "I'm gonna raise high-spirited horses and even more high-spirited sons. I'm going to live a quiet life . . . one so boring that you won't believe it. And I'm going to thank God every day for the peace." Nathan's chin trembled slightly when he spoke.

John rubbed his hand over his mouth and chin. The last thing he wanted was for Nathan to see him cry.

"I'd like that kind of life, too," he muttered, keeping his gaze toward the ground.

In the distance there was a loud boom and the sound of gunfire growing nearer.

Nathan cocked his head and listened.

"Here come the boys," he said with a wry grin. "Guess I'd better catch up with 'em before they leave my butt here."

They both got up and stood awkwardly for a

moment. Then simultaneously they embraced, holding each other tightly for a while before slapping each other on the back.

"Did you mean it about wanting to come back to Tennessee," Nathan asked.

"If Father will allow me back on the place."

"If he doesn't, you'll find another place . . . close by," Nathan said with a determined look in his eye. "It's your home, John. It's where you belong.

John nodded. "If I do head back down that way one of these days, I want to be sure I see your ugly face there, too. So don't go messin' around playing hero and get your fool self killed."

"I'll be there," Nathan said. "I swear it." Nathan reached out his hand and John took it. They each clasped their hand around the other's forearm in an old boyhood pledge.

"I swear it, too," John said quietly, looking into Nathan's eyes.

Later he watched as Nathan rode off, waving his hand over his head.

For the first time in a long while, John felt a spark of hope. About his brother. And about home.

Lida and John were thrown together every day for the next week. But he made sure that they were never alone. The glances they shared at the meetings with Sam were filled with a longing intensity that neither of them could deny. And sometimes Lida thought that was more torturous than not being together at all.

On those nights she would slip away from her aunt and uncle's house to meet Sam and John. And usually when she returned, Christela would creep into her bedroom, demanding to know everything.

By now, her cousin had guessed about the way Lida felt about John Sexton.

"But what will you do about Carl?" Christela asked one night as they sat whispering.

"I can't marry Carl," Lida vowed. "Even if nothing ever comes of my love for John, I could never marry Carl. Or anyone else for that matter."

"Oh, Lida," Christela whispered. "It's so romantic. So . . . exciting, being in love with an English. Remember when we were children? It was always more exciting doing the things we weren't allowed." She frowned at Lida.

"Is that what this is?" Christela asked, her eyes wide with concern for her best friend. "You are grown now. You can't ruin your life just because you want to do something that is forbidden."

"I . . . I thought at first that might be a part of it," Lida admitted. "I thought he was the most exciting, unreachable man I'd ever met. And I must admit that when I realized he was as aware of me as I was of him, I felt this strange, overwhelming power. Like nothing I've ever felt with a man before." She turned and looked at Christela. "But it's more than that, Chrissie. Oh, it's so much more than that now. Remember when we were girls and we talked about . . . you know when we finally married . . . what would happen on our wedding night?"

"You . . . you haven't . . . ?"

"No, no," Lida said. "But back then, I thought it was only something we women *had* to do. A way of pleasing our husbands and of having children to inherit the future. But with John . . ." Lida put her hands to her face. "Oh, Chrissie, I've never felt like this about a man before in my life. I think about him every moment. I dream about him. And when he touches me . . . or kisses me . . ." Lida's voice trailed away as she became lost in the memory of those times.

"It's a good feeling?" Christela asked quietly.

"Yes," Lida whispered. "It's a very good feeling."

"But what will you do? Do you think John will become Amish for you?"

"No," Lida said, frowning. "He's said as much. He said he could never live the way we do. And to be honest, I'm not sure I'd want him to." She turned and took Christela's hands. "You see, I don't want him to change, Chrissie. I love him just the way he is—arrogant and independent. Not wanting to answer to anyone. I don't care that he's demanding . . . sometimes fiercely so. I don't want him meek and mild, tamed by our Amish ways," she admitted, her voice barely above a whisper.

"Lida, do you know what you are saying? Either you must give him up forever. Or you must give up our ways . . . the church, your family . . . everything!"

"I know," Lida whispered. "I know."

* * *

The night before Lida and Christela were to leave to go back home, she and Samuel and John had their last meeting at the little house.

"You can expect the people to be at the farm in two days, Lida," Sam said. "I'm sorry—I know that doesn't give you a lot of time to prepare for them."

"It's all right. I'll be ready," she said.

"I have to go," Sam said. "John, you won't mind driving Lida back to her uncle's house will you?"

John gave him a wry look, then shook his head. He knew exactly what Sam was trying to do.

"I don't mind."

"But before I go . . ." Sam moved across the room and came back with a large package wrapped in plain brown paper. "This is for you, Lida. But I suggest you not open it in front of your parents, or your aunt and uncle either for that matter."

"May I open it now?" she asked, her eyes shining with excitement.

"Of course," he said, handing her the package and stepping back out of the way.

Inside the box, beneath a layer of tissue paper, lay the red dress, along with the satin and lace hat and matching red shoes. Lida looked up at Sam with surprise, her eyes wide, her lips parted.

"Oh . . ." she whispered.

"I hope you don't mind," Sam said, frowning now with worry. "I haven't insulted you, have I?

I thought you might need a disguise at one point or another . . . you looked so beautiful in it, and it seemed . . ." Sam shook his head and reached for the box. "I'm sorry, I wasn't thinking."

"No," she said, holding onto the dress. "No, I want to keep it. And I'm not insulted. I will keep it for remembrance." She stood up and gathered the dress against her and then placed a quick kiss on Sam's cheek. "Thank you."

There was an odd look in John's eyes, but he smiled at the two of them. He didn't think he'd ever seen such a look on Lida's beautiful face before.

Later, as John drove her back to her aunt and uncle's, there was a brooding silence in the coach.

"I'm glad you are the one bringing the slaves in two days," she said. She looked across the coach, waiting for John to meet her eyes.

When he looked up, there was such emotion in his eyes that Lida's breath caught in her throat.

He shook his head slowly.

"I should never have let Sam talk me into this. I should have quit rather than let him convince me to include you in this madness."

"But you couldn't quit," she said, smiling softly at him. "You want to help these people as much as I do. Do you know what I've learned about you these past two weeks, John Sexton?"

"No, what?" he asked, his voice husky and strained.

"I've finally learned the truth about you."

"And that is?" he asked slowly.

"That you are not cold and unfeeling. That you aren't the mercenary you claimed to be."

John's eyes changed then, his jaw tightened, and he sat back against the seat.

"I *am* being paid."

"But that's not the reason you continue doing this dangerous work," she said. "I've watched you, and I've seen the compassion in your eyes when Sam speaks of those waiting in Kentucky. I see the determination and the anger in your eyes when you hear what is being done to the slaves. And I know finally why you do it."

"You think you know . . ."

"I know," she said with quiet insistence. "And I know what kind of man you are. And I'm proud of you."

John clenched his fists, willing himself not to move, not to touch her. He was relieved when they reached her uncle's house and the coach stopped.

When Lida leaned toward him, he was surprised by her brief kiss at the side of his mouth. Then she scrambled from the coach and was gone.

John sat very still in the carriage. His hand moved automatically to the place where she'd kissed him and his eyes held a glazed, bemused look.

This was a different Lida than the one he'd known back at the Rinehart farm. She was less provoking, more understanding somehow. Yet the response he felt at her brief sweet kiss was just as powerful, just as heated as it always was when she was near.

What in hell was he going to do about her?

* * *

Lida was tired. She had lost so much sleep due to the clandestine meetings while she was in Cincinnati. And it wasn't much better when she was in bed. She couldn't sleep, couldn't think of anything or anyone except the mission.

And John. Always John.

But she was glad to be home. Mostly because she was eager to start preparing the Grandfather house for John and his passengers. And, too, because she had worried about her parents while she was away. Their farm was a large one and most Amish farms this size had big families to share the workload. Lida felt guilty that her absence had caused more work for her mother and father.

The plan was for John and his runaways to arrive sometime on Wednesday night. She was so nervous that morning that she couldn't sleep and was in the kitchen long before her mother came downstairs.

"Well," her mother said, her eyes wide with surprise and approval. "This is very pleasant, coming down to a kitchen filled with the good smells of food."

Lida muttered something. She was too anxious about tonight to even talk to her mother intelligently.

"Lida? Is something wrong? Where is your mind this morning my little *Fräulein?*"

Lida smiled at her mother's teasing efforts.

"Nothing's wrong," she said. "I just couldn't sleep, that's all."

"Is the weather," her mother said, glancing out the window. "The heat will be bad today."

Just after breakfast, they heard riders in the yard. Her father stood up and walked to the door, then took his hat and stepped out onto the porch.

Lida peeked through the screen door and saw that it was the sheriff and his deputies. Her heart began to beat a little faster. Had they caught John? And now had they come for her?

Lida was aware of her mother watching her anxiously. Not wanting to appear upset, Lida went about cleaning up the kitchen, but she managed to remain near the door so she could hear what was being said outside.

The sheriff spoke quickly.

"It's the law. Ain't nothin' I can do except uphold the law, even though I don't agree with it. But you see, Mr. Rinehart, what this so called Underground Railroad has done to our part of the country? The land is crawlin' with bounty hunters, lookin' to make a quick dollar by takin' those nigras back to the plantation owners down south."

"It is disturbing," her father said. "Even though we Amish have no intention of getting involved, it seems there is little we can do to avoid it in this case. Those two dead men were found on Amish land."

"Yessir. I'm real sorry 'bout that, too. That's why I come out here so often. Just want you to know what's happenin'. And be cautious. Wouldn't hurt to load you up a shotgun or two."

"Nein," Jacob said quietly. "We do not believe in the use of firearms."

"Well," the sheriff said with a sigh. "Be extra careful tonight and keep your ears open. We got word that there's some runaways comin' through tonight. Word is them paid-for-hire men is gonna be waitin' for 'em over at Strasburg."

Lida's heart was pounding. She could hardly hear for the roaring in her ears. All she could think about was John and that he was about to be met with another ambush just like the one that killed Ephraim.

"No," she whispered desperately.

"What's that dear?" her mother asked.

"Nothing . . . nothing." Lida began untying the house apron she wore over her dress. "Mother, do you mind if I run over to see Christela for a little while? I'll be back within an hour, I promise."

"We have churning to be done today," her mother said with a frown. "And the week's bread-making to get started."

"I know," Lida said, hurrying toward the stairs to go up and change her shoes. She knew her mother would rather she not go. But she had to find some way to warn John. There was no way she was going to stand by and let this happen. She would die before she would stand by and let him walk into another ambush.

"I'll hurry," she said over her shoulder as she left the kitchen.

At the Dietz farm, Lida pulled her cousin outside, quickly telling her what she'd heard.

"Oh, Lida," Christela gasped. "What's to be done? Is there no way you can warn John?"

"There has to be. I'll find a way. But I need your help."

"What can I do?"

"I want to tell mother that I'm spending the night with you. I'll come back here after supper . . . before dark. There should be plenty of time for me to ride to Strasburg and warn John."

Christela's dark eyes were wide with fear. "Lida, you shouldn't. Remember what Mr. Greenhow made you promise . . . that you would limit your activities so that you would be safe?"

"I know," Lida said, dismissing her cousin's fears. There was nothing on her mind now except warning John. "But I can't worry about that now. I just wanted to tell you what I have planned. All right?"

"All right," Christela said. "But I don't mind telling you, this frightens me."

"It frightens me, too," Lida said solemnly. "But it's something I have to do."

Twenty

Lida thought darkness would never come. Finally, just as the sun dipped below the line of trees to the west, she slipped away from Christela's house and out toward the barn. She knew that by the time she saddled the horse and rode to Strasburg it would be dark. She only prayed she would be able to find John in time, before the bounty hunters trapped him and the others. She wouldn't even allow herself to think about what would happen if they caught her, too.

She rode across fields and around fences, making her way as quickly as possible toward the abandoned shack where she thought John would be.

After it grew dark, her horse stumbled several times as it went blindly across the rough, rocky ground. She was forced to slow the pace, even though her heart raced with anxiety. She felt an overwhelming need to find John and have this over and done.

Finally she saw the abandoned house ahead of her. It sat in a clearing and the glint of starlight made the tin roof visible. No other light could be seen.

For a moment Lida sat on her horse beneath

the cover of the trees that surrounded the small meadow. Her body was tensed, eyes and ears alert as she stared hard and tried to detect any movement or sound. There was nothing. No sound except the wind and the crickets.

The quietness was frightening. Lida's heart began to beat even faster as she feared the worst. Was John lying in the darkened house wounded? Dying even?

Climbing down from her horse, she didn't even bother to tie the reins to a tree. The animal probably wouldn't be noticed here in the shadows of the forest, and if something happened, she knew it would make its way back to the Dietz farm and that Christela would come looking for her.

She moved slowly and as quietly as she could around the edge of the trees, intending to go across the open space at its narrowest point. Finally, with a burst of energy that surprised even herself, Lida ran across the opening, feeling as if at any moment a rifle shot would sound, certain that someone was watching her every movement.

When she reached the back of the house, she leaned against the wooden siding, catching her breath and wondering if her pounding heart would ever return to normal. Her knees were trembling so badly she thought she might not be able to take another step.

Finally she forced her legs to move and began sliding along the house to the corner.

Suddenly, at the end of the house, she saw a tall shadow emerge, and before she could react, the man was upon her, grabbing her by the arms and hauling her back against the house.

She started to scream and felt a hand fasten hard against her mouth and nose. She was panic stricken . . . more frightened than she'd ever been in her life. As she kicked and tried to fight her way free of the man's strong grip, it took a long moment for her to understand his fiercely whispered words.

"Lida! God . . ." John cursed beneath his breath. His hand moved from her mouth and he shook her until her hair fell about her face and spilled down her shoulders. "What the hell are you doing here?" he hissed. "Have you lost your senses?"

"John," she whispered. Her arms moved of their own accord around him and despite his gruffness and the rough way he held her, she pressed against him with a loud sigh of relief. "Oh, John, thank God . . . you're alive."

"For the moment," he said, his voice rumbling beneath her ear.

She sensed him turning his head as if listening for something. Then she heard it. The sound of hoofbeats, of riders moving quickly toward them and the house.

Lida gasped and clutched John's shirt.

"It's the bounty hunters," she whispered, her words tinged with desperation. "Where are the slaves? You have to get them away from here and—"

"They're not here," he said. John took her arm and practically dragged her with him along the back of the house. "I sent them in another direction," he muttered as he glanced cautiously around the edge of the house.

"But—" For a moment Lida's mind refused to work. The realization of being in John's embrace, despite his seeming reluctance, had ruined any other chance for conscious reasoning.

She shook her head, knowing they were in danger and that she needed a clear mind. In that split second, she realized that John must have learned about the planned ambush somehow. And that he had sent his "cargo" on in another direction while he rode to the designated meeting place to act as a decoy.

"You knew," she whispered, as the truth of what had happened penetrated her brain. It would be more difficult for him to escape now, having to worry about her. "Oh John . . . I'm sorry. I—"

"Never mind," he said. "It's too late for that. We have to get out of here. Where's your horse?"

"Back there . . . in the woods," she murmured.

"Damnation," John cursed.

She felt his hand move toward the Colt that he wore at his side. And she knew then that it was too late to make a dash for the horse. In only a few moments, the riders would be around the bend in the road. They would surround the house and there would be nothing either of them could do to escape.

Suddenly, with what seemed a miraculous flash of insight, her mind cleared and she remembered the old storm cellar at the back of the abandoned farm. Once, on a trip to visit relatives in Strasburg when she was a girl, they had been forced to stop here and take shelter from a vicious summer storm.

She took John's arm in a strong grip. When he murmured some muffled question, she pulled at him.

"Follow me," she said. "There's an old storm cellar. If it hasn't fallen in completely."

She felt him hesitate for only a moment. Then, taking her hand, he ran, pulling her with him across the open field and glancing once over his shoulder at the sound of the approaching riders.

They were so close now that the noise was almost deafening. Lida thought there must be at least a dozen of them to create such a loud drumming of hoofbeats.

"Please," she muttered to herself when she spotted the slight mound of earth and grass that covered the long-forgotten shelter.

She pulled away from John and fell upon the grass, running her hands over the earth as she searched for the opening in the darkness.

John, realizing what she was doing, dropped to his knees to help.

"There's a door," she whispered. "With a large iron ring for a handle."

"Here," he said. "Here it is."

She heard him grunt as he strained to pull the small wooden door free of the grass and roots that had covered it for years and now almost obliterated it.

She didn't know how they managed to get the door open and clamor down the narrow steps before the riders entered the front yard of the abandoned house. She didn't notice the stinging scrapes on her hands or her ragged broken nails until they were safely down in the cellar with the door closed above them.

Lida had never felt such a feeling as she did then, standing there in complete darkness in the small, cold enclosure. It was like being buried alive.

"Snakes," she said, shivering. "Oh dear Lord, I hope there aren't snakes down here."

Without thinking she reached out for John and immediately felt his warm hand enclose her fingers. Then he pulled her to him and wrapped his arms tightly around her. Nothing had ever felt so good as the warmth and security of his body against hers.

"It's all right," he whispered, holding her to still her trembling. "It's all right. As soon as we can light a match, I'll check the place out. The bounty hunters won't find us here."

She sensed him move his head as if to look upward toward the door.

"Not tonight anyway," he murmured quietly. "But the cellar will be easy to spot in daylight."

"You think they'll wait out there until morning?" she asked, her breathless voice revealing her fright. "Oh, John . . . I can't stay here all night." She could feel her heart pounding, feel the sense of suffocation sweeping over her in one hot rush. "Please . . . I can't," she said, her voice growing louder and more frightened.

"Shh." Gently, John placed his hand over her

mouth, bending his head low until they were almost touching. "I'm here," he said. "I want you to sit here on the steps while I—"

"No!" Her hands clutched his shirt, raking wildly at him as she tried to keep him near. "Don't leave me. God, John . . . don't leave me. Just let me touch you. I'll be all right as long as I can touch you."

In the darkness John frowned. He had never seen Lida this way. Had never seen her lose that quiet, composed dignity that he admired so much. But now, hearing the fear and desperation, he felt his heart turn over in his chest with an odd little lurch.

He reached for her, hauling her against him and holding her so tightly that he could feel her heart beating in rhythm with his own.

He placed a kiss against her temple, then reached back with one hand to find the steps and sink down on them. He pulled her with him, placing her on his lap and holding her like a child, rocking and murmuring soft, soothing words against her hair.

Suddenly the ground shook. John held her even tighter, cradling her head protectively as they heard the shouts of the riders just above them. He held his breath as they rode very close to the storm cellar.

Earth and dust sifted down on them.

Lida cried out softly and John placed his hand against her mouth as he cradled her protectively against him.

"It's all right," he whispered. "Hang onto me, blue eyes."

John knew that if the horsemen rode across the camouflaging mound of earth that covered the cellar, there was a possibility they would notice the hollow sound that indicated an underground opening. It could even collapse beneath them.

Only seconds later, the riders did come across the mound of earth. John and Lida could feel the door above them shake and there was a splintering sound as a horse's hoof almost smashed through the partially rotted wood.

John held his breath, waiting. Would they guess what they had stumbled across? And that someone might be hidden inside?

They heard curses and the sound of more riders.

"What's wrong?" one of them shouted.

"Damned ground's soft. Let's get out of here before my horse breaks a leg."

"They have to be here somewhere," another said. "We'll settle in here 'til daybreak. See if we can find a trail at first light."

Lida closed her eyes and lay her head against John's shoulder. "No," she whispered fiercely. "No."

They heard the horsemen riding away from the storm cellar. But they didn't go far. They were close enough that Lida could still detect the sound of men talking and hear the stamping of their restless animals.

"They're staying," she said with a groan. Suddenly, the dark enclosure and the stale air were too much. She couldn't breath.

Lida tugged at the neck of her dress. Perspiration quickly covered her face and arms.

"I can't stand it," she whispered, her voice panic-stricken. "I can't." She stood up quickly and, despite John's attempt to hold her back, she fought like a wildcat as she tried to scramble up the steps.

"Lida," he said, his voice low and harsh. "You can't. Here . . . come here." He tried to hold her again. Soothe her. But she was so frightened that he knew she was not even hearing him.

Holding her with one arm, he struggled to find a box of matches in his shirt pocket. When he managed to light one, he felt Lida relax against him, although her breathing remained hard and labored.

John glanced around the tiny room that had been built on a slab of solid rock. The walls were lined with stone, and from the shelves placed along two walls, he guessed that the family that had lived on the farm years ago had also used the storm cellar as a storage place for canned goods and vegetables. There was one dusty table in the room and on it sat an old lamp that was covered with pale, wispy spiderwebs.

Holding his hand toward Lida, indicating she should stay still, John moved quickly to the table and lit the lamp. The glass globe was so black that the light barely penetrated through it, but it was enough to illuminate a bunk bed against the opposite wall and to show that there was little else left in the abandoned cellar.

John took the lamp and turned toward Lida. In the flickering light her eyes looked huge and frightened. And he saw her gaze move quickly around the walls and ceiling.

John held the light up, smiling at her for reassurance.

"See," he said quietly. "No snakes. No bugs. No rats."

Lida swallowed hard and tried to smile. She could feel the muscles in her face twitch from the effort. Her hands were trembling.

"I don't mean to be such a baby," she said, her voice soft.

With a murmur, John put the lamp back on the table and went to her. He took her in his arms and held her.

"I didn't think you were afraid of anything, *Fräulein,*" he said, attempting to tease her out of her fear.

"Just snakes," she muttered against his shirt. "I really hate snakes." She shuddered and wrapped her arms around him.

"I'm not crazy about 'em either," he said with a soft laugh. "Believe me, if I'd seen one when I lit the lamp, I probably would have run over you getting up the steps."

"No, you wouldn't," she said, smiling finally. "You wouldn't leave me here alone." She hesitated a moment. "Are you angry with me . . . for coming here this way? You wouldn't be stuck here if it weren't for me."

"Being stuck with you is not the worse thing that's ever happened to me," he said, still teasing.

Tears sprang to Lida's eyes at his sweetness.

John looked into her eyes and his expression changed. The teasing look left his eyes.

"No, I'm not mad," he whispered. "You're the bravest woman I've ever known. To risk going against your family and church this way, coming here to try and warn me and the people with me. All alone." He put his hands on the sides of her head and turned her face up toward him. "You knew the danger and the possibility of what might happen and you did it anyway."

He pulled her head against his chest, cradling her there against him. She could feel his quiet breathing and the steady rhythm of his heartbeat.

"I'm not angry," he whispered. "How could I be angry when you tried to save my life?" John bent his head and looked down at her, and she could see the worried look on his face.

"But Lida . . . sweetheart, I have to tell you something honestly."

"What?" she asked, looking into his eyes and feeling a stab of fear in her heart.

"I'm not real sure either of us will get out of this alive."

Twenty-one

Hearing his words, Lida felt so many raw emotions and thought of so many things she wanted to say to him. She tried not to think about her parents and what it would do to them if she should die here. If no one ever found them or knew what happened to them.

She clung to John, trying not to let him know how weak and shaky her arms and legs felt.

"I'm sorry," he murmured. "Sorry that I ever involved you in this."

"You know you can't take the blame for that," she said, looking up at him. He was so close, the familiar scent of him warm and reassuring. And Lida found that even as she fought the fear and danger, she wanted nothing more in this moment than to kiss him and to be held by him. "I forced my way into this because it's true, I wanted to help. But you guessed the real reason that night in the carriage. It was because I wanted to be with you and know that you were safe. I couldn't bear being at home every day, never seeing you, never knowing . . ."

John's eyes held such tenderness that it took Lida's breath away.

He bent his head and kissed her. The touch of his lips was soft, almost reverent, even though the look in his eyes, when he pulled away, was hot and filled with an exciting desire.

John knew that he was in danger here, in more ways than one. And yet the thought that he might die tonight never knowing what it was like to make love to her, tore at him and made his heart ache.

He'd find a way out of this. For Lida's sake, and her parents, he had to find a way to get them safely out of the storm cellar and away from the bounty hunters.

He shook himself, putting thoughts of lovemaking out of his mind. He wrapped his arms around her, cradling her against him there on the steps.

The lamp flickered against the stone walls. The damp coldness caused John to look with longing at the narrow bed.

"Why don't you try and get some sleep?" he asked, nodding toward the bed.

"No," she said quickly, shuddering as she eyed the filthy mattress.

"I'll be right here. I won't let anything happen to you or—"

"No," she said again. Her small hands grasped his shirt as she looked into his eyes. "I don't want to waste a minute of my time sleeping. If it all ends tonight, I want to spend every last moment looking at you and hearing your voice." Lida's eyes filled with tears and there was a quiet sob in her voice, although she smiled and tried to appear brave.

John closed his eyes against the pain he felt

when he looked in the depths of those beautiful, tear-filled eyes. For a moment he couldn't speak.

But Lida had said it so well. It was what he wanted, too, more than anything. And he didn't intend to insult her intelligence by lying and telling her that everything would be all right. She was a grown woman who knew just as well as he did what danger they were in.

"Tell you what," he whispered, his voice husky with emotion. "Why don't we both sit on the bed—at least it's softer than these steps. I'll hold you and we'll talk."

With a tremulous smile, she nodded and got off his lap. John placed the lamp on the table and went to the bed to turn over the dust-covered mattress.

"No snakes," he said with a teasing self-satisfaction. "No bugs."

She smiled at him, then nodded toward the table.

"What about the lamp? Do you think they can see the light around the door?" She glanced up at the ceiling.

"It's possible. Would you be frightened in the dark?"

"Not if you hold me," she whispered.

"All right," he said, turning toward the light. "We'll probably be safer without it." He reached for her hand as he blew out the light, then both of them sank down onto the bed, leaning their backs against the stone wall.

"There," he murmured. "How's that?"

Lida sighed and rested her head against his shoulder.

"I'll pretend we're at home in the barn," she said.

"Good," he said, putting his arm around her. "Tell me about the barn. Tell me what you did there when you were a little girl. Did you gather eggs, take naps in the hay?"

"Yes," she said, laughing softly. "Ephraim and I would wrestle in the hay and Papa would come in and scold us for strewing the hay everywhere and not working. Of course I don't think he really cared. He was usually smiling when he left."

They talked for a long while, holding one another, laughing softly at their stories of childhood mischief.

Finally they sat quietly until John spoke.

"My mother was the peacemaker in our family, always trying to make sure that Father wasn't too harsh in his punishments. Always reminding Nathan and me that we were brothers and family." Lida could feel him turn his head toward her and she felt his breath against her hair. "Your mother reminds me of her a lot."

"All mothers are that way . . . aren't they?" Lida asked.

"I think so," he said thoughtfully.

"So you see," she said. "We aren't so very different after all."

John said nothing, and Lida could almost feel his thoughts there in the intimate darkness.

"You miss your mother a great deal, don't you?"

"Yes," he said, without hesitating. "I miss her."

"And your father?"

"I miss him, too. But I'm not sure things will ever be the same between us. He's a stubborn, unrelenting man and he hasn't forgiven me for what I did. Last time I heard from Nathan, he said Father was ill . . ." His voice trailed away.

Lida heard the pain in his voice, the longing that he had not been able to disguise this time.

She felt John move, restlessly shifting his weight on the lumpy bed. When he spoke again, his voice was lighter.

"And what about you?" he asked. "Do you long for the day when you'll be a mother with four or five children trailing along behind you?"

"Four or five?" she asked, trying to mimic his lightheartedness. She groaned, then laughed. "I don't know about that."

"What about Carl?" John asked, his voice suddenly becoming deeper . . . quieter.

"I decided some time ago that I couldn't marry him," she said. "I should never have told him I would."

John knew why. Even though Lida hadn't said it. Even though she was being very careful with her words, John knew exactly how she felt. It was the same way he felt.

Against his will, he felt his body responding to her soft, sweet words. To her unspoken declaration of love. Being here with her, holding her, talking about every detail of their lives, made him want her more than he ever thought possible. But there was a difference tonight.

It wasn't just the danger, or the not knowing if there would be a tomorrow.

He knew this woman better than he'd ever known any other. Yet, oddly enough, some of the women he'd hardly known had ended up in his bed. *This* was different. Because Lida was different.

And he was beginning to think that knowing her had changed him, too. And although he still wasn't so sure that was a good thing for either of them, he found pleasure and hope in that knowledge.

For the first time in a long while, he felt a glimmer of peace. A sense of belonging. Maybe the difference with Lida was spiritual. That odd harmony that sometimes happened between lovers. A blending of not only the physical and mental, but of the soul as well.

And for the first time, that thought didn't bother him. In this moment of not knowing if either of them would live to see the sunrise, he welcomed it.

Now that they were warmer and more comfortable, John could feel Lida relax against him. Her breathing was slow and steady and he thought she might be drifting off to sleep.

"Lida?" he asked softly.

"Hmmm?"

"There's something I meant to tell you before."

He felt her snuggle against him.

"What?" she murmured softly against his shirt.

"In that red dress the other night . . . you were the most beautiful, exquisite creature I've ever seen." His voice was a whisper, a soft declaration made with a hint of wonder.

Lida went very still for a moment, reveling in the acknowledgment of his words. Then with a sigh, she laughed softly and snuggled closer to him. Her head moved to rest against his chest.

"Thank you," she whispered. In the next moment, she was asleep.

After a while John slept, too.

Neither of them could be sure what time it was when the sound of gunfire erupted. It was all around them it seemed, echoing off the rock walls of their prison, thudding into the ground above them with frightening, heart-stopping explosions.

Their first response was to reach for one another.

"My God," John muttered, his voice still raspy with sleep.

"They know we're here," Lida said, her sleepy words panic-stricken. "John . . . they know we're here."

"No," he said, listening carefully. "Wait . . . I don't think they do. Listen."

They could hear shouts and raucous laughter from somewhere above. The gunfire continued, although John doubted the shooters had any particular target or cared, for that matter, where they were shooting. He suspected that they were only drunk and bored.

Suddenly a bullet hit the earth-covered door with a splintering crack. The sound was loud, echoing in their ears and causing a spray of dirt and dust to fall down into the room around them.

John's body curved around Lida's automatically, shielding her from the debris. Lida cried out, clinging to him with all her might and fighting the terrible fear that swept over her in the darkness.

Her body was trembling and John could feel the desperation and fear in her. If the truth were known, he was afraid, too. Afraid of dying. Afraid of seeing her die in his arms . . . afraid of losing her forever.

It was that fear and desperation that made him seek her mouth in the darkness. He was crushing her against him, needing to find reality, needing to convince both of them that they were still alive.

Lida's arms moved around his neck and, with a quiet groan, she responded to his hungry, demanding kiss.

In that moment when danger crowded in around them, all the control, all the holding back that John had endured for so long was gone. He didn't care anymore about what was right or wrong. He didn't care that Lida was Amish and he English. He didn't even care that she was forbidden to him. All he cared about was holding her, loving her. His need to make love to her was so violent that he felt as if he could actually absorb her body into his.

Lida recognized his surrender with an instinct born of love. She felt his letting go and his need and with a wild little cry of elation, she welcomed him.

"Lida," he whispered, feeling her body arch against his.

Neither of them knew when the noise above them stopped.

By then, Lida was lying on the rough bunkbed

with John beside her. His thigh was across her legs. The heat of his body seemed to envelop her as he held her, kissed her. His hands, exploring . . . seducing, set her on fire.

Lida clung to him, knowing that wherever he led, she would follow. For a second, that night in her bedroom flashed before her eyes. She'd thought that experience was sensual and erotic. And now she found it was only a tiny, sweet taste of what was to come.

The pleasure of his kiss and his touch was all she ever wanted. It was slow and sweetly insidious, pushing away all other thoughts, all doubts. She wasn't sure of the moment when something changed between them into a wild storm that left her nerves shattered and her muscles trembling. All she knew was that it had.

Her body quivered with the intensity of what was happening. And now, as if John sensed it, too, his hands became more demanding and purposeful.

His movements were no longer meant to calm and soothe, but instead seemed design to arouse and send her rushing headlong toward some mysterious shattering moment that she hardly understood.

The darkness was so complete that it made his touch even more erotic and electrifying. Quickly John unfastened her dress and impatiently pushed the material away from her shoulders and down to her waist. His mouth found her nipples, and the feel of his tongue and teeth made her cry out with pleasure and surprise. She moved instinctively against him, her hips lifting, her body urging him on.

John pushed his clothes out of the way, his skin burning with the need to feel her naked body against his own. For a moment, he held himself away from her, letting the scent of her body intoxicate him.

When he pressed down against her and felt her breasts against his chest, he couldn't help the groan that escaped his lips. She was hot . . . so hot. And her skin was as smooth and soft as the red silk dress she'd worn.

John wished he could see her. Wished he could see that silken fall of hair against the bed as her head moved back and forth in sensual torment. He wanted to see the wild longing in those deep blue eyes.

Lida's hands clutched at him with an amazing strength. She moaned and whispered against his neck.

"I want you to . . ."

John felt his stomach muscles contract with an almost unbearable need. He didn't want to wait. Every instinct of his male being urged him to go on, to find relief. But he had to wait. For Lida. He had to slow down, be more patient. No matter how desperate she was to have him make love to her, he was the knowledgeable one and she still a virgin. He couldn't let himself forget that.

"Soon, love," he whispered against her mouth. He practically ripped away her dress, pushing it down over her feet before helping her remove her underwear.

Lida was trembling violently, like a small leaf in a windstorm. She wasn't afraid anymore. She was past that. Now, she only wanted the fulfillment . . . an end to this desperate longing she felt. And she didn't care what the consequences were.

She felt herself responding, felt a wild, pounding rhythm that seemed to wrack her entire body.

"John," she cried. "I can't . . . I don't . . ."

"That's it, love," he whispered. His hand moved lower to help her, to ready her. "Just let it happen. Let me—" He groaned. The heat of her body was unbearable and her hoarse cries sent him spiraling over the edge of self-control.

"Now," she urged. Her hands moved over him with restless impatience, pulling at his shoulders, raking down his chest.

John couldn't stand the sweet torture any longer either. His entire body was on fire from wanting her.

"Please," she whispered.

"Yes, now, angel . . . God . . . I've waited so long for this," he murmured. "So long."

He pressed her down into the mattress and pushed himself against her soft intimate flesh. He had half-expected Lida to pull away at this first invasion of her body. Instead, after the first penetration, she welcomed him with a quiet cry, holding onto him with a wild pagan intensity that surprised and delighted him.

She was no typical maiden, given to swooning and crying. She was his match in every way. Meeting his body after that first hesitant moment. Taking, demanding.

John braced himself on his arms above her, wishing once again that he could see her, could see the wild sensual look on her face. The feel of her was exquisite . . . earth-shattering.

He let himself go, pulling her into his arms, feeling her mouth and teeth against his neck. Her voice, desperate and hot, urged him on and on as her hands moved down to the small of his back to feel the sensuous rhythmic contraction of muscles there.

His chest raked again and again over her soft breasts, torturing him, driving him insane. He slid his hands under her, lifting her, causing her to gasp as she clung to him.

His voice held a guttural quality as he whispered to her, instructed her. Until finally she was sobbing his name, half-crazed with pleasure and desire.

When he heard her frenzied cries and felt her body trembling, he lost all control. The pleasure of their wild, sweet ending hit him like a sledgehammer. Surprising. Plowing into him like a train and causing a hoarse cry to rip from his own throat. His heart was pounding, his throat and lungs dry.

Nothing had ever prepared him for such a feeling. He'd made love to many women, but he'd never felt anything like this in his life. Nothing . . . no one had ever taken him to such heights.

"God," he whispered. "Lida . . . my beautiful Lida."

Twenty-two

Lida had been afraid. But now, lying quietly in John's arms, hearing the beat of their hearts, she thought she had never been so happy in her life. His lovemaking had banished even the sound of the drunken bounty hunters that waited for them. Had pushed away the terrible thoughts of their impending deaths.

"Are you all right?" John murmured. "Did I hurt you?"

"You didn't hurt me," she said, touching his face in the darkness.

Lida wanted nothing more than to declare her love for him. It was the most joyous feeling she'd ever experienced. And even under the circumstances, she was filled with a contentment that made her feel as if she could lie there forever. She wanted to talk about that feeling. But suddenly she felt shy, as if she were afraid she'd say the wrong thing.

John cradled her close, his muscular body still heavy across hers. The wild passion that had gripped both of them moments ago had abated somewhat. But feeling her warm naked body against his, he thought that wouldn't last long.

"Lida," he whispered. "I'm amazed. I don't think anything like this has ever happened to me."

Lida laughed softly, pleased beyond reason that she had not disappointed him.

John thought he'd never been filled with such a fierce sense of protection. And a bit of awe. He'd known Lida was strong, and that she was different from any other woman he'd ever met. But he hadn't really expected her to give herself to him so completely. She'd held back nothing, had made no protests, seemed to have no reservations about what was happening to her. And that amazed him. And delighted him.

He probably should be ashamed, disgusted with himself for making love to her and taking her virginity, when he knew all the possible consequences. But he had denied his hunger for her for so long. The sheer intensity of the situation they were in had only heightened their desire for one another and had left no room for regrets or reservations. If this was to be their last day on earth, he was glad he had spent it this way. With Lida. Loving her. And being loved by her.

John realized that Lida was asleep again. She muttered something softly and cuddled up against him. As they lay there in the darkness, he listened to the sounds outside their hiding place.

It was quiet above the cellar now. There were no hoofbeats, no gunfire, although he thought he still heard intermittent laughter and talk.

He cradled Lida against him and pulled her

dress up to cover both their naked bodies. Then he slept, too.

It was hours later when they woke. John wasn't sure what it was that woke him, but there was a tiny sliver of light filtering down through the weeds and grass around the door. Their underground prison seemed very quiet and still.

Lida nestled her face against his neck and instinctively John's hands moved down her body, caressing her smooth skin. He could feel the bones beneath her skin. Strong bones. For all her slenderness, Lida was not a delicate woman. She was healthy and strong . . . and more stimulating than any other woman he'd ever met. For a moment he wished he could stay there with her forever. Hide from what waited outside. And from what he knew she might face from her community if they did make it out of this alive.

If they did make it, he intended keeping their passionate alliance from her church if he could. He'd never wanted to be responsible for a break between Lida and her family and friends in the first place. That was the main reason he'd fought so long and hard to keep this from happening. But now that it had, he meant to do everything within his power to keep the Amish from finding out and Lida from being hurt.

"What is it?" she asked, noticing his stillness. "Do you hear something?"

"I'm not sure." John turned to her for one last sweet moment, kissing her slowly and laughing when he felt his body stirring to life again.

"I wish we could stay here forever," she murmured, echoing his own thoughts. She trailed her fingers down his chest, pleased that now in the faint glimmer of light, she could see him. All of him in full masculine glory. "You are a beautiful man, John Sexton," she said, her eyes moving over him without a trace of false shyness.

John let his eyes move over her, too, reveling in the sight of her full hips and lush breasts. Her waist was so narrow he could almost span it with his hands, her stomach feminine and slightly curved. But her legs were strong and muscular. He let his gaze move down those long legs and he shook his head with wonder.

"Damn, but you are a beautiful woman, Lida Rinehart."

They fell into each other's arms, holding one another and murmuring quiet endearments. But both of them knew they couldn't afford the luxury of making love again. There was no more time.

"Put on your clothes, angel," he said.

John dressed quickly and climbed the steps, pushing open the cellar door only the slightest bit. He could see three men at the house. The rest seemed to have disappeared. The men who remained sat on horseback, talking. And now one of them motioned first toward the west and then the east, and the other two riders moved away in those directions.

There was a worried look on Lida's face as she stood in the room, watching John. Her hands were clasped tightly together as she waited and prayed silently.

Last night she knew finally and with certainty that John wanted her, that there would be no turning back from the passion they felt for one another. She had thought then that she could die freely and with contentment if only God would grant them that one night of love. But now, in the light of day, she knew that wasn't true. Looking at John, feeling the love in her heart that their physical completion had brought, she knew she'd never be ready to die and leave him.

She didn't want to die. She wanted to live. She wanted to live for John and what they'd experienced together last night.

Only then did the realization hit her. Even if John told her that he wanted to spend the rest of his life with her, she'd have to make a decision. He'd already said he could never live Amish. If she didn't want to lose him, she'd have to leave the Amish community, never to return. Some people who left and went English were never able to see their families or speak to them again.

"They're leaving," John whispered, backing down the steps. He turned to Lida and took her arms, pulling her to him for a brief moment. "We have to go now, before they circle back and find your horse."

"Oh," Lida said. "I didn't tie him up. I thought if something happened, he would go back to Christela's . . . where I spent the night. All the noise and gunfire last night . . . it probably scared him away."

"That's all the better. Let's just hope they didn't see the horse first or pick up his trail. Don't worry about it—we'll walk back to the Dietz farm. If we're lucky, your folks won't know you've been missing all night."

John hugged her tightly against him, then pulled away to look down into her eyes.

"About last night . . . Lida, I—"

Lida saw the worried look on his face and she put her fingers against his mouth, then reached up to kiss his chin.

"Don't say it," she whispered. "Don't say you're sorry, or that we shouldn't have made love. I'm glad it happened. I wanted it to happen. So please . . . don't say anything to spoil what I'm feeling."

John shook his head and sighed heavily.

"When this is over, we have a lot of talking to do."

"I know." she said, agreeing. At least he hadn't said it was over or that he never wanted to see her again. As long as he didn't say that, she held onto the hope that he might one day love her as much as she did him.

"Are you ready?" he asked. He took her hand and glanced around the gloomy room before pulling her toward the steps.

"Ready," she said with a firm nod of her head.

Pushing up on the door only slightly, John blinked his eyes, squinting in the bright sunlight. He hesitated a moment, letting his eyes adjust and looking toward the abandoned house to make sure there were no other bounty hunters waiting.

He pulled Lida up and beside him on the steps,

still holding the door open a small crack above their heads. He nodded toward the woods.

"You hold the door. Leave only a very narrow opening to see through. I'm going to make a run for it. If you hear shooting, you close this door and stay put. Even if you have to stay here for another night. If they find me, they'll think I'm the only one. Wait it out and you'll make it."

Lida was staring at him with a look of horror.

"No . . . John," she whispered.

"Here," he said, shoving the box of matches into her hand as he pulled himself up out of the hole. "Do as I say. Promise me, Lida, you'll do it."

"I don't care what happens to me if—" Her blue eyes were large and filled with disbelief at his suggestion.

"Do it, angel. You have to," he demanded. "If I make it, count to a hundred before you follow."

He kissed her hard then and, with one backward look, leapt up and away from the storm cellar.

He ran in a crouched position across the open field. Lida was almost afraid to watch. Her heart was pounding, muscles tensed as she waited for the sound of a gunshot.

John disappeared into the shelter of the woods and Lida breathed a sigh of relief. She saw him wave once from behind a large tree. Then she waited almost a full minute, holding her breath until she thought her lungs would explode. Finally, with a silent prayer, she pulled herself through the cellar opening and followed John's path across the open field.

Lida could hardly believe it when she entered the woods and there were no shots. Being free, outside in the sunlight, and feeling John's arms around her was the most wonderful feeling in the world.

"Let's go," he whispered. "They could be anywhere."

It was almost noon when they reached the boundaries of the Dietz farm. Lida saw some of Christela's family in the fields. They stopped what they were doing and stared at John and Lida as if they were specters, risen from the grave.

Lida looked down at her dress and apron, covered with dirt and grime. She'd lost her cap and her hair, whipped by the wind, fell in tangled strands about her flushed face. Her hands were scratched, nails torn. She must look a sight.

Self-consciously she reached to push her hair out of her face. She glanced up at John and saw him watching her from the corner of his eye.

"You look fine," he murmured. "We'll say you were lost and I just happened to find you."

Lida shook her head in agreement, but she felt the sting of tears behind her eyelids. She didn't want to lie. She wanted to be able to tell everyone that she had been with John. That she loved him and belonged to him. And knowing she couldn't do that hurt more than anything.

She knew why John was doing this. He wanted to protect her, to keep her from being shunned by her church and family. But was it what *she* really wanted? At this point she wasn't sure.

When Lida saw the crowd of people in Christela's front yard, she thought her heart might actually stop beating. She moved closer to John, catching his hand for a moment while they were still too far away for the others to notice. They looked into each other's eyes, aware now of what they were about to face. Her parents were there and they knew.

For John, he couldn't have felt worse if he were the one being scrutinized and judged. Damn, but he'd *rather* it be him.

"Lida," he murmured beneath his breath. "I didn't want this for you. I never wanted to come between you and your beliefs."

"You haven't," she said, gritting her teeth. She stopped before crossing the short distance to the people waiting for them. She didn't care now what they thought or what they saw.

"I'm the one who came to you, remember? I'm the one who sneaked away in the night to find you. And I wanted you to make love to me. You've known that for a long time and you tried to protect me. And I know that you would have continued resisting the idea last night, too, if things hadn't been so frightening and dangerous, so . . ."

She paused, not wanting to cry. She had no idea how this day would end or when she'd ever be able to see John again. She didn't want their last moments to be filled with tears or regrets.

"No matter what happens to me with my family

and my church," she said, swallowing her tears, "it's not your fault."

When Lida saw Christela running toward her, she stepped away from John.

"Lida! Oh, Lida," Christela said, coming to grip her cousin in a fierce hug. "I was so afraid. I was afraid you were dead. I didn't know what to do." Her eyes were filled with guilt as she glanced from Lida to John. "I'm sorry. I had to tell them that you'd gone to find John."

John gritted his teeth and stood very still. Lida could see the clenching and unclenching of his hands. She knew he wanted to help, to protect her the way he had last night. But there was nothing he could do here. Whatever happened now was between her and the Amish church.

When she and Christela turned to walk back to the gathered crowd, John caught up with them, refusing to let Lida face this alone. Despite his rumbled clothes and the dirt on his hands and face, Lida thought he had never looked more handsome and proud than he did at that moment, walking straight and tall beside her.

Seeing that made her lift her own chin and take a deep breath. Whatever was to be, would be. She couldn't change it, any more than she could change her overwhelming love for this man.

Twenty-three

Her mother and father were standing at the front of the group of people watching John and Lida and Christela come toward them. Now that she'd seen her daughter alive and safe, Anna Rinehart seemed hardly able to contain herself. She ran forward, coming to take Lida in her arms as if she were a child.

"Mein Schatz," she cried. "Oh, Lida, my little girl. I thought I had lost you forever."

Lida hugged her mother, stroking her hair and murmuring assurances that she was fine.

Finally Mrs. Rinehart pulled away and stood for a moment studying Lida's face before turning to stare into John's eyes. Her look was one of hurt and betrayal, a look almost too painful to see.

"Mrs. Rinehart," John said apologetically, reaching a hand forward.

"Nein! Do not try to make things right, John Sexton. It is too late for that. Too late for my daughter's reputation."

"Mother . . ." Lida began. "Please, it's not—"

"You are blinded by love, child," her mother whispered for her ears only. "It is best you say nothing. This man has fooled all of us. And from what I can see in your eyes, my daughter, he has fooled you most of all."

When Lida turned to John, it was with a pleading look. That look touched him and wounded him to his very core. This was what he had been trying so desperately to avoid. This was the very reason he had pushed Lida away time and time again. And now it was here—the moment he had always known would come if he let himself give in to those forbidden thoughts and desires that he'd had for her from the beginning.

He shook his head and sighed. At that moment he wished Lida could know what was in his mind, what was in his heart. He should have told her last night. Confessed all the feelings he'd kept bottled inside for so long.

Now it was too late. All he could do was hope that she understood.

Lida's father stood waiting with the others, making no attempt to come to her as her mother had. Now her mother took Lida's arm and pulled her impatiently toward the group. When Lida turned back as if to reach for John, her mother pushed her hand away.

"Don't," Anna Rinehart said, her face harder than Lida had ever seen it. "Do not shame me any further, daughter."

Lida bit her lip and walked forward to face her father. Seeing the look in his eyes, she actually thought for a moment that he might strike her. And he had never done that in his life. Glancing briefly at the group of people, she saw her Uncle Levi and her aunt, little Adam Frederick and the rest of her cousins. Some of their neighbors were there, too, and far in the back, she saw Carl.

She wanted to run and hide from the hurt and accusation in his eyes.

"We will hear your explanation now," her father said. He didn't touch her, didn't offer any sympathy with his bright blue gaze. The anger and disappointment were clearly visible on his face.

Lida sensed that John had followed and that he was standing behind her. She felt his presence and, for a moment, she could hardly resist the urge to turn and fling herself into his arms. She would beg him if she had to, to take her away from here, away from the disapproval and accusation she saw in the eyes of everyone she'd grown up knowing and loving.

"Mr. Rinehart—" John began.

"Not you," Jacob said, his face turning dark with rage. "I will hear the words from my own daughter."

When she'd been with John at the abandoned farm, Lida had felt so sure about what they'd done, about her love. She had made her choice and there had been no regrets. There were none now about that. But she felt confused. She had let love blind her to the reality of what returning to her family meant. She'd thought she could hide what had happened, at least until she decided what she would do. But she hadn't counted on Christela's revelations to everyone.

"I went to warn John, Father," she said, her voice very low.

"Why?" he said. His voice sounded low in the still and sultry noonday air. "Why would you concern yourself about this war issue, when you know you are not to be involved?"

The sun beaming overhead was hot against Lida's bare head. And for a moment she felt weak and faint. She hadn't eaten and they had walked a great distance. She swallowed hard and tried to concentrate on what was happening.

"When the sheriff came to the house yesterday, he said there was to be an ambush." Lida gazed directly into her father's skeptical eyes. As much as she loved and respected him, she wondered how he could distance himself from the war and all its problems. How any of them could.

"I had to warn him, Father. I couldn't let him die the way Ephraim did."

"You could have told the sheriff what you knew."

"No," she said, shaking her head. "I couldn't do that. I wasn't sure I could trust him."

"And how did you know where this man was?"

"I—" Lida knew the moment for the whole truth had come, and she wished with all her heart that it did not have to be here in front of everyone. But that was the Amish way. Bearing burdens together. Sharing everything. Even shame and the admission of sin.

"I was working with him, the way Ephraim was." Lida's voice rang clearly in the hot summer air.

There was an audible murmur of disbelief among the people listening. Then they began whispering to one another, and looking at Lida as if she had indeed committed an unpardonable sin.

In their eyes, she supposed she had.

Turning her gaze back to her father, Lida's breath caught in her throat. There was a violence there she'd never seen before. An anger so deep that it frightened her. His eyes glinted with it, and his face had turned a dark blood red.

"You would do this to me?" he shouted. He waved his hands in the air, losing all attempt at controlling his fury. "To your *Mutter?* You, an *unverheiratet Madchen,* would traipse over the countryside, stay the night with a man . . . an English man?"

"My being unmarried has nothing to do with it, Papa. You don't understand. We were in danger. We—"

"Nein, gern!" Her father was trembling in his anger. For a moment, Lida actually feared for his health. "It has everything to do with it. You do not care for these slaves. You do not care for the work as you say."

"But I do," Lida protested, taking a step toward him. "I do care."

"Even if your church forbids involvement in such violent things?"

"Father, I—"

"Pah! You do not fool me. Your caring is for this man only!" he said, stabbing his finger into the air toward John. "I should have seen it. I should have known what was happening." He took a deep breath, puffing his chest out and stiffening as if he were about to hand down a sentence.

"You have disgraced us. You have disgraced yourself. And worst of all, you have disgraced your church." He turned his wrath then toward John. But all the fury seemed to have been spent. He faced the man he had cared for like a son, with only a cold anger.

"You came to my house and we took you in. We fed you and tended you . . . nursed you back to health. I behaved toward you as a father toward a son."

"Yes sir," John said quietly. "I know. And I appreciate it."

"Appreciate," Jacob said. *"Gern!* You appreciated nothing except my daughter and her inexperience. You have brought this disgrace to my family. Can you stand here and tell me honestly that there has been no intimacy between the two of you?"

Lida glanced toward John. Her lips were trembling as she saw him frown, wavering between telling the truth or lying to this man that he liked and respected.

"You cannot deny it," Jacob said. *"Mein Gott!"* Jacob Rinehart slammed his fist against his open palm. The sound of it rang through the air and echoed against the house. "And even if you did, I can see it in your eyes. And yours, daughter," he accused, glancing at Lida.

Some of the other's moved back a step, away from Jacob Rinehart's quiet anger. Lida's mother stepped forward and placed her hand on her husband's arm.

"Jacob," she said quietly as if to calm him.

But he shrugged away from her and continued staring at John.

"There is only one way you can atone for what you've done, and keep my daughter from further disgrace. You can marry her. You must repent your sins before the brethren, put aside your worldliness forever. The Amish church welcomes any outsider who truly repents and wishes to live according to God's discipleship. You know our ways—they are not so hard."

Jacob's last words were given more softly. There was almost a note of wistfulness there, as if he wanted to forgive John and welcome him if he would only agree to Jacob's offer and do the right thing in the eyes of the church.

Lida closed her eyes. She could feel her face burning with embarrassment. Her humiliation was complete. She could feel the others staring at her, wondering, condemning her for what she had done. Even Christela looked at her as if she were someone she hardly knew. And she couldn't bear to look into her mother's eyes and see the pain and humiliation there.

The silence seemed to go on forever. The fact that John said nothing for so long actually made Lida's heart tremble.

Finally she could stand it no longer. She opened her eyes and turned around to face John. But she knew. She already knew what he would say. Hadn't he made it clear from the beginning how he felt about the Amish church?

His gray eyes were stormy as they met hers and held.

"Lida . . . I'm sorry," he said, shaking his head, still looking at Lida. "The Amish are a good and kindly people, but I can't . . . I could never truly accept all of your beliefs. If there were any other way . . . I'm sorry," he added softly.

Lida's lips began to tremble. Her entire body was trembling as tears slowly fell from her eyes and down her cheeks. She felt as if she were barely breathing. As if she were dying.

Suddenly she turned and ran. Pushing her way through the crowd and running as if death itself followed on her heels.

"Lida!"

She heard John's shout behind her, but when she turned and glanced back over her shoulder, she saw the men surround him and keep him from following her.

She ran with all her might, past the Dietz's barn and out into the wide pasture that separated their land from her father's. Finally, weak and exhausted, she fell into the tall clover, feeling its coolness against her skin even as the dirt beneath dug into her hands and knees.

"John," she said, sobbing wildly. "Oh, John, why couldn't you love me the way I love you? Why couldn't you just have told my father you loved me and would do anything to be with me?"

No one followed Lida. Even if they knew where she was, they left her alone to cry and to sort through her feelings. And to decide what she would do.

She knew in her heart that there would be no choice now but to shun her from the church. The *Meidung* they called it. An ugly-sounding word for a harsh, ugly sentence.

She cried until she felt there were no more tears left. Until she was numb with grief. Finally, she became more aware of the earth beneath her, of the cawing of crows as they flew above the field and the singing of birds across the meadows.

She sat up, feeling tired and dirty. The touch and smell of the clover soothed her somewhat. Being outdoors on the farm always made her feel better. Finally she got up, thinking about John and the look of sadness in his eyes when he had told her and all the rest that he could not marry her.

And last night. Always the memories of last night came to her. Haunting her, teasing her with thoughts and wishes of what might have been. Being with John, loving him, was one of the most wonderful experiences of her life. How could she bear to give that up? How could he?

Finally Lida forced herself to walk toward home. It wasn't what she wanted. She dreaded facing her parents alone, having to hear again how she had disgraced them. But she was bone-tired. She needed a bath and she was more hungry and thirsty than she'd ever been in her life.

She had never intended to disgrace anyone, least of all her parents who had always been so good and loving to her. But how could it be wrong to love someone? To fall in love with a man and want to spend the rest of your life with him?

Her newly discovered love for John, an English, made her feel like a stranger in her own land, among her own people. Because of that she would pay the penalty of shunning by her church. She would be an outcast, isolated until she repented publicly and vowed never to repeat her sin. And since John refused to marry her, they would expect her to marry Carl and settle down to the life they approved.

Now, gazing across the wide, beautiful green fields, seeing the pristine white fences and barns, for the first time in her life Lida felt as if she didn't belong here. She was a prisoner surrounded by beauty and peace and serenity.

But a prisoner nonetheless.

Twenty-four

When Lida arrived back home, she felt as if she'd been gone for weeks instead of hours. Everything looked the same, and yet it was different. *She* was different and now she saw everything in a complete contrast to the way things were before.

She had hoped that by some miracle her parents wouldn't be home yet. But they were. She saw her father working near the barn and when she walked into the kitchen, her mother was there.

She turned when Lida came inside.

"*Liebling,*" she said softly, seeing Lida's swollen eyes and dirt-stained clothes. She came and put her arms around her. "I am sorry you are hurting. You have done a wrong thing, but I am sorry it must be so hard for you."

"Why does it have to be this way?" Lida asked, looking into her mother's eyes. "Why does everything have to be so difficult with the Amish? Sometimes I just wish we could be like everyone else."

Oddly enough there was sympathy and understanding in her mother's eyes. Lida hadn't expected that.

"One day, when you're older, you will learn to accept the way we live. You're young. It is the way of the young to question everything and everyone."

Her father came into the kitchen then. He placed his hat on a peg and came to sit at the table. His eyes were pained and brooding. He looked old.

"The news about what you have done will travel fast," he said, as if Lida were only an acquaintance instead of his daughter. "You may expect a meeting soon to decide if you will be shunned or not."

"I know," Lida said.

She didn't know why his words didn't frighten her or fill her with regret. She felt more anger than anything, that a group of people—even her own kinsmen and neighbors—would set themselves up as judges to tell her that she had sinned.

She didn't feel what she'd done had been a sin. What happened between her and John had been beautiful and sweet, tender beyond anything she'd ever experienced. She would never believe it was wrong. Never.

She lifted her chin and faced her father's fierce gaze.

"Where is John. They didn't hurt him, did they? They didn't—"

"John Sexton is English. He is no longer your concern."

Lida's eyes widened. His cold pronouncement was all it took for the anger that had been simmering within her to suddenly spring to the surface.

"Not my concern?" she gasped. "How can you say that what happens to John is not my concern? I love him, Papa. I will always love him. And nothing any of you say or do is ever going to change that. Tell me where he is."

Her father pushed himself away from the table and stood. He was shaking as he addressed her.

"You will not speak such words in my house! Love!" he said disdainfully, practically spitting the word at her. "In our society, love is sacred. It is what is between a mother and her children. It is what a man feels for his church and his land. But it is not the basis for tearing one's life apart."

"If I were not Amish—" she began, still angry.

"If you were not Amish, John Sexton still would not marry you," he said bluntly. "You know his name—the Sojourner. Does that not tell you anything about the man? He is a wanderer, a man obsessed with adventure and glory. He is not for you, little *Schwester.* You must forget this man and marry Carl Miller as you planned. John Sexton is not for you."

"I won't marry Carl," she stormed. "I won't marry anyone here."

She ran from the room, forgetting her hunger. Forgetting everything except her father's hurtful words. He had voiced the greatest fear that lay in her heart. That John didn't love her and would never want to marry her. Now, away from John and the reassurance that his desire gave her, she wondered if her father could be right.

Would John have said yes if she had been an English like him? Or had he taken his pleasure with her merely because she was so willing and because she had pursued him? What man would turn down such an offer from a woman?

Moments later, while she lay across the bed in her room, she heard the bedroom door open. Her mother came in carrying buckets of steaming water. She looked at Lida not so much like a mother, but as a woman who understood.

"I thought you'd like to bathe here in your room, *Liebling.*" she said, her voice filled with love and tenderness. "I will bring you something to eat."

"Thank you, Mother," Lida said. "You are so good to me—I don't deserve it."

"Of course you do," her mother said. For once the gentle woman's voice was stern and filled with a strong resolve. "You deserve all the goodness anyone can give." She stood for a moment watching her daughter's eyes. "You must realize—sometimes a man doesn't understand what's in a woman's heart . . ."

She hesitated and began again as if the words were hard for her. "What your father said about John . . . that was wrong. Men do not always understand how it is with a woman when she is in love."

Lida was surprised.

"Were you in love, Mother . . . when you married Papa?"

"Oh, yes," she said, her eyes becoming soft. "I thought if I could not marry him, I would most likely die."

"And . . . and did he love you?"

"He said he did. But I think it was several years before he truly knew what it was to love and be loved. Men are different from us, dear," her mother said wistfully. "Sometimes they're all bluff and smoke. Sometimes I think they don't know themselves what it is they want or what they feel."

"Do you think what I did was wrong, Mother?" Lida asked softly. "Going to John that way?"

"According to the church, you were wrong."

"But do *you* think I was wrong?"

"I worry that a child might be the result of this love you have for the English."

"I wouldn't care," Lida said with a stubborn lift of her chin. "At least I would have something of him to remember."

"Child," her mother scolded. "Don't say such a thing. If there is a baby and you are unmarried, you will never be allowed back into the church. It would be an outcast and so would you."

"I could live somewhere else. Would that be such a horrible thing?" Lida asked. It was something she'd wanted to ask her mother for a long time. An idea she'd often toyed with as a child. But now, even as a grown woman, she wanted her mother's approval.

"If the love you feel for John Sexton is real. And if he loves you in return, then there is nothing horrible about it. And you know I would be sad to see you leave us. But you must choose your own life, dear. Your father and I will be gone one day, and you will be left with either the life you wanted or the one someone else chose for you." Her mother's smile was sad and wistful as she put her fingers to her lips to indicate that they shared a secret. "But do not tell your papa I ever said such a thing."

Lida got up off the bed and went to her mother. They embraced, and her mother kissed her cheek and ran her hand down her daughter's long silky hair.

"Have your bath now," her mother said, moving toward the door. "I will bring you something to eat."

There were tears in Lida's eyes as she watched her go.

"I love you, Mama," Lida whispered.

Her mother turned and smiled, then closed the door.

The next few days, Lida worked hard. She spent her days in almost complete silence, especially when her father was around to make his disapproval known. And although she knew she had her mother's sympathy, she also knew that there was nothing she could do to make things easier for Lida. For the first time, she was alone.

She had been hoping that John would come. That he would just ride up to the house one day, sweep her into his arms, and carry her away with him. Even though at this point, she had no idea how that would be a solution to anything except her longing. She just wanted him. She wanted to see him and touch him, feel his lips on hers, revel in his strong arms about her.

She supposed she was thinking about him the morning that she heard the sound of wheels in the drive behind the house. Lida quickly dried her hands and ran from the kitchen, stopping short when she saw Carl climbing down from a buggy and coming toward the house.

Her father was working on a broken board at the end of the back porch. He straightened from his work and stood waiting as Carl walked toward the house. Jacob's gaze focused on Lida and the look in his eyes warned her that this was her chance to make everything right.

Lida waited on the porch.

"Morning," Carl said. He stood in the yard, looking up where Lida stood on the porch.

"Good morning, Carl."

"I've come to talk," he said.

"Would you like to come inside?" she asked, waving her hand back toward the door.

There was an odd look on Carl's face. She'd seen it that day at the Dietz farm, when it was revealed to everyone where she'd been all night and with whom.

He shook his head and took off his black hat, turning it round and round in his hands as he gazed down toward the ground. He kicked the toe of his shoe in the dirt before speaking.

"I've come to ask out of our arrangement," he said quietly. His head lifted then and he looked into Lida's eyes. There was a quiet anger in his gaze, and resentment.

And there was something else, too. Something that surprised Lida. There was a disapproval, disgust even as he stood staring at her.

"Of course," Lida said. "I understand." It was

what she wanted. But his look, and the fact that her father stood listening, made her feel sick.

She had been judged by them all and found guilty. But it wasn't the guilt that hurt Lida so much. It was the disapproval and the ugliness she saw in their eyes when they looked at her.

"I guess everyone knows by now what's happened," Carl continued. "So I hardly think it necessary to make an announcement." His lips clamped together in a thin, disapproving line.

"Yes, I agree," Lida said quietly. "I'm sure it isn't necessary."

Carl slapped his hat against his thigh. He looked as if he wanted to say something else. But instead he nodded and turned away.

"Guten tag, Herr Rinehart." he muttered as he headed back toward his buggy.

"Guten tag, Carl."

Lida wasn't sure why she stood watching him go. Something perhaps in the way he had looked at her. Or just a feeling of intuition. When Carl reached the buggy, she saw him speak to someone who waited there, half-hidden by the black top, and she guessed that his odd behavior was because he'd brought a girl with him.

When Carl got into the buggy and turned the horse around, she saw who it was he had spoken to and who sat now so close beside him.

It was Christela. Her own cousin.

Chrissie turned her face toward the house and Lida met her sheepish gaze. Not that she cared that Carl had turned to Christela. It was natural and good. They would make a good couple. In fact she was surprised she hadn't seen it before.

But it hurt. The judgment and isolation against her had already begun. With her father. With Carl. And now even with Chrissie, the person who'd been her best friend since childhood.

Lida turned then and saw her father shaking his head. His look said it all. He thought Lida had ruined everything. And now she was letting the most eligible young man in the area get away because of her disgraceful behavior.

That night when they ate supper, her father seemed to make an effort to discuss something besides Lida's dishonor. He mentioned that someone would need to watch the sheep in the south pasture for the next few days.

"There's been wild dogs spotted in the area. I'll go to my brother's house tomorrow morning and ask if Adam Frederick and one of the older boys can come."

"I'll do it," Lida said quickly. She needed some reason to get away from the house. The thought of spending the entire day outside, away from her father's constant disapproval, sounded glorious.

"You, daughter? Well," he said, rubbing his chin. "I hadn't thought you might . . ." He glanced across at her. "You'll have to take a rifle, in case the dogs come. I can have your cousin Adam come, too, if you'd like."

"No," she said. "It's not necessary. I won't be afraid. Or lonely. I'll take a book to read."

Her mother nodded toward Jacob. "It might be

good," she said. "This week has been very hard for her."

Lida expected him to say that she deserved any hardship that had come. But instead. he only nodded, and the subject was settled.

The next morning was clear and very warm. Lida spent her time walking about in the pasture, trying to keep the sheep together and just enjoying the outdoors. There had been no sign of the wild dogs, but still she was cautious, making sure not to wander too far from the rifle that sat against a large elm tree in the middle of the pasture.

Around noon, clouds began to move across the sky. Intermittent sunlight and shadows raced across the billowing sage grass that the sheep had left standing. Several times Lida thought she heard something in the grass, but seeing nothing, she eventually went back to the tree, intending to eat her lunch.

When she heard someone call her name, she jumped up from the ground and whirled around toward the sound. Her mouth flew open and she stared at the man coming toward her. Her heart began pounding, a loud, rhythmic beating, a sound that obliterated everything else.

"John," she whispered, still unable to believe he was there.

He was just at the edge of the tall grass as he walked toward her. She let her eyes take in every muscular inch of him, from the top of his shining black hair to the long legs that stretched out as he walked.

He wore a white shirt, open at the throat, and suspenders that she recognized as belonging to her brother. He was handsome, breathtakingly so, and Lida thought he was the most wonderful sight she'd ever seen.

He stopped and, with a questioning look, stood watching her, as if he weren't sure how she would react or whether she would welcome him.

When she began to run toward him, he smiled and opened his arms. His gray eyes sparkled and there was such tenderness in their depths that Lida felt breathless.

"Oh, John," she cried. "You came."

Twenty-five

Without saying a word, he caught her up in his arms and took her mouth hungrily, like a man long past the bounds of any self-control. As if he had been waiting for her all his life.

"I shouldn't have come," he murmured, trailing kisses down her neck and pushing at the material that covered her full, tantalizing breasts. "I should have stayed away from you forever and let you live your life in peace."

John knew they were only words. Words that should strike some cord within him and make him think with reason before he lost himself in her nearness. But even as he said them, he knew they were meaningless. He'd never missed anyone in his life the way he missed Lida these past few days. Never wanted anyone the way he wanted her now. He couldn't have stayed away from her any longer if his very life depended on it.

The other night had been magical, and he'd thought he wanted her then beyond anything he'd ever known. But it was nothing compared to this. The desire he experienced now had been fueled by nights of thinking about her, nights of remembering the feel of her body against his, the touch of her hands. Long moments during the day when he would be in a daze, drunk with the memories and the feelings.

Saying he shouldn't have come were only words. He *had* to come. Been compelled with a white burning urgency to seek her out and bury himself against her soft white breasts.

"Lida," he groaned against her mouth. "My sweet Lida. I couldn't blame you if you never spoke to me again. Or never wanted to see me again."

He heard her murmur of protest and felt her hands tug at the buttons of his shirt, pushing the suspenders away from his shoulders.

"I'm glad you came," she whispered urgently. "I was so afraid . . . afraid you'd never come back."

He took a deep breath and held her face between his hands, forcing her to look up at him. For a moment they both were still as they gazed into each other's eyes.

"Did you really believe I could leave you? That I could go away forever without kissing you and holding you again? Oh, angel, I've been crazy wondering about you. I came to your father's farm almost every day just to catch a glimpse of you. I tried to stay away . . . I knew I should for your sake. I thought I could be content if I could just see you one last time." He kissed her mouth quickly.

"It almost killed me—watching you, not being able to touch you . . ." His mouth moved to her ear. "Seeing how hard you worked. Knowing you were alone and scared." With an impatient groan he kissed her again, opening her mouth and feeling an overwhelming need to have her naked and warm against his body.

He almost laughed with delight when he felt Lida pulling his shirt away from his chest. He closed his eyes and groaned when her mouth moved down his chest to his nipples, and her hands moved restlessly down to his stomach. He felt her sharp little teeth, nipping, teasing. Her mouth felt hot and sent arrows of desire racing through him.

John knew her well and he had known instinctively that she wouldn't be shy and reluctant today, anymore than she had been that first time. But he was still filled with awe at her straightforward honesty about their lovemaking. The fact that she wanted him just as much, just as boldly as he wanted her, made him feel wild with pleasure and made him want to take her with an impatience that was almost unbearable.

He pulled the white cap from her head and freed her hair to fall softly about her shoulders. He buried his face in her hair, smelling the freshness, the clean scent that was hers alone.

Only when he untied her apron and began to unbutton her dress did she hesitate, looking up into his eyes with questioning wonder. Her hands moved up to cover his.

"Here?" she asked, her blue eyes glittering.

"Yes, here," he said, his voice husky with impatience and need. "Now. God, angel, I want to make love to you right *now.*"

He moved her toward the cloth where she had begun to place her lunch. With one quick movement he dashed everything away and laid Lida down on the ground.

As she looked up at him with trust in her eyes, he hesitated, holding himself above her until his arms began to shake.

"If you want me to go, tell me now . . ." he said. "If—"

"No," she whispered, her hands moving urgently to touch his chest. "Don't go," she said. "I never want you to leave me again."

John didn't even bother removing his clothes, or hers. He pushed her dress up out of the way and took her swiftly then and there. The way he wanted it. The way he knew she wanted it, too.

Lida welcomed him, her body quickening as she cried out her pleasure.

He loved this about her. Her heated response, the lack of self-consciousness, feigned or real, about the act of lovemaking.

He heard her breathing against his ear, the air coming faster and faster from her lungs as she moved with him, urged him on with her small hands and her heated welcoming body.

"So sweet," he whispered, his hands digging into her hips. "So sweet and—" He groaned, unable to contain himself. He had to concentrate, had to focus or—

Lida's body was trembling beneath him. Her movements were quick and frantic as her hunger for him accelerated, as she felt the delicious release coming closer . . . closer.

"Ah . . . *God!*" he whispered, his voice hoarse and fierce as she matched his hard quick rhythm.

Lida grabbed his shoulders, her head arching back, holding on as her entire body seemed on fire.

John caught her up in his arms, holding her tightly as he joined her in their quick, heart-stopping climb to the heavens. His voice was deep and husky as it mingled with her quiet, sobbing little cries.

Afterward John lay against her in exhausted silence. Her hands moved to his hair and he kissed her softly against the side of her mouth. They became aware of the wind in the tree above them, and of the rustling grass and the quite murmur of the sheep nearby.

John smoothed her damp hair away from her temples and moved to lay beside her, pulling her dress back down and then taking her in his arms.

Lying there in the still peacefulness with the gray clouds racing by above them, John took her hand and brought it to his mouth.

"I wasn't sure I'd ever see you again," he murmured softly against her skin.

"I was afraid they had hurt you," she said, turning her head so she could look into his gray eyes.

"No," he said softly. "They just wanted to make sure I didn't follow you, or cause you any more problems than I already had."

"They're wrong. They just don't know you the way I do."

He took her hand, feeling the calluses on her small palms. "You've been working hard."

She pulled her hand away, suddenly feeling self-conscious and keenly aware of the kind of woman he was used to. She doubted his fiancée Katherine ever had calluses or broken nails.

He took her hand again and frowned at her as if to chide her for her actions.

"My hands are rough," she murmured apologetically.

"No. They're good hands," he said, kissing her fingers one by one. "Strong and steady. I love your hands."

"When were you watching me?" she asked. "I didn't see you or—"

"I didn't intend for you to see me. In fact I told myself I'd get out of your life completely. That I'd never let myself come to you again."

Lida frowned, holding her breath against what he might say next.

"But I couldn't stay away," he said, looking into her eyes. "God, I just couldn't stay away from you."

"But how did you know I was here today?"

"A little *vogel* told me," he said, smiling at her mischievously.

"Ah, your German is improving," she said, grinning back at him. "Would the little bird's name be Adam Frederick?"

"It would," he said. "I've managed to find him several times lately, and he is always willing to give me information. He likes his cousin Lida a deal, I think."

"The little rascal," she said, laughing. "Papa must have told them I was here. He wanted Adam to help me today. I just hope the boy doesn't say anything to Christela about seeing you. Carl came to the house yesterday to ask out of our arrangement. Chrissie was with him. She's turned against me, John," she said with a slight catch in her voice. "My own cousin thinks I'm nothing more than an Amish whore."

"Lida," he muttered, frowning at her. He cursed beneath his breath and sat up, looking down at her and shaking his head. "I don't ever want to hear you say such a thing about yourself again."

"It's what I will be called," she whispered. "That and a lot worse besides."

"Do they intend banishing you then?"

"Yes," she whispered. "I'm almost certain of it." She lifted her chin and sat up beside him, staring out across the waving grass.

"What will happen?" he asked, his voice harder.

"I will be set apart from everyone. I will live alone, eat alone, work alone. These past few days will be nothing compared to the isolation of *Meidung.* I won't be allowed to attend church, of course, or any other Amish functions. No one may speak to me, not even my own family."

John cursed again. "It's too cruel," he muttered. "It's cruel blackmail, that's all it is."

"It is our way," she whispered. "There's nothing I can do."

"Come with me," he said, turning to catch her shoulders and pull her toward him. "I'll find a place for us nearby. Where we can be together." He didn't dare actually say the word marriage. He wasn't sure how she would react to his asking her to leave her Amish world forever and live English with him in marriage. But he assumed she knew that was what he meant.

For a moment Lida's heart leapt at his words. Then she realized that he had not mentioned the word marriage. Only a phrase she didn't fully understand—a place where they could be together. What did that mean? A place for both of them to live together without marriage? Make love together every night? As much as she longed for that part, she couldn't. It wasn't enough.

She wanted John Sexton. But not for a month or six months. She wanted him forever. And now, after the fire of their lovemaking had died down to warm, banked embers, she realized that a commitment for a lifetime was not what he'd had in mind when he came to her today.

"I . . . I don't think so," she muttered. She stood up, walking away from him and smoothing down her dress as she turned her back.

"Lida?" he asked. John stood up and went to her. Her shoulders were stiff, her arms hugging her body as if for warmth. "I thought that was what you wanted. We can be together. You can—"

"Be your Amish whore?" she asked, turning to face him with glittering fury in her eyes.

"Dammit," he said, clenching his jaws together. He took her arms and shook her. "Why do you say such things? What did I say to make you so angry?"

"Nothing," she said. "You didn't say anything.

I have to go now. The sheep have to be taken to a new pasture."

"You want me to become Amish, is that it? You're still angry because I refused to join the church. Sweetheart, I don't blame you for that, but—"

"No, of course I don't want you to do anything you don't want."

She turned away and began putting the scattered lunch items into her basket. And as John watched in stunned dismay, she quickly folded the blanket they'd lain on only moments ago.

"Dammit, Lida," he said, coming to take the items from her hands. "Look at me." He took her chin, forcing her to look up into his face. "What's this all about? Why are you behaving this way?"

"What way?" she asked with a stubborn glint in her eye. "I have to go, that's all. I'm sure you have things to do, now that you got what you came for. That is why you came here today, wasn't it?" For a second, her eyes almost gave her away as she glanced quickly toward the spot where they'd made love.

"Lida," he said, his voice soft with disbelief. "Is that what you think? You think the only reason I came to you today was to—?"

"Isn't it?"

"You know it isn't," he said angrily. He wanted to shake her. Kiss her until she lost that stubborn look and listened to what he was saying.

"You stubborn little . . . dammit, you wanted this as much as I did. You can't deny that."

She looked away from his accusing eyes then. He was right. She couldn't deny it was what she'd wanted. Neither of them had been able to say a sensible word to one another before they were in each other's arms, kissing, impatiently pushing away their clothes in order to be closer. To find the ultimate pleasure that both of them sought.

"No," she whispered. "No, I can't deny it."

John frowned at her and at the odd little catch in her voice. He loved her lack of deception and her refusal to make excuses for what she wanted. But now for the first time, he thought there was a hint of shame in her words.

"When will I see you again?" he asked.

John could feel his heart pounding with some ancient fear that he didn't quite understand. Now that he had finally given in, had finally let himself feel, let himself love, he didn't want to lose it.

He didn't want to lose her.

"I can't," she whispered. Her lips were trembling and she couldn't stop the tears that filled her eyes. "I . . . I can't see you again, John. Not if I ever intend to be brought back into the church. Please . . . don't ask me."

John watched with stunned amazement as she turned and ran across the field. All he could see was the bright glint of her hair as she bounced through the tall grass. He reached down to the ground and picked up her cap that she had overlooked.

He brought it to his mouth, taking a long deep breath and inhaling the familiar scent of her hair into his nostrils. He closed his eyes against the unexpected pain that washed over him in one hot wave.

"God," he muttered. He felt as if he'd been kicked in the chest. And he wasn't sure he would ever be the same.

Twenty-six

John stood in the clearing beneath the elm tree long after Lida was out of sight. He was aware of a quiet, an emptiness that left him feeling oddly annoyed and impatient.

Lida had surprised him with her refusal to go with him. It was what he thought she wanted.

What he really wanted was for her to leave Ohio completely, marry him and go with him to Tennessee. He had spent many long sleepless nights wishing for that impossibility. The thought of Lida working side by side with him on his farm, in the beautiful valley along the Nolichucky River, had been on his mind more and more since that night in the storm cellar. He thought sometimes it was the dream that kept him going.

But it was only a dream. A fantasy. She was Amish and he wasn't. Her reaction today had proven just how impossible their ever being together was.

He had suggested moving to a nearby town only because he felt guilty about taking her away from her Amish family. She would still be an excommunicant from the church, but at least she would be near her home, still be able to see her mother and father, if only from a distance. It tore at his heart to think of Lida being unhappy. And he was willing to sacrifice more than he'd ever given to anyone—his own home—if it would bring a smile to her beautiful face.

He shook his head, staring into the distance where she had disappeared. The wind shook the long graceful limbs of the elm above him and brought with it a sprinkle of rain.

John gritted his teeth and turned to walk back through the tall grass to the fence where he'd tied his horse. He wasn't going to give up on Lida. No matter what she said. No matter how fiercely she swore that they could never be together.

John Sexton wasn't used to losing. He wasn't used to having things denied him. But this time, the one thing he sought and wanted most in the world seemed to be slipping further and further away.

Lida Rinehart. When he first saw her, he'd seen a sweet, simple Amish girl. But he'd learned about her tenderness, even when he'd given her more reason to hate him than anyone. He learned about her strength and courage, her intelligence and compassion. He wasn't sure when it happened, but Lida had become the most beautiful, most desirable woman he'd ever known. She was more than sweet and she certainly wasn't simple. And he was finding that he didn't want to live his life without her.

The Amish elders had set the meeting about Lida's behavior for the weekend. Adam Frederick had told John that much. He'd said it would be held at the Dietz farm. And John intended being there.

Early on Saturday morning, John met the young Dietz boy in the pasture beyond their barn.

"It's going to be in the barn," the boy whispered, his eyes bright with excitement. Helping a man like John Sexton was an adventure beyond Adam's wildest dreams. He thought the English was the bravest, most daring man he'd ever met.

"Are you sure?"

"Ja. I heard *mien Vater* say it. He said there will be too many people for the house."

"And did your father say that Lida would be there?"

"Oh, *nein,"* Adam said, frowning. "The member being shunned cannot be present. Everyone else is there. It will be a sad day."

"Right," John grumbled. "If it's so sad, why do they do it?" he muttered beneath his breath.

Adam shrugged his shoulders and looked up at John with wide eyes. John patted the boy's arm and smiled.

"It's all right," he said. "I'm just trying to understand. Do you think I can slip into the loft without being seen?"

"Ja," Adam said, his eyes twinkling with adventure again. "No one will go to the loft. It is filled with hay."

Well before the meeting, John was hidden in the Dietz hay loft, just as he'd planned. He waited silently, listening as the Amish members began to file into the barn and take their places on the long benches below him.

The crowd was silent and then John heard a man's voice, ringing loud and clear in the big open barn.

He was speaking in German, but John had learned enough to manage and make out the gist of his words.

As the bishop talked about Lida, John gritted his teeth. He was glad that she wasn't present to hear the accusations. It made what was between him and Lida sound so ugly. And it wasn't.

The man's voice rose as he continued.

"Dem Tuefel und allen seinem Engeln ubergeben," the man said, practically shouting the words of condemnation.

Now John could hear women weeping, and as he looked down through the cracks of the loft, he saw the faces, stern and solemn. He saw Lida's father seated near the front. He was looking straight ahead, his face blank, as if the bishop's words did not touch him.

The bishop repeated the phrase in English. "Lida Rinehart has confessed her sins and is committed to the devil and his angels. She will not be allowed to eat with us or speak to us; we will give her no help, no favors. Kindness of spirit is permitted, but nothing else until this member repents and promises to commit the sin no more."

John sighed and sank back into the hay. He could hear the sound of the people below, some crying openly, others whispering and murmuring with a hint of horror at the necessity of their actions. And then he heard the shuffling sound of movements as they began to move quietly out of the barn.

So it was done. The dreaded *Meidung* was begun. They would shun her, put her away from them as if she were a leper. And it was his fault. Everything bad that had happened to Lida was his fault.

All he could think about was seeing her, holding her. Begging her to forgive him.

Lida lay awake long after the house was quiet. It was a hot night. The curtains at her windows hung limp and still in the night air.

Lida kicked the sheets away from her and lay in the dark, thinking about what her father had told her. Knowing that this was the last night she would spend here until she had repented and paid for her sinful ways with cold silence from those she loved. By the morning it would have begun. She would not be allowed to live with her parents or even eat a meal with them. When her father had said she could move into the *Grossdawdy*, it had been it with a sadness that tore at her heart. This obviously wasn't what he wanted either; she knew that. But her father believed in his church and in following its rules.

And yet, lying there awake, trying to think of how she could have done anything different, she couldn't seem to find an answer.

Nothing could have kept her and John apart.

Lida thought she had known that from the very beginning, even when she'd blamed him for Ephraim's death. There had been an undeniable spark there even then. An overwhelming bond that kept drawing them together time and time again. In her heart she probably knew all along where it would lead and how it would end. With their lovemaking. And with this terrible shunning.

But she wouldn't change anything. Except perhaps the fact that John hadn't asked her to marry him.

Lida heard a noise and lay very still. She was used to the night sounds of the farm and the house. She knew every one of them by heart and was not frightened by them.

But this was different. She wasn't sure why, but it was a different sound.

She heard it again. A very quiet sound, one that probably wouldn't even have wakened her if she'd been sleeping. She sat up, her body moving into the thin strip of moonlight that fell through her window and across her bed.

When she saw her bedroom door open, she gasped and felt her heart begin to race furiously.

"Shh." She recognized John's deep voice even though he had not said a word. And she thought she would never be able to breathe normally again.

She couldn't believe he was here in her room. Hadn't let herself believe she would ever see him again. She had told herself that he believed her that day in the sheep meadow. That he believed she did not want him and didn't want to go away with him. Telling herself that was the only way she thought she'd be able to survive.

But now that he was here, her heart fought its way free again. Refused to listen to the warnings that swirled around in her head.

She found herself moving off the bed. Going to him with no false denials and with nothing held back.

"John," she whispered, going into his arms.

"Lida . . . oh, angel," he murmured, kissing her eyes and her cheek, nestling his face against her hair and breathing in the scent as if he might memorize it.

"You shouldn't have come," she began. "I told you—"

He stopped her words with his mouth, unable to temper the urgency he felt when he held her and kissed her this way.

Lida couldn't keep from touching his big hard masculine body, from letting her hands move over him. It seemed like a lifetime since they'd kissed. After nights of remembering and nights of being without him, she felt her body begin to ache with frustration and need.

As they kissed, hungry beyond words, Lida moved a little toward the bed.

John pulled away with a quiet groan and took her face in his hands.

"I was afraid you'd already be gone," she whispered. "What about the slave movement? Has Sam—"

"It's been suspended. Here in Ohio at least. They're rerouting through other states."

"I'm glad," she cried. "I shouldn't be, but I'm so glad that you won't be in danger anymore."

"I couldn't stay away from you," he whispered. "God help me, but I can't."

His words thrilled her.

"The church has made it final. I'll be moving to the grandfather house tomorrow," she said, her words soft and sad.

"I know. I was at the meeting today," he said.

"You?"

"I was hiding in the barn loft. Adam Frederick . . ."

"That little *snickelfritz,*" she said. But there was a note of affection in her voice as she spoke of her young cousin.

"Lida, I'm sorry I hurt you. This shunning is all my fault. I should never have—"

"No," she whispered, touching his mouth. "No regrets. Promise me."

But he didn't promise. He couldn't. Not after what they had done to her.

"You'll come to me at the grandfather house?" For the first time, safe in his arms, Lida found the idea of her isolation bearable.

If fate had declared that she and John would never marry, then at least she could have this. She didn't care about the need to hide, to deny from the world what they felt. If only she could see him this way, touch him, love him, then she would be able to live.

"Lida, sweetheart," he whispered, touching her

face with tenderness. "Is that really what you want? Having to meet in secret?"

"It's the only way," she said quietly, knowing that he could never agree to be Amish.

"I came to ask you one last time. Let me find a place for you in Millersburg. If you are to be shunned anyway, what does it matter where you live? Wouldn't it be better to—"

She reached out to touch his face, unable to resist touching him when he was so near, so accessible.

"I've already disgraced my mother enough," she said, hoping he would understand. "I can't hurt her further by moving to the city, away from the Amish community. She has hopes that I will be returned to the church one day, and I can't take that hope away from her."

John took a long slow breath.

"I see," he said quietly.

"Please understand," she said. "When you came to me the other day at the meadow and I said I couldn't see you again . . . I didn't mean it. It's awful without you. If the only thing we can have are meetings like this, then I don't care."

"But it's not what I want for you," he said, shaking his head in frustration. "You deserve more than that. You deserve a husband and children, respectability."

"I'll never marry," she said. She wanted to add the phrase, unless I marry you. But she couldn't. She had been more bold with this man than she'd ever imagined she could be. But she couldn't bring herself to ask him to live a life he didn't believe in and couldn't be comfortable with. She would never ask that of him.

And she couldn't bear having him refuse her again.

John looked at her sadly in the dim light from the windows. In her white cotton gown, with her hair down, she looked so young and innocent. And for a moment, he wished with all his heart that things could be different.

"I should go," he said. His glance took in her rumpled bed and he was well aware that he shouldn't be there, in her father's own house, lusting after the only daughter the man had. Why couldn't he get it through his head that he'd caused them enough trouble already?

"Don't," she whispered. Her eyes glittered at him; her mouth looked so soft and vulnerable. "Don't go. Not yet."

"Lida," he warned, knowing he wouldn't be able to resist, but telling himself he should. "I'll come to the grandfather house tomorrow night."

"How can I wait until then?" she whispered. She moved her hands up his chest. Her arms entwined around his neck, letting her fingers curl into his hair at the back of his shirt, and she drew herself against him until their lips were only inches apart.

"I need you," she said. "I need you tonight . . . here . . . now."

Her voice had a languid air, a breathlessness that rang through John's mind, turning and twisting until he knew he would face death rather than leave her tonight. No woman had ever held such power over him. Such sweet, irresistible, undeniable power.

"Tell me you need me, too, John," she whispered, raining light little kisses on his mouth and jaw. "Please tell me."

Finally, with a soft groan, he swept her up in his arms, crushing her against him and letting his hands move down her back to her hips. He could feel every soft sensuous inch of her through her gown. So great was his need that he wanted to rip the gown away and take her right where they stood.

"Need you?" he muttered, his voice rough with desire. "God, woman, I've never needed anything or anyone the way I need you. Do you know that? Do you have any idea how it feels?"

"Yes," she whispered, her voice soft. "Oh, yes, I know exactly."

Lida pushed the material of her gown away from her shoulders and down until it fell to the floor with a splash of white around her feet.

John closed his eyes and groaned softly before taking her mouth. His desire was strong, so wild and out of control that he was actually afraid he might hurt her without knowing it. But he couldn't stop. Not now. Not ever.

They sank to the floor on the soft braided rug. He couldn't believe the heat of her body. It surpassed even the heat of the sultry summer night. It surrounded him, urged him on until he thought he could die from the sheer pleasure of it.

She met him eagerly, matching his every movement with no limits and no holding back.

"I love you," she whispered, her voice becoming urgent with desire. "Oh John, I love you so much."

Twenty-seven

Afterward, John picked Lida up in his arms and carried her to bed. As he slid in beside her and held her close, he found himself wishing that he didn't have to go. He hated leaving her to face the isolation from her family and church. And he wished he could stay with her forever.

She'd said she loved him and he knew it, felt it with every instinct he possessed. And yet he couldn't seem to find a way to tell her that he loved her. Not like this, when everything he did seemed to hurt her more and cause her disgrace. Not until he could make everything right for her.

Lida nuzzled against him. Despite all that had happened to her recently, she felt happy. Elated to have him here in her bed, in her arms. She had felt a momentary twinge of fear when she'd whispered the words I love you moments ago. He'd told her before not to love him.

But they hadn't frightened him away this time. She was acutely aware that he also had not said that he loved her. But at least he hadn't turned from her with revulsion or disgust. He was still here. Warm and strong and sensual.

John kissed her neck and murmured quietly against her skin.

"Perhaps I should go," he said. "Before someone hears us."

"I don't care," she said, turning to look at him. "I don't care if the entire world knows. I'm not ashamed of how I feel about you."

He laughed softly, feeling an odd pleasure race along his spine at her fervent declaration.

"Neither am I," he said. "But that's hardly the same as having your parents find a man in their daughter's bed in the middle of the night."

"I'm a brazen woman," she whispered. "And you made me that way."

John touched her face and made a quiet growling noise of protest. He wished he could see her expression clearer.

"John," she said, taking his hand and laughing. "I'm teasing. Don't you know I'm only teasing?"

"Good," he said. "I'm glad. I feel guilty enough the way it is."

"Don't," she said. "Don't feel guilty about me." She stretched her arms over her head, letting her body arch like a contented cat before relaxing against him again. "I have loved every moment of it. God forbid, but if something happened this second and we never see each other again, I will never regret what we've shared together."

"Oh angel," he whispered, kissing her lips. "I wish it could be different for you. I wish—"

They heard a noise in the house. Squeaking boards, as if someone walked across the wood floors.

For a moment they lay very still, holding each other and not speaking. Then there was only silence again.

"That does it," he murmured, pulling reluctantly away from her and swinging his legs over the side of the bed. "I have to go. I don't want to upset your father more than he already is."

Lida loved him for that. She loved his impetuous nature and the fact that he could not resist slipping secretly into her room to make hot, passionate love to her. But she also loved him for his concern about her father's welfare and peace of mind.

She lay in the bed, taking great pleasure in watching him dress. She could see the glint of moonlight against his dark skin and the way his muscles moved. She could almost feel those muscles now beneath her hands, could still smell the lingering scent of him on her pillow. She loved his smooth-shaven face and for a moment she felt her breath catch in her throat. Was there a more beautiful man anywhere in the world than he was to her? She thought that was completely impossible.

He came back to the bed, holding his arms on either side of her as he bent to kiss her.

"I hate to leave you," he whispered.

"What will you do, now that Sam has closed the operation in Ohio?" She held her breath, waiting . . . hoping he would tell her he intended to stay.

"I'll be here for a while yet," he said. "Until we decide on another route, or more likely another state. I'm not sure I'll be involved in the actual processing though. Sam thinks it's getting too risky for the Sojourner to continue."

"You want to go back to Tennessee," she said softly.

"I'd like to . . . I told you about my father's illness."

"Yes."

He kissed her again and stood up, staring down at her where she lay on the bed. She was still naked and she hadn't bothered to cover herself. John allowed himself a moment to let his gaze wander down her body and her long shapely legs.

"You'll come back soon?" she asked. "To the grandfather house where I'll be?"

John shook his head and grunted softly.

"Lady, you won't be able to keep me away."

That night, despite it being Lida's last night in her parents house, she felt happier than she'd ever been. She fell into a deep, untroubled sleep, waking just before dawn, smiling at the night's memories. She put her hand on the pillow, closing her eyes and breathing deeply, hoping to recapture a sense of John's presence.

She looked sleepily toward the large rug on the floor where they'd made love. Then she smiled and drifted back to sleep, waking again only when her mother knocked on her door.

"It is time," her mother said softly. "Your father has hitched the horses to the wagon, even though he knows the bishop would not approve of his helping you. By rights, I should not even be speaking to you now."

"No one will know, Mother," Lida said, sitting up in bed and looked sadly across the room at her mother. "But your kindness means so much and I promise I won't put you in the position of going against the church again."

Her mother's eyes grew cloudy and she nodded from the doorway before quietly closing the door.

The next few days were busy ones for Lida. She spent her days cleaning the grandfather house that had been vacant for years. By the time she went to bed at night she would fall quickly to sleep, too exhausted to think about anything for long.

Soon the house was clean and bright. Her grandparents' furniture was still there. All she needed were new curtains and perhaps new rugs on the smooth wood floors. But she could do that—it would be winter soon—a good time for making rugs and curtains.

But despite all the hard work, Lida felt good and happy. Oddly enough, the shunning seemed to be just what she needed. For once she didn't have to face anyone's disapproval. She could do as she pleased. Spend the day anyway she wanted.

Of course her entire life had been attuned to work, as with most Amish girls. That part didn't change. But the work was different now, more meaningful because it was her own home that needed cleaning, her duties that needed doing.

Once the house and yard were in order and supplies bought and stored in the kitchen cupboard, Lida felt a contentedness she'd never experienced in her life.

Now all she needed was John. And when he came to her a few nights later, she felt as if her life were truly complete.

Over the next month, Lida saw her mother only once, when she happened to be out picking berries. It was an awkward moment for both of them and sad for Lida when her mother turned away without speaking. Anna Rinehart would often walk across the meadow and come to the fence dividing the two properties. Sometimes she would leave milk beside the fence for her daughter, or something special she had baked, even though technically she was supposed to have no association with Lida until she repented and the church saw fit to take her back.

But Lida had been thinking more and more lately about her exile from the Amish church. It wasn't so bad. She had everything she wanted—a house and garden, a cow that would come fresh in the spring. A man who came to her at night and swept her away to heights of wonder and almost unbearable pleasure.

Life was good. Until one morning in August when Lida woke up feeling sicker than she'd ever felt in her life.

She hardly made it to the chamberpot before she was violently ill. And although by afternoon she was feeling somewhat better, the same thing happened the next two mornings.

It was only a coincidence that John came to Lida's that third day. He usually waited until late evening or nighttime. But he wanted to tell her that he was going home. And he wanted to ask her to come with him.

He found her outside, lying in the grass near the well.

John ran to pull Lida's limp body up into his arms.

Her face was deathly pale and there was a thin sheen of perspiration above her upper lip.

"Lida," he whispered. "Angel, please, open your eyes . . ."

Seeing her lashes flutter and then open, John thought the sight of those big beautiful blue eyes was the most wonderful thing he'd ever seen. It took a moment for her to focus and realize that it was John who held her.

She smiled faintly and put her hand up to touch his neck.

"God, sweetheart," he murmured, breathing a sigh of relief. "What happened? Did you fall? Did you—?"

There was a strange light in her eyes as she looked up at him. Then she shook her head and hid her face against his chest.

"What is it?" he asked, feeling his heart begin to pound. "Tell me."

"You're going to hate me," she whispered.

"Hate you? I couldn't hate you. Lord, blue eyes, don't you know by now how I feel about you?" He reached beneath her chin, forcing her to look at him. "Don't you?"

She couldn't believe the look of tenderness in his eyes. She thought it was the one thing that gave her the courage to tell him.

"I must have fainted because I . . . I think I'm going to have a baby," she said, watching his face closely.

John's mouth opened, and for a moment he seemed too stunned to speak. Too stunned even to understand what she had just said.

"Baby?" he whispered. "A baby." he repeated, shaking his head.

Lida closed her eyes and gritted her teeth, waiting for his reaction.

"This is my fault," he said. "I should have known. Hell, what did I expect? I've come to you almost every night since . . ." He looked down at her, seeing the fear in her eyes. "How long?" he asked.

"I . . . I don't know. Not long I suppose. I've only been sick the past three days."

"Oh Lida, honey . . . I'm sorry," he said. He helped her to her feet and walked with her slowly back toward the house. "I should be horsewhipped."

Lida frowned at him. He wasn't pleased. She'd been terrified that he wouldn't be.

"John . . . don't . . ."

He took her by the arms and pulled her around to face him. His expression was fierce as he spoke.

"I've done nothing but cause you pain since I first walked onto your father's farm. I've been a fool," he said. "Blind and self-indulgent, thinking only of what I wanted and what I needed. It wasn't enough that you lost your brother. I couldn't leave you alone until you were disgraced, and now—" His eyes were hard and filled with self-loathing.

"John," she murmured, touching his face. "Don't do this. Don't—"

"You've been kicked out of your church," he said, gritting his teeth. "Isolated from a mother and father that you love dearly. Left to live here alone, away from your friends, while I visit you at night like you were nothing more than some—" He shook his head, cursing himself. "I should have known." He stared into her eyes. "I'm a bastard for putting you through this," he said. "I should have married you when your father asked me that day—"

"Stop this," she said. But despite her resolve, Lida felt her lips trembling. She could hardly speak. "I understood why you couldn't. I still do."

With a quiet groan John drew her into his arms, cradling her head against his chest and stroking her hair at the nape of her neck.

"You're too good," he whispered. "Too sweet and giving . . . more loving than I ever deserved. And I swear to you, Lida," he pulled away and took her face in his hands, looking straight into her eyes as he spoke. "I swear I'm going to make things right. No matter what it takes, this time you won't be the one who suffers."

When he pulled away from her, Lida was stunned. She watched him walk quickly across the yard toward the small barn where he'd left his horse.

"John . . ." she called.

He waved his hand over his shoulder, but kept walking.

"I'll be back." He turned around then, pointing at her. "You go inside and rest. Don't do anything 'til I get back. Promise me," he shouted.

"I . . . I promise," she said weakly, staring after him.

She continued standing in the yard, feeling the hot wind against her skin. She was still standing there when John rode away toward her father's farm.

Twenty-eight

Lida could hardly contain herself as she waited inside the house for John. She alternately paced the floor and went to the windows to look outside.

Where was John going? And what was he planning to do?

It wasn't long until she heard the sound of a buggy approaching the house. She ran out to the front porch and shaded her eyes, looking in the direction that John had disappeared.

Then she shook her head in disbelief.

Coming across the field was her father's buggy. Her parents were inside and John was riding just behind them.

Lida felt numb as she stepped off the porch into the yard. It was the first time she'd seen her father since the shunning began. When her father and mother got out of the buggy, her mother came running to her, stopping a short distance away, but looking at Lida with such sweetness in her eyes. Her father approached more slowly. When John joined them, they stood facing Lida.

"John," Lida said, her voice soft with worry. "What have you done?"

"He has done the right thing," Jacob said. "He

came to us like a man, in the proper Amish spirit of truth." There seemed to be a ring of pride in Jacob Rinehart's voice as he said the words.

Lida's gaze darted toward John. His look was serious and his teeth tugged at his lower lip as he stood watching her. Lida stared at him, frowning, still unable to believe he had gone to her parents. Was he saying he wanted to marry her now?

Lida turned to her mother. "Mother, I'm sorry. I know I told you—" Lida turned to her mother.

"A baby," her mother said, her lips trembling. She clasped her hands together and took a step forward. "My own little girl is having a baby."

If her mother's response to the news was joyous, her father's was less than so. His eyes were still just as accusatory, just as hard as before.

"But . . . I don't understand," Lida said, looking from one to the other. "This will only make things worse. The church will never take me back now."

"*Nein,*" her mother said. "It is a blessing. The answer to our prayers."

Could it be? Had John actually asked their permission to marry her . . . and take her back to Tennessee with him?

She turned toward him, her eyes shining, a smile on her lips.

"John has agreed to join the church; he will be Amish now. As soon as you are married and both of you have confessed your sins—"

"No," Lida gasped. Her mouth dropped open and her eyes sought John's. "No, John. I don't want you to do this. Not this way. Not because of me."

"I'm doing this for our child, Lida. For my son. Do you really think I'd allow him to be born a bastard?"

"John," she whispered, frowning and shaking her head.

Suddenly the sky above her seemed to be spinning. The trees that lined the yard began to whirl in a fast pattern. Lida put her fingers to her eyes, and she heard only her mother's murmur of protest before she sank to the ground.

She awoke later in her own bed upstairs in the farmhouse. She felt a cool wet cloth on her forehead and turned her head to see her mother sitting beside the bed, smiling at her.

"You will have to be careful for a while, *Liebling.* It was the same with me before you and Ephraim were born. I'd never fainted in my life until then. But it will most likely go away when the morning sickness leaves you."

"Mother," Lida whispered, reaching out her hand. "Where's John? I have to see him. I have to speak to him."

"He is downstairs with your papa. They are making plans."

Lida groaned and closed her eyes. She didn't want this. And she knew in her heart that it wasn't what John wanted either.

"I have to get up," she said, pushing the cloth away and sitting up in bed.

"Mein Schatz," her mother murmured. She moved to sit on the bed beside Lida, putting her

arms around her. "You should rest. What is it? What is troubling you? Is it John? Don't you love him?"

"Yes," she whispered. "Oh, yes, I love him. With all my heart. But, Mother, I can't imagine him being Amish. He's not like us. It isn't his nature to be meek, to turn the other way when he sees something wrong. I'm just afraid . . ."

"Afraid?" her mother said with a quiet laugh. "What is there to be afraid of? This will make everything right at last."

"I'm afraid being Amish will destroy him, Mother. He is an intense, impatient man, full of life and energy. He won't be content to—"

"Ah," Anna Rinehart scoffed. "But he will learn, my dear. The Amish church will teach him to be meek and patient. He will learn." Her mother stood up, looking down at her with great tenderness. "Now, let's hear no more of this talk. It is only pregnancy nerves that makes you talk this way. Everything will be fine. Once you and John are married and living Amish, everything will be fine. You'll see."

She walked to the door and looked back at her daughter.

"I will go downstairs and tell John you would like to see him. Your father and I will take care of everything. We will speak to the bishop, make plans to revert the shunning, just as soon as John has joined the church. Then you can be married. You are in such early stages of your pregnancy that no one will guess why you married."

Lida sat on the bed, feeling stunned. Feeling sick at heart.

When John stepped into the room moments later, she looked up at him with her heart in her eyes.

He came quickly across the room to her and knelt beside the bed. He put his arms around her hips and looked up into her face.

"What is it?" he said, his voice soft. "Are you still sick? Should I—"

"Why are you doing this?" she asked. She touched his face, letting her fingers trail down his smooth dark skin. Her eyes were filled with warmth and tenderness. She could hardly believe that this man—her strong, masculine lover—was humbling himself this way.

John took her fingers and brought them to his mouth. Then he pulled her off the bed onto his lap on the floor, leaning his back against the bed as he supported her in his arms.

"I told you," he said. "For our son."

She smiled. "Are you so sure it will be a boy?"

"I'm certain of it."

"Would it matter if it's a girl?"

John looked deep into her eyes and when he kissed her there was something different about his touch. It wasn't that he had never been gentle or tender. He had. Often. But this was different.

"Not at all," he assured her. "But I just always thought that our son would be first, then a daughter."

"You . . . you've thought about this before? About us . . . having children together?"

"Of course I have," he murmured, smiling at her. His eyes sparkled, then turned warm as he bent to kiss her again. "Is that so hard to believe?"

Lida studied his eyes, trying to decide what it was she saw there. Could she have been wrong about him? Had their love changed him so much that he could now agree to live Amish?

"What is it?" he asked, seeing her look.

"I don't know. It's just . . . this has all happened so fast. You came here this morning—" She stopped, and a little frown appeared between her eyebrows. "Why did you come this morning? Was there something wrong?"

John hesitated, thinking of the reason he came. To ask her to marry him and go back to Tennessee with him. Away from her family and her church. Away from the excitement he saw in her mother's eyes when she learned her daughter was pregnant. Now that there was to be a child, he couldn't do it. Children were everything to the Amish. He simply couldn't take what should be the happiest moment of Lida's life and turn it into what he wanted.

"To see you," he said, jostling her in his arms and smiling at her. "Why else?"

"In the morning?" she asked suspiciously, turning her head and looking at him oddly.

"In the morning," he whispered, kissing her ear. "In the afternoon . . . any time of the day."

When he kissed her that way she could barely think straight. She felt so confused that she just wanted it all to go away. She wanted to believe that they could be happy living here. That he could be happy.

"John," she whispered against his mouth. "Tell me this is really what you want."

"It is," he said firmly, without hesitation.

John wasn't lying. If he had serious doubts about becoming Amish, there was one thing he had no doubts about. He wanted to marry Lida. He wanted to sleep with her in his arms every night. Wake up every morning to see her beautiful face and work beside her every day. He wanted to walk with her through the fields with their son between them, holding both their hands. *She* was what he wanted. And that much was no lie.

For a moment Lida looked at him, studying his eyes and his face as if she might find the truth there. Then she threw her arms around his neck and rained kisses against his hair and ear.

"Oh, John," she sighed. "I swear, I'll make you happy. I will be the best wife you could ever wish for. And the best mother your sons could ever want."

"I know that already," he whispered, his look growing tender.

When he hugged her close, he closed his eyes, saying a silent prayer that he could make *her* happy here in this strange country, surrounded by people he barely knew and hardly understood. For he knew that her happiness depended on how well he managed to join the Amish and convince all of them that he was sincere.

It was decided that the wedding would take place in two weeks. First the bishop would have to lift Lida's shunning and then publish the news of the marriage to the congregation. That would all take place on Sunday.

"Normally weddings are held in November or December," Lida explained to John. "After harvest." They were sitting in the kitchen of her home with her father and mother present. Her face felt hot and she could barely meet John's gaze. He seemed so different as they discussed the requirements of the church. So quiet and distant.

"Since there is no church building, where will the wedding take place?" John asked. He sounded polite and matter-of-fact.

"In our home," Anna Rinehart said proudly. "It will be an all-day celebration with lots of food and visiting the *Freundschaft* . . . the kinship," she added with a shy smile. "You and Lida will spend the first night at our house and then you will come back here to live. You and Jacob will farm the land together, and one day it will be yours and your children's.

John nodded solemnly.

"Two weeks is not a very long time," Jacob said. "But it cannot be helped," he added, his gaze going with accusation to John. "At least it will be enough time for you to grow a beard."

John's eyebrows lifted and he looked from Jacob to Lida.

It was something Lida had thought about often. She had been glad John didn't have a beard like all the young men she knew. She loved his smooth clean face and the way his skin felt and smelled after he shaved.

"I wish that weren't necessary," she said wistfully.

"Every adult male must have a beard," Jacob said stiffly. "But no mustache."

The room was quiet. They all sat awkwardly for long moments.

"Anything else?" John asked.

Lida's eyes grew sad. He hated this and she hated it for him. She could see it in his eyes . . . sense it in every look and every word he said.

"You and I will go to the bishop today, John" Jacob said. "It will be necessary to tell him the circumstances. But I'm sure he will agree to all the arrangements and we will see to your baptism and clothing. The shunning will be lifted by Sunday and the wedding will proceed on time."

John stood up when Jacob did. He looked down at Lida and there was a mixture of sadness and tenderness in his eyes.

Lida wanted to go to him and put her arms around him. Tell him everything would turn out better than he thought. That they would be happy here together.

But she couldn't. Because she was afraid herself that this would ruin everything between them. All she could do was stare into his stormy gray eyes and hope that he understood what was in her heart, and that she would do anything on earth to make him happy.

Twenty-nine

The wedding was held on a beautiful morning at the Rinehart farm. The long service began early and included wedding hymns from the Amish *Ausbund.* There was a long sermon on marriage that was illustrated from the Old Testament and then simple vows were made by John and Lida. There were no kisses or rings. No flowers to decorate the house. Afterward they were escorted into the living room where a wedding table, called the *Eck,* had been prepared for them in one corner. It was brightly decorated and held colorful dishes of food as well as a fancy layer cake and bowls of fruit. Other tables in the room were occupied by other couples, who ate, then left to be replaced by someone else.

It should have been the happiest day of Lida's life. Yet for her it was one filled with confusion and guilt and awkwardness. She and John hardly spoke, except for meaningless chatter.

They had barely seen one another since that day at her house when he had learned so suddenly of her pregnancy.

The guests stayed all day and for a wedding supper, after which singing continued until late in the evening.

Normally a newly married Amish couple would not set up housekeeping until spring. But in John and Lida's case, that would be overlooked.

Everyone had learned about her clandestine meeting with John that night of the intended ambush and the scandal her actions had caused. Now, from the sly looks, Lida sensed that despite what her mother thought, most of them already knew about her pregnancy as well. But she knew how forgiving the Amish were and she expected them to accept John into the fold as if he had always been one of them. And to accept their child as well.

That night she and John stood at the door, telling all their guests goodbye. She was surprised when Carl and Christela came to shake their hands.

"I wish you the best," Carl said. But even as he spoke, his lips had a stiffness, his eyes were lackluster and distant. He made a slight bow to her and nodded to John before turning away.

Christela stood for a moment as if she did not quite know what to do. Then she stepped forward, put her arms around Lida, and hugged her. There were tears in her eyes when she pulled away.

"I know you will be happy," she whispered. "He is the one you wanted."

"Yes, he is," Lida said, not looking at John.

Upstairs in her old room, where she and John had made love on the floor, there was a sudden uneasiness separating them that had never been there before. If there had been one constant between them, it was their intense physical attraction. That had never failed. But now, as she undressed on one side of the room and John on the other, she wondered if things would ever be the same between them again.

She watched out of the corner of her eye as John shrugged his broad shoulders out of the Amish split tailcoat called a *Mutze.* He looked different with his short black beard. She thought he was even more sensual-looking than before. The beard made him look like a pirate and emphasized his startling gray eyes and dark skin.

She heard him mutter beneath his breath, cursing she thought, as he struggled with hooks and eyes on his vest and then the buttons of his Amish barn door britches.

"Do you need some help?" she asked.

"No," he murmured, glancing at her with a dark look in his eyes.

"You'll become used to all the buttons and hooks after a while," she said quietly.

John said nothing but went to the bed where he sat down and pulled off his shoes and trousers, then slid into bed. His gaze moved toward her where she stood in her white gown and he turned the sheets on her side of the bed down for her.

When she got into bed beside him, she heard him sigh. His hands were beneath his head as he stared at the ceiling. Both of them lay there for a long while, the silence of the room surrounding them like a tomb.

"Do we stay here only one night?" he asked, not even turning to look at her.

"Yes, one night," she said. "Tomorrow it is our duty to help clean up from the wedding. Then we can go home."

"Good," he said. His voice was a deep quiet rumble, and Lida thought there was a hint of his usual impatience in it.

When he turned his back to her, she was stunned. For a moment she started to touch his bare shoulder, ask him if things could ever be the same between them. But she couldn't. She had already humiliated herself enough, and she simply could not bear the possibility of his rejection. His actions made it clear to her that he only married her because he had to, not because he loved her.

She held herself rigidly in the bed until she heard his quiet rhythmic breathing and knew he was asleep. Only then did she allow the tears to come, not even wiping them away when they ran down her face into her hair.

It was not the way she had imagined her wedding night would be. Not the way at all.

By the time they arrived home the next day, Lida was exhausted. Even though her mother had given her different home remedies for morning sickness, she still felt nauseated most of the time.

John carried in all their weddings gifts and she went up to her bedroom. She didn't even remember when he came to bed much later, but during the night she felt him move and she turned automatically toward him.

John, half-asleep, took her in his arms. Lida murmured softly and snuggled against him. When he began kissing her, she felt a little tingle of delight. Things would be better now, she told herself. Here alone in their own home, things would be much better. They had to be.

Their lovemaking was as powerful as ever, except that she sensed a new tenderness in John when he held her. He seemed more careful, even though his desire fully matched her own.

And it was different. Not less exciting—Lida thought their lovemaking would never lack that. Just different.

And at the end, as both of them reached the highest peak of pleasure, John slid his hands beneath her and pulled her up hard to meet him. And finally she heard him whisper the words she'd been longing to hear for such a long time.

"Angel," he groaned, his powerful body trembling with desire. "My angel, I love you. I do love you."

It was all she needed. All she thought she would ever need for the rest of her life.

It was only after the next few weeks that she began to doubt that. As she and John worked, she began to think that she needed something more to make her life complete. She needed his happiness.

He was so quiet. He worked hard from daybreak until past dark most days. And although they made love often and with the same intense passion, there was a distance between them that she couldn't explain.

They tended to limit their conversations to the farm and the work, and the baby they would welcome in the spring. When they spoke of the child they had made together, it seemed the only time John was animated and happy. The only time he seemed his old self.

He spoke of his son as if he already knew what the boy would look like and how he would be. He was so excited that Lida began to pray that it would be a boy, just so he wouldn't be disappointed.

She would watch him sometimes, rubbing his beard, or tugging at the Amish clothes. She knew he hated living Amish and she thought that if the bishop and the others knew how John really felt, he would surely be excommunicated. But only she knew that he had not truly accepted their ways and their religion. It was not even something they discussed between them. And that was the way it would remain.

Once he came in from the fields where he and some of the other men had been cutting firewood for winter. Lida was alarmed when she saw him come in and go to the washbasin to splash water on his face.

There was a cut on his lip and a dark bruise on his temple. But it was the look in his eyes that upset her most.

"John," she murmured, going to hand him a towel. "What happened?" She reached out to touch his face, and he jerked away from her as if she were someone he despised.

When he turned, his eyes were hard and filled

with the same distrust she remembered from when they first met.

"What is it?" she asked, her voice soft and pleading. "Please, John . . ."

"Nothing," he said, throwing the towel down and stalking toward the table where she had his supper ready.

"You can't tell me it's nothing," she said, standing with her hands on her hips and staring at him. "Was there an accident? Did you fight?" she said, frowning at him with worry.

"The Amish don't fight, remember?" he said sarcastically. "They're much too righteous and civilized to do such a thing. Only the unenlightened English fight."

Lida sighed and sank down into a chair across the table from him. She reached out to place her hand on his and he looked up, meeting her gaze.

"Don't shut me out John," she whispered. "Since our marriage, I hardly know you. You've changed. You—"

He grunted and slid his hand from beneath hers.

"Well, that much is obvious," he snapped, running his hand over his dark beard. "But then that was the general idea, wasn't it?"

She sighed heavily. She had no idea how to reach him anymore.

"How long are you going to punish me?" she asked, drawing her mouth into a flat, angry line.

John put his fork down and took a deep breath, letting the air out of his lungs with a loud, impatient rush.

"For what, Lida? For getting pregnant? You hardly did that by yourself. For being Amish? That wasn't really your choice either, was it? Anymore than it was mine." His words came quickly, harshly, as if he'd been holding them back for a long time. He looked into her eyes, and his own were troubled and dark. There seemed to be the weight of the world on his shoulders when he spoke again, but this time his voice was softer and tinged with a quiet regret.

"For making me love you?" he asked. "You couldn't help that either. I think I fell in love with you that very first night, in your parents' barn when you stood so defiantly in front of me and ordered me to leave." His smile turned sweet and wistful as he continued to look at her across the table.

John thought she had grown more beautiful than ever the past few weeks, if that were possible. Late summer had left her skin a warm peach color and her eyes sparkled a bright, clear blue that matched the autumn sky. Even her hair had a fresh new glow that glinted in the sunlight and made him long more than once to stop what he was doing and take away her *Kapp* and pins. Some days just looking at her made him want to forget everything and take her to their bedroom right then and there to make love.

"John, is this what you really want? Living here among people you don't understand? Was it Carl and the other men who did this to you today?" She glanced at the cut on his lip, noticing how he winced as he sipped his coffee.

"It was an accident," he said. "Carl said he shouted before the tree he was cutting fell my way."

Lida's gasped. She knew Carl had lied. Even though he and Chrissie were together now, he still resented John for coming to the Amish and taking his place with Lida.

"Oh my God . . . John! You could have been killed."

"I don't think so," he said wryly. "I think it was more of an initiation . . . or a warning, I'm not sure which."

Lida stood up, her hands clenched at her sides. Her face was flushed with anger.

"I'm going to speak to him. I—"

"No," John said, standing up and reaching across the table to take her arm. He pulled her back down into the chair.

"That's the reason I didn't want to tell you in the first place. I don't want you upset. And I sure don't need you fighting my battles for me. I can handle anything Carl Miller has to offer," he said, his eyes glittering dangerously. "Next time I'll be prepared."

"Oh," she sighed, shaking her head. "So now what's between you and Carl is a matter of male pride and superiority. You men. You're all the same."

"Forget about it," he said, turning to his supper. "Everything's fine."

But it wasn't fine. Lida knew that and she thought John did, too, if he weren't too stubborn to admit it. When she tried to question him about his home, to try and learn if he really did want to go back to Tennessee, he ignored her or changed the subject. She didn't know his reason for pretending everything was fine. All she knew was that it wasn't.

Over the next few weeks the weather grew progressively worse. The short days were often dark and filled with rain. There were even early flurries of snow.

John would come back into the house, shielding his face from the blustery winds, rushing in to take off his rain-soaked coat and hat. Those days were the worst. When he was stuck indoors he would pace the floor, silent and brooding, drinking coffee and staring out the windows toward the barn.

Lida's heart ached for him on those days and she couldn't help feeling guilty that she was the reason he was like a caged animal. He grew quiet and thoughtful. Withdrawn from her.

One afternoon when darkness came early because of an approaching storm, Lida was bringing soup to the table when she stumbled and spilled the contents of the tureen all over the kitchen floor.

"I'm sorry," she whispered, glancing at John where he sat at the table. "I'm sorry . . . I'll fix something else." She took a towel and fell to her knees on the wood floor, trying to push away the unexpected tears that came to her eyes.

She wanted things to be nice for John. She wanted that more than she had ever wanted anything for herself.

"God," he muttered, coming to his feet. He took her arm and pulled her up from the floor. "My god, get up. You're not my maid or my slave. You're my wife." He was furious and as he held her arm he pulled her toward him, staring into her eyes like a man possessed. "Do you think I care what we eat? Do you think I want to see my wife crawling on the floor like an indentured servant, trying to please the great master of the house? For God's sake, Lida," he said, shaking her.

Lida couldn't believe the depth of his anger and bitterness over something so trivial. He had never spoken to her that way. Never looked at her with such uncontrollable fury.

"I . . . I'm sorry," she whispered again, unable to stop herself and unable to make sense of anything that had happened between them lately.

He cursed and turned away from her, raking a plate off the table where it went flying across the room with an ear-splitting crash.

He grabbed his coat and hat from the hook by the door and turned to her, his gray eyes filled with a wildness and fury that frightened her.

"And for God's sake, don't keep saying you're sorry," he shouted.

He strode to the door and slammed it so hard as he went out that the windows rattled. Lida saw him running through the pouring rain toward the barn, and she slumped into a chair with her face in her hands. She hoped that he only intended working in the barn a while. It was growing dark and the weather was much too unpredictable to be out in. But moments later, she saw him ride out of the barn, his head down against the beating rain as he rode like a demon away from the farm. And away from her.

It was well past midnight when she heard him come back. She had laid awake in their bed, lying stiffly, listening for him, and praying that he was safe.

It seemed like hours after she heard him downstairs that he finally came up to their bedroom.

She lay quietly as she listened to the sound of his breathing across the room. She could hear him removing his clothes and then his footsteps on the floor toward the bed.

His body was shockingly cold as he got into bed beside her and pulled her into his arms. She went into his embrace with no questions and no words of protest, happy just to have him home safely.

"I'm sorry," he murmured against her hair. "I'm the one who should be saying those words," he said. "Not you . . . never you."

"You're freezing," she murmured, holding him close and letting her warmth penetrate into his skin. She loved his sweetness, the way he tried to apologize for what had happened. But it broke her heart, too, and as she held him, she tried to be strong and not cry.

"You feel so good," he whispered. "So good."

"Where did you go?" she asked, touching her fingers to his damp hair and beard.

"Nowhere," he said. "Riding . . . thinking."

"What were you thinking?"

"About you. About how good and sweet and

giving you are. About what an ungrateful fool I am and that I don't deserve you or your love.

"John," she protested, snuggling her face against his neck and kissing him. "I want you to be happy. That's all I want."

"I am happy," he said. "I have you and we're going to have a child together."

"You have this place, too—it's yours now," she said, frowning at the hint of reservation in his voice. "It's a good farm," she added.

He said nothing and for a moment she thought he was asleep. She moved so she could see his face.

"John?"

"It isn't mine," he said, his voice soft and restrained. "I don't feel as if it's mine. This land is beautiful, the soil is rich and good, and I know I should be grateful. But it isn't mine Lida. And I'm not sure it will ever be."

Lida bit her lip to keep from arguing. She didn't know what else to say to him. And she didn't know how to take away the deep pain she heard in his voice and saw in his beautiful gray eyes.

She lay quietly, holding him, feeling his body warm to the same temperature as hers and finally hearing his steady breathing as he fell asleep.

That night for the first time since her wedding night, Lida cried herself to sleep.

Thirty

After that night there was a quiet, unspoken truce between them. John still rode away from the house sometimes when he was angry or impatient or when he could no longer seem to stand the tension between them. But he never stayed away from Lida at night anymore. And although she still wanted to please him, she was more careful about the way she did it.

They often had visitors on cold winter weekends. Their house became a popular retreat for young people in their Amish district. Part of it was because John was still a mystery and a novelty. But Lida knew that they genuinely liked him as well. And that pleased her.

Just as many had predicted, President Lincoln issued the preliminary Emancipation Proclamation. The fact that it only referred to those slaves held in territories deemed rebellious had caused a flurry of controversy. Some northern abolitionists felt it was too little, while unionists believed the war had wrongly changed course—from saving the Union to ending slavery. And that very idea seemed to confirm what many Confederates had felt from the beginning—that ending slavery in the South and breaking their hold on prosperity was the North's real jealous purpose in going to war.

General Lee's victorious efforts of summer had been forgotten. He was back in Virginia and feeling frustrated with the war, many said. Lida knew that John was worried about his brother Nathan, who was also in Virginia. He'd told her about their meeting near Cincinnati and about how Nathan had promised to return safely to Tennessee. But she knew John still worried about him.

And even though John's father had rallied against his illness somewhat the past few months, he was still very ill according to the letters they received from John's mother.

By January, Lida was feeling big and awkward and unappealing, though John assured her every day that she was beautiful. And his tender lovemaking at night seemed to prove that he really meant it.

Still, when they received a message that Sam Greenhow would visit, Lida grew anxious and self-conscious about his seeing her. She had always known instinctively, as a woman knows such things, that Sam found her attractive. And now, seeing her big with child, she wondered what he would think and if he would be disappointed.

When they heard him ride into the yard, John went out to greet him and Lida stood in the kitchen waiting. Despite John's protests, she had baked and cleaned until she was exhausted. She was wearing one of her prettiest dresses, although Sam's visit made her think wistfully of the red silk dress that was hidden away upstairs in a trunk. She wasn't sure why she still kept it, except that some nagging little thought in the back of her mind told her she might wear it again one day.

When Sam came into the warm bright kitchen, he stopped, his eyes sparkling when he saw Lida.

"God, Lida," he murmured. "You're even more beautiful than ever. And I didn't think that was possible."

Lida's face softened and she could actually feel the tension leaving her neck and shoulders. She walked forward, smiling, and placed her hand in Sam's, leading him toward the living room.

She felt him tug at her hand and turned back to see his odd, familiar teasing smile.

"Can't we stay in the kitchen? I like it here. Besides, it smells too good to leave."

Lida laughed and looked at John. He seemed pleased and he didn't even seem embarrassed that his friend was seeing him dressed in Amish clothes and wearing a beard.

They ate and laughed and sat talking afterward. John and Sam couldn't seem to stop talking. Lida thought it was the most enjoyable time they'd had since moving to this house.

"There are a lot of Union forces in your home state now, John," Sam said.

"Where exactly?" The only news John received about the war was when he went into Walnut Creek, and with the bad weather, those visits had been infrequent lately.

"A little place called Murfreesboro—Stones River. I believe its near Nashville."

"Yes, it is," John said, frowning.

"It's a good distance from your home, isn't it?"

"Yes. Mother's last letter said there had been very little activity near Greeneville, thank God. It's not a strategic area. Not now anyway."

"Lincoln is still upset with the way the war is dragging on," Sam said. "And the criticism of his army and generals never seems to end. I don't envy the man."

John nodded in solemn agreement. "What about you?" John asked. "Not still hiding slaves are you, now that the Emancipation is done?"

"No," Sam said with a wry smile. "I am representing some former slaves in court, though. Some could be landmark cases. But I must admit, it's not nearly as exhilarating."

John laughed. "You're getting too old for such excitement anyway. You should marry and settle down."

Lida's gaze moved to her husband. Did she detect a note of pride and contentment in his voice? He turned then and met her eyes and smiled.

And yet during the evening, she noticed his enthusiasm when he and Sam spoke about the war and about politics. He missed it. And when he spoke about Tennessee, there was a wistful quality in his voice that he couldn't hide.

After Sam left, John was very quiet. When Lida started up to bed, he was still sitting at the table and there was a distant look in his eyes, almost as if he didn't even know she was there.

"John?" she said quietly. "Are you coming to bed?"

His smile was sweet and affectionate, even though he seemed faraway. "Not yet. You go ahead. I'll be up in a little while."

After she was in bed, Lida lay thinking about their evening. About the difference in John when he was with Sam talking about something besides farming. After all, he had been trained as a military officer at West Point, and although he loved farming, she thought he had always intended to do something else with his life.

She couldn't imagine John becoming like her father. With all his intensity and passion tamped down and hidden away. That wildness and his often-lost attempts at self-control were a great part of what had excited her about him. She had always pictured John as a spokesman for other people, as a fighter for something he believed in and would fight for with all his heart and soul.

Had becoming Amish broken that spirit and banished his fierceness forever? The very thought of it made her heart turn over in her chest. What could she do? She felt helpless now with the baby coming. It simply broke her heart to think that the requirements of the Amish church would change John into a man like her father, making his spirit quiet and causing it to wither like the green Ohio hills in winter.

After that night, Lida began to think about what it was she really wanted. And what John wanted. She wanted him to be happy more than she wanted anything else. And for him to be the way he was before—full of life and interest. As for herself, she had glimpsed an entirely different life through his eyes and Sam's. And she was beginning to think more and more about it with interest and envy.

It was then that she began to formulate a plan in her mind.

In March the weather was still cold and blustery. Lida felt good. Her sickness was completely gone and she worked almost as hard as she ever had. But one morning, she felt different, and by noon, she realized what it was.

The nagging pain in her back and legs had grown stronger. And now it wrapped around her and seemed to envelop her entire body.

When John came back from the barn, she was feeling frightened and a little desperate. And she was practically gasping through her first painful contractions.

"Lida," he said, seeing the expression on her face and coming immediately to her. "What is it? Is it the baby? Why didn't you call me?"

"Yes," she whispered. "I . . . I think it is."

"But it can't be." He frowned at her as if she had lost her mind. "Can it? Isn't it too soon?"

"Mother says first babies sometimes come early." There was fear and dread in her eyes, even though she wanted to be strong for John. "I think you'd better go find her and have papa fetch Mrs. Jaberg."

"Here," he said, putting his arm around her waist. "Let me get you upstairs first. Wouldn't you feel better in bed?"

"Yes," she said, gasping at the pain when she walked. "But I didn't want to try the stairs alone."

"I'm here, blue eyes," he whispered, kissing her hair and her face. "I'm here now. Everything's going to be fine. By this time tomorrow, we'll have our new baby. We'll be a family, angel," he said. "Just the way you've always wanted."

But the baby wasn't there by the next day. Lida's labor seemed to go on forever. For hour after torturous hour, she thrashed about in bed, listening to her mother's instructions and those of the midwife Mrs. Jaberg.

By noon Lida was exhausted and weak. Her skin was pale and her eyes seemed huge and bright. She had seen the fear in John's eyes when he came into the room, and if she had not known before how much he loved her, she knew it now.

Something was wrong. Both of them thought it, but neither of them dared speak the words out loud.

Please. she prayed silently. Please God, don't let it end now that he loves me. Not so soon. Not like this.

Later Mrs. Jaberg prepared a potion for Lida, something she said would speed up the birthing process. When she brought it to the bed, Lida held up her hand.

"Wait," she whispered. "Not yet. I . . . I want to speak to John first."

The midwife and her mother looked at one another. She could see the worry in their eyes and she knew, as they did, that she could not continue this way much longer.

"Just for a minute," she said, taking her mother's hand.

"All right, *Liebling,*" Anna said. She smoothed Lida's hair back from her forehead. "He's downstairs with your papa. I'll get him."

When John came to the bed, his eyes were troubled. He sank to his knees beside Lida and took her hand, bringing it to his lips and looking into her eyes.

"What is it, angel?" he asked. "God, Lida, this is killing me. I wish there was something I could do . . . anything—"

"There is," she whispered. When she reached to touch his face, another pain hit her and she closed her eyes, wincing and gripping his hand until the agony subsided.

She held John's hand so tightly that her fingers became numb. He glanced toward the door where the midwife waited outside and his look was one of impatience and frustration.

"Can't they give you anything?" he growled. "Isn't there something you can take for the pain?"

"Shh," she said, trying to smile. "Listen to me. There's something I have to tell you before . . . in case—"

John's face turned ashen and his eyes slowly filled with horror.

"No," he whispered. "Don't say it. I don't want to hear—"

"I . . . have to," she said. She closed her eyes, trying to concentrate on the words instead of the pain. "I've loved you from the beginning," she said, her words a mere whisper in the quiet room.

"More than my church, more than my life even. I would have done anything for you. I still would."

"I know that," he said, his voice still impatient with worry. "Sweetheart, don't tire yourself. You don't have to—"

"I do," she said, fiercely squeezing his fingers. "I have to say this. If anything happens . . ." She saw his look and frowned at him before continuing. "I want you to take our baby and go home to Tennessee."

"God . . . Lida, don't." John took both her hands then, bringing them to his mouth. There were actually tears in his eyes and that more than anything, broke Lida's heart. He had always been so strong, so unmovable. She couldn't believe his tears were for her.

Tears flooded Lida's own eyes as she continued. Everything had been so hard for them. Life hadn't turned out the way either of them wanted it.

"I mean it," she whispered. "Don't stay here because of me. Don't stay Amish. Our child will be a Sexton, and he should be a Presbyterian like his Father. It's right that he grow up in Tennessee, where his roots are. Where his grandparents and great grandparents lived. Where there's Sexton land that will be his one day. Promise me," she said, breathless with exhaustion. "You have to promise me."

"Lida, I can't—"

"Please," she whispered through dry, parched lips.

John bent to kiss her. Her mouth and skin were

hot, and her eyes were pale and so clear that they looked like a doll's eyes.

"I promise," he murmured against her mouth, then lay his head against her breasts.

Lida sighed and touched his hair.

Another pain struck her and she arched her back, groaning in agony.

"Tell them," she gasped. "Tell them I'm ready."

John's eyes were stricken as he reluctantly moved away from the bed and out of the room.

"She can't die," he murmured to himself. "She can't."

After the midwife administered the potion, the contractions began to come faster and faster, until they were one long continuous torment. At the end, when her delivery began, Lida fainted from the pain and was mercifully unconscious when the child was finally born.

Outside in the hallway, John heard the baby's first cry. He rushed inside the room as the cries grew louder and stronger.

"A boy," the midwife said, looking triumphantly toward John.

John closed his eyes and breathed a sigh of relief. He could hardly see the child as the woman wrapped him in a blanket and held him toward his father. John touched the baby's forehead with one finger.

"Is he all right?"

"He's fine," she said. "A strong, healthy son."

John nodded and started toward the bed, but Lida's mother stepped in front of him.

"We're not finished yet," Anna said, touching

John's arm gently. "Why don't you go downstairs and tell papa. Have a cup of coffee, and then you can come up and see your wife and son."

John's face was tortured as he looked toward the bed. Lida's eyes were closed, as if she didn't even know he was there. And she was so pale and still.

He backed out of the room and leaned against the wall outside in the hallway. Only then did he finally give way to the despair and fear he felt.

"Please God," he whispered. It was the first sincere prayer he had made in a very long time. "Please . . . just let Lida and my son be all right."

When Anna Rinehart came down to the kitchen later, John saw something in her expression that frightened him. He came up from the table and went to her.

"Is she all right? Is—?"

"John," Anna said, her face solemn. "Lida has a fever. It's not uncommon for some women after such a long hard labor. Mrs. Jaberg has given her something that should help but—"

"A fever?" he said. His gaze darted toward the stairs, then back to his mother-in-law. "What exactly are you trying to say?"

"I mean . . . she fainted just before the baby was born and I'm afraid the fever has weakened her and caused her to remain . . . unconscious. Mrs. Jaberg isn't sure if there is anything else wrong or not but—"

Without another word, John raced up the stairs, taking them two at a time. When he entered the room, it was almost dark and there were lamps lit. He'd been so distracted and worried about Lida that he had hardly looked at his son. The midwife held the baby and as John approached, she turned down the blanket so he could see its face.

"Isn't he handsome?" Mrs. Jaberg asked.

John saw the dark little face and the black hair and he smiled and shook his head with wonder, hardly able to believe that he and Lida had made this miraculous little creature.

The baby's eyes were open and he stared up at John almost as if he knew who he was.

"He has blue eyes," John said, taking the baby's small fist. John laughed. "He's strong."

"His eyes will probably change later," Mrs. Jaberg said.

"No," John said, shaking his head fiercely. "They'll be blue, like his mother's." He turned then and went to the bed, his heart aching at the sight of his strong, passionate Lida lying so still and quiet.

"Mr. Sexton," the midwife said. "I thought you should know, the baby will be all right through the night as far as feeding is concerned. We can give him sugar water while Lida is so very sick. But tomorrow . . . if Lida isn't better, I'm afraid we'll have to find a wet nurse for the little one."

"No," John said firmly, turning to stare at the woman. "We won't need one. She'll be fine." He pulled a chair close to the bed and reached to take Lida's hand. "By morning, she'll be fine," he whispered.

The midwife shook her head sadly and sighed

as she watched the tall handsome English grieving for his wife. She couldn't think of him as Amish, even if he did wear a beard and dress in black trousers and a white shirt. He still had the pride and arrogance of an English. And she for one doubted he had ever really embraced their religion. Or that he ever would for that matter. She clucked her teeth quietly, seeing his misery and knowing how hard this life must be for someone who didn't truly believe in it. She thought he didn't even realize how dangerously ill his young wife was. Perhaps it would be better for all of them if poor Lida did die and John Sexton took his little boy back to Tennessee

"I'll take the baby down to the kitchen where it's warmer," she said.

But John didn't hear. He was hardly aware of anything except Lida's small hot hand in his and the sound of her labored breathing.

He loved her more than life. And whatever he had to do, whatever promise he had to make to God for her life, he would do it. He took her hand and, with his elbows propped on the bed beside her, he brought her fingers up against his forehead, whispering soft words, and making quiet, desperate promises.

"I love you, Lida," he whispered. "Don't leave me. I don't think I can live without you. Whatever you want from me, I'll do. Whatever God wants, I'll give it gladly and without pride. Just get well. Please, just open your eyes, sweetheart, and look at me."

Lida moved and her eyelashes fluttered, but she didn't wake.

John continued talking to her, pleading with her to get well.

"Do you know how much I love you?" he asked. "How much I would give just to make you and our son happy? I'll do anything, blue eyes. I'll sacrifice my entire life if it's what God requires. I'll live Amish and never complain another day. I don't care anymore. All I care about is you, sweetheart. You're all that matters to me now."

Thirty-one

When Lida opened her eyes the next morning, she felt strange and oddly disoriented. She couldn't move and felt as if a great weight held her down. Then she saw John's dark head against her shoulder, where he was slumped over in his chair. His muscular arm lay across her shoulders and was what she felt weighing her down.

Lida let her gaze move around the dimly lit room, frowning as she tried to remember what had happened.

She touched John's hair and he jumped.

He sat up and stared at her, sleep still evident in his eyes. His mouth was open as if he couldn't believe what he was seeing. Then he took her face in his hands and kissed her.

"Lida," he whispered, his voice husky and filled with some emotion she'd never heard before.

"The baby," she said, looking into his eyes. If something were wrong, wouldn't she be able to see it in her husband's eyes?

"He's fine," John said, smiling and touching her forehead. "A strong, healthy, blue-eyed boy. Just wait 'til you see him. How are you feeling? You had a fever and—"

"I feel good," she said, shrugging her shoulders as if she were just as surprised as he was. "I'm tired, but I feel really good. I want to see him."

John could hardly breath for the joy that clutched at his heart. He actually felt light-headed with happiness. He shook his head at her, marveling at her seemingly miraculous recovery and praying silently that this was for real.

"Let me get your mother. She'll tend to your needs and make sure you're all right. And then I'll bring your son up to see you."

Lida bit her lips and nodded. She couldn't take her eyes off him as he left her side and walked out of the room.

Later, when Anna Rinehart came back down to the kitchen, she was grinning broadly.

"It's amazing," she said, her eyes large and shining. "I don't think I've ever seen anyone recover so quickly from this kind of childbirth fever. We'll have to watch her carefully and keep giving her the medication, to make sure the fever doesn't come back."

"What about the baby?" he asked. The boy had begun crying and when his mouth found his fist, he nuzzled back and forth against it hungrily. "He seems hungry. Will Lida be able to feed him yet?"

"We'll see," she said. "Why don't you take him up and let her try. I told her we could get a wet nurse until she's feeling stronger, but like you, it isn't what she wants."

John had concentrated on Lida so completely last night that he'd hardly had time for his son. Now, as he carried him upstairs, he gazed down at him, feeling the soft warm weight of him in his arms and looking with wonder into those small intensely blue eyes.

"My son," he whispered reverently. "There are so many things I have to tell you. You're going to have to be much wiser than your father."

The baby began to cry loudly then and John laughed.

"Let's see what your mother can do about that," he said, opening the door to Lida's bedroom.

When Lida saw John at the door, she pushed herself up in bed, her blue eyes large and expectant as she waited for her husband and son. When John neared the bed, she couldn't take her eyes off the tiny bundle in his arms and she held her arms out with loving impatience.

Lida cradled him to her breasts, her face filled with awe and solemn with concentration as she pushed her nipple into the baby's searching mouth. When he began to nurse with greedy, satisfied little noises, Lida looked up at John, and when she smiled, there were tears of joy in her eyes.

He sat on the bed beside her, marveling at the sight before him. Nothing had ever moved him as that moment did. And for the first time in his life, he felt as if he'd come home.

Home wasn't a house or a certain part of the country. It was this. Lida and his son.

"What's his name?" she asked.

John shrugged, then laughed. "I guess we were so worried about you, we forgot to name him. You said before he was born that you wanted to wait until you saw him before you decided."

"He looks like you," she said, running her hand over the baby's black hair.

"He has blue eyes like yours."

"I had thought about naming him Samuel," she said a bit shyly. "Would you mind? I want him to be like you and Sam. Strong and certain about what he wants. Interested in the world around him and intelligent about his choices."

"You think I've been intelligent in my choices?" he asked, his gray eyes teasing.

"You chose me, didn't you?" she teased back.

"The smartest thing I ever did."

He laughed and reached out to touch the baby and her.

"Sam will be fine with me. Unless you would prefer Ephraim after your brother." The look in John's eyes was one of sad memories and of regret.

"Both," she said with a nod of satisfaction. "Samuel Ephraim Sexton. It sounds strong and noble. Like his father."

"Noble?" he said with a lift of his brow.

She nodded, smiling into his eyes.

"You are the bravest, most noble man I ever met."

Over the next few days as Lida recuperated and grew stronger, she began to remember bits and pieces of that night when she was so sick. She remembered hearing a man's voice—John's. She even remembered some of his words.

He seemed to have changed since Samuel's

birth. He worked hard, but there was a new intensity and purpose in him that hadn't been there before.

When she finally remembered all that he had said to her that night she almost died, she knew the reason.

"I'll sacrifice my entire life if it's what God requires." She was sure she'd heard him say those words. Somehow she'd heard it through her fever-induced sleep, and she remembered it as plainly as if he stood in the room now and repeated the words to her. *"I'll live Amish and never complain another day."*

"Oh, John," she whispered. Her eyes grew dark and troubled as she realized what he intended to do.

As soon as she was strong enough, she wrote to John's mother, telling her about the baby and about how happy she and John were. And without telling John, she also told Mrs. Sexton that she thought John was truly homesick for Tennessee and his own home. She explained quickly about her own thoughts over the past few months and how she only wanted John to be happy.

"I do not have to remain Amish to be happy," Lida wrote. "But I do require loving John and having him in my life for my happiness. If you feel his father could accept him now . . . and us, then I would like nothing better than to come home with John and try and start a new life for ourselves there. This is not something I have told John yet. So when you write, please keep that in mind."

With the war and the inconsistent mail deliveries, it was almost a month before they received a reply from John's mother.

She expressed delight at the birth of her first grandchild and told them she could hardly wait to see Samuel. She asked a lot of questions about the baby and about Lida as well. And at the end of the letter, when the tone grew more serious, she told John that his father was still ill and would like to see him. Lida had her answer.

"Your father has changed his thinking in many ways since this horrible war began, John. He says he needs nothing so much as to see you before he dies. He speaks of you almost daily and when we received Lida's letter, you should have seen the excitement in his eyes. He was even able to be up and around for a few days afterward, and I know it was from sheer determination to get well enough to see his first grandson. Won't you come home to see him, son, before it's too late? Let him make his amends so there will be no regrets for either of you. I realize that traveling by train is a long and tiring prospect, especially with a baby. And now with the war invading every state it could be dangerous as well. But if you feel it's safe and if Lida agrees, I hope you will come soon."

Lida had already read the letter before John came in, and now as his eyes scanned quickly over his mother's words, he sank into a kitchen chair. She could see the changing expression on his face and the way his eyes darkened. But when he looked up, there was a repressed happiness on his face that made her heart sing.

"I think she's right," she said. "It's time for you and your father to reconcile. Do you want to go?" she asked.

"More than anything," he said, his voice soft and filled with a longing she hadn't heard in awhile. "What about you?" he asked. "Will the trip be too tiring? Do you think—?"

"I want to go," she said. "And by the time we make all the arrangements, I'll be as strong as I ever was. But it's up to you, John. I will do whatever you wish."

"We won't make the trip if I think you or Samuel will be in the slightest danger."

"I know that," she said. "I've always felt safe with you."

"Let me talk to Greenhow about it. He'll know all the latest troop deployment. If he thinks it's safe, we'll go."

"All right." Lida turned away so that John wouldn't see the glitter of happiness in her eyes. She had a lot to do before the trip.

A few days later John received word from Samuel that he thought it would be safe traveling by train to Tennessee. Lida could barely contain her excitement as she began to make preparations.

"Lord, woman," John said once when he watched her packing trunks. "It looks as if we're staying in Tennessee forever." But his smile was tender and indulgent and she knew he didn't really mind how much they took. He was even more excited than she was, but in his new Amish nature, he struggled to repress it.

The night before they were to leave, they visited with Lida's parents. The one thing that held any regrets for Lida was that she knew how sad they'd be, living apart from her and their grandson.

Before they left, she pulled her mother out onto the porch and told her the news that if things went as she planned, they would not be coming back to Ohio.

"I know this will hurt both of you," she said. "But I promise I'll come and visit as often as I can. And you might come see us, too. Tennessee is not that far away."

Anna Rinehart took her daughter in her arms.

"It's all right. I've seen this coming for quite a while now," she said quietly.

"You have?"

"Child," her mother said. "Did you think I couldn't see how unhappy John was trying to live Amish? And how much it bothered you that he was unhappy. I'll admit he has changed since Samuel was born. He's been trying harder. But knowing you, you've seen through that just as quickly as I have."

"Anna Rinehart," Lida said, looking at her mother with a new respect. "You are an extraordinary person. I'm so lucky to have you for a mother." She pulled away with a slight frown. "But what about papa? Will he be terribly angry with me? I don't think I could bear it if he never speaks to us again."

"Don't worry about your father. He'll be fine. We've talked about this a great deal lately."

"You have?"

"Yes, it's something I've warned him might happen. I tried as best I could to prepare him for it, and I think he had reconciled himself to the fact that it would happen soon or later, just as I did."

Lida shook her head and smiled at her mother. "Oh, you don't know what a relief it is to hear you say that."

When Lida went inside to tell her father goodbye, she thought he already had guessed that this parting was to be longer than he'd been told. He held his daughter for a long time and kissed Samuel again before they left.

The next morning was a warm, beautiful spring day. The sun sparkled through the windows of the farmhouse as Lida and John carried everything out and placed it in the wagon. Once everything was ready, John took Samuel out to the porch to wait while Lida went upstairs to change clothes.

Earlier she had pulled the red silk dress out of its wrappings and hung it in one of the bedrooms where John wouldn't see it. Now as she took it from its hanger, she could feel her heart beating with excitement and anticipation.

Would John understand? Was this really what he wanted, too?

"Well, if it isn't, we'll just come back," Lida said with a smile and a shrug. She really had changed since meeting John. And she knew in her heart that she could be happy anywhere, doing anything, as long as she was with John and Samuel.

She stood before the mirror, smiling at her image and pleased that the dress fit as well as it did, considering the changes her body had gone through recently. There was a new snugness in the bust, but she thought that it was hardly noticeable.

She spent her last few moments going from room to room, touching items that had belonged to her grandparents, saying goodbye to the house where she and John had begun their marriage.

Then she stepped out onto the porch.

John turned and saw her standing there in the red dress and his mouth dropped open. Slowly he rose from his chair and placed their sleeping child in a nearby crib.

With a look of stunned disbelief he walked to Lida and stood before her, not touching her or speaking, but simply letting his gaze move over the silk dress and back up to the sparkle in her blue eyes.

"What are you doing?" he asked with a slight shake of his head. "Where's your *Halsduck* and *Kapp*?"

Lida smiled. He had mastered their language and their habits as quickly as he had mastered her heart. She thought it was the one thing that had pleased her the most, the way he'd made himself learn and try to adjust to her way of life.

Because he'd done it for her. No one had ever loved her the way he had, or been willing to sacrifice so much for her.

"Going to Tennessee, I believe," she said.

"Lida . . ." He stared into her eyes as if not knowing what to think or what to say.

"We're going home, John," she whispered. She couldn't help the tears that filled her eyes. For, despite his stunned look of disbelief, there was a dawning pleasure and excitement in his eyes as well. Something she hadn't seen there in months.

"Remember the night I was sick . . . the night Samuel was born?"

"How can I ever forget it?" He stepped forward placing his hands at her waist and looking into her eyes.

"I heard you talking to me that night, John. Somehow, through the fever, I heard what you were saying."

John frowned and shook his head, looking at her with love and disbelief.

"I know you would have been willing to live here forever. To become Amish forever, even though it wasn't what you wanted. You did it to please me, because you thought it was the only way I could ever live. But it isn't. Because I love you, John, more than life, more than anything. Don't you know that I couldn't let you give up your home, the life you dreamed about? I can't be happy unless you are."

"But what about you? I never wanted you to sacrifice your life and your religion for me."

"Sacrifice?" she asked. "Lord, John, don't you know by now that it's no sacrifice? I'm not a saint. I hadn't exactly planned on spending my life in a nunnery. Mother told me a long time ago that I had to make my own choices in life. She didn't want me to live a life based on someone's else dreams. But I don't think I really understood what she meant until I had a child of my own."

John shook his head as if he still didn't believe her.

"Loving you and spending the rest of my life with you is no sacrifice, John. It's a dream come true. It's what I want, too." She smoothed the red silk dress and smiled at him. "Besides, I'm beginning to like red."

"I can't believe you did this," he said, amazed. "That you planned all of this and I didn't know."

"I was afraid if you had time to think about it, you would say no."

"Are you sure about this? Really sure? What about this farm . . . your family?"

There were tears glittering in his gray eyes as Lida reached up to touch his face. The face that she loved most in the world.

"You are my family now," she whispered, her lips trembling. "You and Samuel."

"I don't know what to say," he whispered.

"Say yes," she said, putting her arms around him and holding her body tight against his. "Say you want to go home to Tennessee and that you want me and Sam to go with you." She was breathless and waiting as she looked into his eyes.

"Lida, sweetheart," he scolded. "Surely you don't think . . . Don't you know by now that I do, that I love you?"

"Say you would have married me anyway, John. Even if there had been no baby."

Her voice had grown so soft that John could

barely hear her words. And the look of uncertainly and vulnerability in her eyes struck straight at his heart.

"God," he muttered, a dawning light of realization in his gray eyes. "Don't you know . . . no," he whispered. "Of course you don't. I haven't bothered telling you, have I? Because I was too busy with my own thoughts and problems."

"Then tell me now," she whispered.

"God yes, I would have married you," he declared with all the fierceness she remembered so well. "I can't imagine spending one day . . . one *minute* of my life without you. I've been a fool about so many things in my life, Lida. But I'm not fool enough to ever have let you go. Even before there was a baby in our lives, I had already decided that. On whatever terms, I meant to marry you and keep you for my own. I'm only sorry it took me so long to tell you."

Lida threw her arms around his neck, laughing and crying at the same time.

"God," he said, choking back his emotions. He buried his face against her neck, breathing in her sweet familiar scent. "I love you. I've never loved you more than I do at this moment."

He drew back and looked at her, wiping away her tears as he smiled at her.

"I'll make you happy," he said. "I swear. I intend to spend the rest of my life making you happy."

"We'll make each other happy," she said.

She reached up and kissed him and felt his own tears warm against her face.

"Then we'd better get started," John said with a husky laugh. "We have a train to catch."

With a mischievous smile, Lida pulled a pair of scissors and a straight razor from the pocket of her dress.

"Not yet. We have time for one more thing before we go," she said, smiling at him. "Just enough time to get rid of that scratchy beard once and for all. I want to be able to look at your strong handsome face all the way back to Tennessee."